FACED WITH THE AFTERMATH OF A LIFE ALTERING DECISION, A NINE-YEAR-OLD BOY SEEKS SOLACE IN THE KENTUCKY FOREST IN PURSUIT OF HAPPINESS, LOVE, AND ACCEPTANCE.

After a life time of abuse, nine-year-old Rusty Travis and his older brother Bo decide their father must be stopped when, in a drunken rages, he goes after their six-year-old sister. After their vengeance is complete, they seek refuge in the tall oak forest where the stumble upon a mysterious runaway orphan. This leads to uncovering secrets about themselves and their family they never imagined leading Rusty to question everything he thought he knew. With his brother by his side, they battle with the demons that shatter their world in the sleepy town of Plum Springs.

The screen door on the porch of the trailer smashed against the post again, temporarily paralyzing him. Instead of seeing his father on the porch, Rusty saw Ruby, and she was running toward him and Bo. It sounded as if she were crying, but Rusty couldn't tell for certain through her high-pitched screaming. A shiver of horror ran through Rusty's body when her voice hit his ears. Something was wrong, and he feared the worst. He couldn't get himself to believe it to be true, though. Ruby was too young. He knew it must have been something their father did, but he didn't want to imagine the possibilities. Rusty dropped the hoe and ran to where Bo was, closer to the trailer and to Ruby.

Ruby didn't stop until she ran into the outstretched arms of Bo, who caught her and wrapped his arms around her petite frame like a blanket. It was only a moment later when Ruby pulled away, looked up, and Rusty saw her face up close.

He threw his hands over his mouth and gasped.

"*Plum Springs* is one of the most intense novels I've read in a long time … Equal parts captivating and heart breaking, I found myself living each vivid moment right there with the likeable nine-year-old protagonist. Dan Lawton is a name to know!"—*Chad Zunker, Amazon #1 bestselling author of The Tracker (The Sam Callahan Series).*

"A poignantly told coming-of-age story of three young children who overcome abuse, finding love and happiness despite all odds. Heart-wrenching and uplifting."—*Sibel Hodge, Award winning and #1 International bestselling author of Look Behind You, Untouchable,* **and** *Duplicity.*

Plum Springs

Dan Lawton

Moonshine Cove Publishing, LLC
Abbeville, South Carolina U.S.A.
First Moonshine Cove edition May 2018

This book is a work of fiction. Names, characters, places and incidents are products of the author's imagination or are used fictitiously. Any resemblance to actual events, locales or persons, living or dead, is entirely coincidental.

ISBN: 978-1-945181-351
Library of Congress PCN: 2018941750
Copyright 2018 by Dan Lawton

All rights reserved. No part of this book may be reproduced in whole or in part without written permission from the publisher except by reviewers who may quote brief excerpts in connection with a review in a newspaper, magazine or electronic publication; nor may any part of this book be reproduced, stored in a retrieval system or transmitted in any form or by any means electronic, mechanical, photocopying, recording or any other means, without written permission from the publisher.

Book cover design by Moonshine Cove Staff, images public domain.

Acknowledgment

A big thanks is owed to my three initial draft readers – Carol, Caryn, and Elizabeth. I can always count on you to ask questions and for your strong opinions, both of which greatly enhance the manuscript.

To Elizabeth – my dearest wife – thank you for listening to me during my times of doubt, or during my moments of confidence, and to all of my ideas. Thank you for vetting the bad ideas and encouraging the good ones. Thank you for giving suggestions, or helping with character name creation, or asking questions that prompt me to fill plot holes. Thank you for being my number one, in so many ways. I love you.

Thank you to Duncan Shippee for assisting me with time consuming marketing tasks – you've made my life a hell of a lot easier. I hope you enjoy seeing your name in print. Brag proudly.

I'd also like to thank Gene Robinson and the entire team at Moonshine Cove for their belief in the manuscript and all of their efforts in getting it ready for publication. I'm looking forward to a long and prosperous partnership.

And finally, to my fellow writers – some of you I now consider friends – thanks for being there to share trials and tribulations with, for understanding the triumphs and disappointments that come with being a writer. Here's to us all achieving success in our own ways.

Previous Works

Amber Alert

Operation Salazar

Deception

About the Author

Dan Lawton is a thriller, suspense, and mystery writer from New Hampshire. He's an active member of the International Thriller Writers (ITW) Organization. *Plum Springs* is his fourth novel.

Dan's first two novels were self-published, and he signed his first book deal for his third novel, *Amber Alert*, the day before his twenty-seventh birthday. Six months later, he signed with his first literary agent. His first novel, *Deception*, was named one of the best thriller novels of 2017 by the Novel Writing Festival. Dan lives in central New Hampshire with his family, where he is hard at work on his next story.

Dan can be contacted directly via: **info@danlawtonfiction.com, @danlawtonauthor on Twitter, or on Facebook.com/danlawtonfiction.**

For a free sample of his other works, regular updates, or to sign up on his mailing list, please visit: **www.danlawtonfiction.com.**

Dedication

For Mom, who has always been my most vocal supporter. Thanks for birthing me.

Plum Springs

CHAPTER ONE

The calluses on the palms of Rusty's hands were split, the loose skin sodden, the pink underneath covered by a creamy white cap. It was warm to the touch, the raised mound ready to erupt. The excess skin bubbled like it'd been burned, but it hadn't — only by the summer. The bandages covering the old calluses were soaked with blood that was so dark it could've been black, the scabs underneath trying to form as the darkness crusted to the skin. The edge of the adhesive curled, the fabric crisped by the afternoon. It was August.

The hoe's wooden shaft was splintered and kept together with silver duct tape, but it hardly worked. On more than one occasion, a loose sliver of wood would free itself from the bundle and stick Rusty like a dull knife. If he was lucky, it would miss his calluses. If he wasn't, it wouldn't. His hands ached constantly.

The garden hoe Rusty used was the same one he'd been using since he was seven-years-old. That was two years ago. Every summer, Rusty and his brother, Bo, would spend their afternoons in their father's field, touching up the soil and replacing the old fertilizer with a new, fresh batch. They would build small mounds around each of the tobacco plants in the rows and fertilize them with the homemade concoction their father made up in his shed. Whatever it was, it kept the pests away and the leaves grew faster and thicker every year. It sizzled when the sun hit it just right, and it smelled something awful.

Rusty's hands weren't as strong as Bo's were. Bo was four years older than his brother and had been working in the field for nearly three times as long. The skin on his palms had permanent scars from where the calluses once were, and the dark stains under his fingernails were permanent. Rusty was still getting used to it. He'd learned to let his nails grow past the edge of his fingertips to avoid getting anything stuck underneath. He couldn't get his cuticles clean, no matter how much he scrubbed them. The infection he got under his thumbnail during the first summer in the field nearly caused his thumb to be amputated — that was the low point. The homemade fertilizer wasn't meant to touch the skin, he learned.

The sweat on the back of Rusty's neck helped him stay cool, but the sensation would be only temporary. The pint of muddy water he was permitted to bring with him was supposed to last from lunchtime until supper, but it never did. Bo learned to ration his portion to conserve it for when he needed it most, which was something Rusty tried to do too. But his willpower was still a work in progress. Temptation was hard to ignore sometimes.

Rusty looked up into the sun and shielded his eyes with one hand, squeezing onto the splintered handle with the other. The blue horizon was cloudless above him. There wasn't a lick of wind. Time stood still, as if the earth had stopped rotating on its axis. Rusty wondered where the edge of the world was as he drove his hand further into the splinter, ignoring the tugging against his skin that followed. He swatted away a pesky horse fly. It'd been circling him as if it were sizing him up for hours, tantalizing him with its bulging eyes that shone like emeralds. Rusty thought he heard the fly laughing at him as it made a figure-eight in the sky with its tiny wings.

A warm liquid ran down Rusty's wrist and tickled his skin. At first, he thought the fly had finally made its move and was prepared to attack, but the trickling down his forearm made him think otherwise. His hand felt wet, cooler than the rest of him, even the back of his neck. He looked down, ignoring the faded bandages and damaged skin that covered his hand, and saw a trail on his wrist where the liquid washed away the soil. It looked like a water droplet swimming down a window the way it did after a shower when the overhead fan stopped working, and Rusty wondered if rain was coming. He looked up again but was still unable to find a single raincloud. August sizzled against his skin. He put his hand to his forehead and wiped his brow with the inside of his thumb, and more liquid oozed down his wrist. It was pus.

Then he felt the pain.

It was a burning sensation, like his hand caught on fire or was thrown into an incinerator and held there. His hand shook as he looked at it, his eyes unable to stop his muscles from spasming. Using the nails on his thumb and forefinger on his other hand, he grabbed the edge of the curled bandage like it was a delicacy. The pain was severe, numbing, and he wanted to see how bad it looked. The blister in the center of his palm hurt the worst.

"Don't touch it," Bo said. He stood next to Rusty and hovered like a hawk. Rusty didn't notice the shadow.

"It hurts," Rusty said, clenching his eyes shut and flexing his jaw. "It hurts really bad."

"No shit it hurts. But it won't get any better if you keep tearing that off. Do you want it to get infected?"

Rusty shook his head. He remembered what it was like when his thumb got bad.

"Then stop touching it."

Rusty opened his eyes and nodded, even though it still hurt.

"Hurry up and get back to work before dad sees," Bo said, then turned and went back over to his row of plants. The mounds of soil surrounding the base of the tobacco plants he worked on were much cleaner than the ones Rusty made. That wasn't unusual.

Rusty held the side of his hand against his chest and pressed. He clenched his eyes shut again and slid the inside of his cheek between his teeth, biting down as hard as he could without drawing blood. More warm pus slid out from underneath the wet bandage and dripped onto his skin. It was as thick and hot as melting wax, and it left a layer of grime where it traveled. The first droplet from before rolled all the way to his navel now, but he fought the urge to scratch it.

Before getting back to work, Rusty turned and looked over his shoulder. Their father's shed was less than a hundred yards from where he stood, and Rusty knew there was a jug of water inside — the clean kind. Their father took trips into town to buy a few gallons of imported spring water each week, but he always kept it for himself. Rusty, Bo, and their little sister, Ruby, were left drinking the well water. All the extra iron made it look and taste like metal. It was as clean as mud.

Before Rusty could consider making a run for the shed, the screen porch on the trailer slammed, sending a flock of farrows scrambling. His head jolted back around and he stood at attention, his muscles tensing as he waited for his father's wrath. If he made him mad, Rusty knew he might take away the rest of his water for the day — it wouldn't be the first time.

Lenny Travis, his father, stepped out onto the porch with a Budweiser in hand, sporting his usual white tank top with yellow-stained armpits. Lenny was the meanest bastard east of the Mississippi, and all the townsfolks agreed. Rusty couldn't say for sure if that was true, but he'd heard someone say it once. It resonated with him. While everyone else in Plum Springs, Kentucky — population: 473 — was kind and friendly and would give you the shirts off their backs in a second, Lenny would take it from you. Then he'd spit on it and throw it in the river, just because he could. That's just the type of man he was. Rusty was scared of him.

Lenny burped once into the air and smiled at the echo that boomeranged around him. Even from a distance — it was maybe fifty yards from where Rusty stood to the front porch where his father was — Rusty thought he could smell the beer on his father's breath. It was early afternoon on a Tuesday, and Lenny was already piss drunk. Rusty got that uneasy feeling in his belly, the same one he felt every time his father called his name, and he did all he could just to stay standing upright. He clutched onto the rounded part of the wooden handle in his hands for extra support.

"Rusty!" Lenny yelled. "What the hell you lookin' at, boy?"

Rusty stiffened and shook his head.

"Speak up, boy."

"Nothing, I was just —"

"You was just nothing. Don't you lie to me."

Rusty looked toward Bo in search of his support, but his head was facing downward and his arms were hard at work with his own hoe. As strong a Bo was, he tried to stay out of it, and Rusty understood why. Lenny was mean and vicious and tougher than them both combined, and Rusty knew he was on his own. The scratchiness of the sandpaper that formed in his throat made him choke as he tried to swallow. His tongue stuck to the roof of his mouth as if it were attached there. Rusty's words eluded him.

When he looked back toward the porch, his father was already halfway toward him. A scowl blanketed his face with rage, sending anxious jolts rushing through Rusty's body like crashing waves against the shore. Rusty tensed, his boots like cinder blocks against the dirt. The beer can in Lenny's hand was dented in the middle and missing the tab from the top, like they all were. Rusty squeezed the handle of the hoe even harder, but the pain in his hand returned and he dropped it, leaving himself defenseless. Both he and his father watched the silver of the duct tape disappear under a cloud of dust.

Lenny grinned.

Rusty cradled his injured hand in his free one and kept it close to his chest, as if he were a crow cradling a wounded wing. It was pulsating, his skin on fire. His chest was puffed out only to give his heart enough room to beat as hard as it needed to — he knew he was no match for his father.

Lenny pulled up when he was only a few feet away and stared at Rusty as if he were deep in thought. Rusty squirmed at the thought of what was on his father's mind. He avoided Lenny's eyes and found himself staring at the day-old stubble that covered his father's face and neck. For the first time, Rusty noticed a touch of gray starting to penetrate the black, and he thought it made him look angrier. To Rusty, his father looked older than he actually was, and he wondered if that meant he would die young. Part of him wished that to be true. A big part of him.

"What's the matter with you, boy?" Lenny said. His voice slurred already.

Lenny's hot breath almost made Rusty gag. It smelled of rotten cheese and stale beer, and it took all the restraint Rusty had not to turn away. He knew he'd get backhanded if he did.

"My hand hurts."

"Snake getcha?"

Rusty shook his head.

"Coon trap? Bullet hole? Pipe bomb?"

Rusty said nothing. The pain in his hand was starting to numb.

Lenny motioned to the sad mound of fertilizer that rose up the base of one of the tobacco plants. "Get some of that stuff on ya?"

Still nothing.

"Then what, boy?" A snort crawled out from somewhere in the back of Lenny's throat as he inhaled sharply through his nose. He sniffed once.

Rusty pulled his hand away from his chest and opened his fingers to show his father. For the first time all day, a small gust of wind came along and blew directly into the callus. It provided Rusty with a moment of chilled relief, but the pain came back with a vengeance, even worse than it had been before, once it disappeared.

"You got a little blister? That's what you're cryin' about out here?"

"I ain't crying."

The beer can made a noise that reminded Rusty of tin being crushed. It was like that time his father had an old clunker Ford smashed up and set on fire instead of having it towed to the scrap yard. The metal twisted and popped then, just like the beer can.

Lenny scowled again. "Don't you talk back to me, boy."

Rusty lowered his hand and stood as straight as he could. His shoulders rose and his lower back arched, and he flexed his pectorals, even though they were flatter than his sister's chest. One day, Rusty thought, he'd be strong enough to take on his old man. But until then, he wasn't sure what to do. Backing down only seemed to make it worse.

Lenny leaned forward and grabbed Rusty by the wrist, his man fingers like tentacles around Rusty's boyish skin. Rusty tried to yank his arm away, but the clasp around his wrist tightened. Unblinking, and with the muscles in his jaw flexing, his pupils widening, Lenny twisted until Rusty couldn't bear the pain anymore. Rusty finally gave in, nervous sweat pouring down his face, and let his father flip his hand over. His fingers were only loosely opened, but Lenny squeezed even harder on the pressure point until they spread out completely. Rusty refused to let his eyes close, refused to let his father know he was in pain.

Without hesitation, Lenny took his open beer and poured it over Rusty's callused hand. The sting that swept through Rusty's hand and wrist was worse than anything he'd ever felt before — worse than when the infected thumbnail separated from his skin; worse than when his pinky got stuck in the pencil sharpener at school; worse than when he stepped on a piece of scrap metal in the driveway and split open the bottom of his foot. The pain was worse than all of that. His hand trembled as the cold liquid swallowed the bandage whole. A tiny air bubble pushed out the beer in gushes, the pressure of the thrusts like a vacuum against his wound. Rusty cried out in silent agony as his lungs begged him for relief.

Lenny's grip tightened.

The tin can crunched between Lenny's stout fingers as he squeezed, and Rusty could do nothing but bite on his tongue and wait for the pain to pass. Rusty wanted to scream and fight against his father's overpowering strength, but knew he shouldn't; screaming would only make Lenny want to inflict more pain. It had so many times before, as if being in control of it put him in a state of ecstasy. The need for that high had gradually gotten worse since Rusty's mom left for the last time, and that was when Ruby was just a baby. Bo took the brunt of the outbursts up until recently. Rusty couldn't remember being hurt by their father before he started working in the field.

Rusty turned his head and closed his eyes and wished the can would be empty soon. He would have prayed to the sky God for the pain to stop, but he questioned if it was real. Bo told him it was, but Rusty wasn't so sure; he couldn't understand why God would let his father hurt them the way he did. Bo suffered through the pain for much longer than Rusty, which confused Rusty even more. Bo accepted the sky God as being real, even with all the bad things that happened to them. Rusty, on the other hand, wasn't as quick to accept something that wasn't there to help him when he was too weak to help himself. He thought the sky God was supposed to be there to protect him.

The flow of liquid eventually slowed and the grip around Rusty's wrist loosened, but the pain didn't subside right away. Rusty grabbed onto his wrist with his free hand and fell to the dirt, writhing in pain, still refusing to let his father know how much it hurt. He felt moisture on his face and realized he was crying, but he could do nothing to stop it.

He buried his face into the pit of his elbow and hid behind his t-shirt. He wished he could disappear. He'd been searching for his own wardrobe for years, for his own Narnia, but he was still looking. The tobacco field didn't offer him up much in terms of material to daydream about. He always wondered if the shed might lead to that place for him, but the shed was forbidden.

The empty beer can landed next to Rusty's head, the crushed center creating a pointed edge that could have sliced his face.

Rusty rolled onto his stomach and let the sharpness of the soil scratch his exposed skin. The patch underneath him was as dry as chalk, and it smelled like dust.

"Told you you was crying." Lenny spat at the ground, causing a puff of dust when it hit, and laughed. "Wussy boy."

When he thought his father was gone, Rusty used his shirt to wipe the water from his cheeks. As he did, something warm and wet poured over his boots and socks, making his already sweaty feet like a swamp. Before he figured out what it was, Rusty curled his toes to try to stop whatever it was from seeping in between them. There was already something starting to grow in the pit between his pinky and ring toes, and he knew something wet would only worsen it. When he took his socks off at night, the stink made him sick to his stomach.

Rusty stayed on the ground, belly down, until he heard the door to the screen porch bounce against the door frame — he knew for sure his father was gone when he heard it. Then he heard a muffled voice coming from inside the trailer, his father's, yelling out for Ruby. His sister was only six-years-old, but Rusty feared her time was coming before long. He hoped she'd be working out in the field too, where he and Bo could keep an eye on her. Being inside that trailer wasn't safe, especially for girls — just ask his mom. If their father ever put his hands on Ruby, Rusty's not sure what he'd do to him; he'd never gone as far as imagining it would ever happen, although maybe it was because he was trying to pretend it wouldn't. But he knew, deep down, it eventually would.

Just thinking about it made his skin hot.

CHAPTER TWO

While still face down in the dirt, a haze of dust clouding his vision, Rusty felt Bo's presence hovering over him again. A shadow appeared in the periphery and blocked out what Rusty could still see, sending the orange sun into hiding behind the lurking darkness. Bo wasn't big, but his shadow seemed it; he looked like a giant with oversized, thinned legs, and a long and narrow torso that was stretched beyond what was normal. Even his head was a miniature version of what it should've been, outlined with a smoky gray hue. Rusty's entire body was covered by the giant shadow, and he was amazed at its size. It almost made him forget about the pain in his hand.

Using his good hand, Rusty rolled himself onto his back, coughing away the cloud of dust, until he looked up at his older brother. Bo's face was smeared with soil and his hair was just as greasy as it usually was, and he looked like a working man. Rusty saw the outline of what looked like a mustache starting to grow above his upper lip. When Bo extended out his arm to help Rusty to his feet, the clump of slicked underarm hairs stuck out too. Bo, unquestionably, was becoming a man; his changing body was proof of that. Rusty wondered how long it would be before Bo would be strong enough to stick up to their father.

Rusty took Bo's moistened hand, felt the coarse, chapped skin on his own, and was pulled to his feet. Rusty wanted to thank his brother for looking out for him, but when he looked at him and saw the sorrow in his eyes, he decided against it. Bo seemed to notice too, because he looked away, as if to hide his face, and his tears.

But no tears came.

Even so, the gesture told Rusty more than any tears could have. Bo, while definitely growing into a man, wasn't one quite yet. His body may have been well on the way, but there was still something missing — it was the emotional strength that men possessed that boys did not. Bo hadn't found that yet. Even though Rusty was four years younger than his brother and not even in double digits yet, he could recognize that. The sadness in his older brother's eyes told Rusty they both still had a long way to go before they'd become men, before they could stand up to their father. They would be spending many more years in this field.

The tobacco field was their father's business. He kept some plants for himself and smoked the finished product like he was a chimney, but on his weekly visits into town — the same ones where he'd pick up fresh water for himself — he'd drop off a truckload of plants to be manufactured and sold. Rusty didn't know much about the process, and he didn't care to know, either. All he knew for sure was he and Bo were the ones to do all the work in the field — planting and preserving and harvesting the tobacco plants — while their father sat inside smoking, drinking Budweiser, and staying out of the sun. It didn't seem fair.

Bo tore off a portion of the bottom of his t-shirt, which once was a bright white but was now stained brown, until he had a piece as long as his arm. He tore through the cotton with his hands, and the harder he pulled the further the t-shirt rode up on him. By the time the piece of filthy cotton was torn, Bo's navel was showing. Rusty saw a small trail of hair there too, leading from the bottom of his button to the top of his jeans.

"Let me see it," Bo said as he held out the loose piece of cotton.

Rusty knew what his brother was talking about, but he pulled his hand away and hid it from him. The pain resurfaced when he moved it, and it was like being jabbed repeatedly with a dull blade. The only comfortable position was to keep his fingers bent slightly, allowing the remaining skin to ravel like a rolled up carpet on his palm. He could smell the Bud soaking into his skin as if it were a sponge.

"Give it here." Bo reached for Rusty's hand.

Rusty didn't move his hand toward Bo, but didn't fight him either. He knew it was the best thing for the wound, but he also knew it was going to sting. Bo's moistened fingers grabbed onto Rusty's wrist and forced his hand toward him. Rusty offered up only minimal resistance, which was really only to satisfy his ego — he hated not at least fighting back, even if he knew he wasn't going to win. The pain that exploded through the open callus made Rusty scream into the openness of the field. It was a relief to do so, having kept it in so his father wouldn't hear it up close, but it didn't help to ease the pain. Bo kept his grip firm while he wrapped the torn piece of t-shirt around Rusty's hand as if it were a bow. There was just enough material remaining after going around thrice to tie a small knot, which he did.

"It's too tight," Rusty yelled, his hand pulsating. "It hurts!"

"It'll be fine. It's the only way it'll heal."

"It's just gunna split open again anyway."

"Don't you remember what happened last time you got an infection?"

Rusty nodded. The scare with his thumb.

"Then quit your bitching."

Rusty scrunched his face and pursed his lips at his brother, even though he knew he was right. Bo shook his head and turned back toward his plants, not engaging. He picked his hoe up off the ground and got back to work as if nothing happened.

Rusty bent over and stretched for the handle of his own hoe, grabbing onto the duct taped portion with his good hand. He'd forgotten all about it, but when he did, the wetness in his socks squelched. He felt the liquid starting to penetrate the holes in his work boots, saturating the socks underneath. He knew the smell between his toes would worsen before it got better. Rusty felt parched.

Next to the hoe and close to the empty beer can was the bottle of water that was supposed to last him the rest of the day. Rusty bent over again and picked it up, then brought the muddy rim to his lips and leaned his head back. Not even a single drop remained. He pulled the bottle from his lips, looked into the hole with one eye, and saw nothing but plastic staring back at him.

Empty.

Anger boiled under Rusty's skin, and he threw the plastic bottle to the ground. He stomped on it with the heel of his boot until the plastic shrunk into the shape of an accordion, leaving a broken tamper ring and no cap. Rusty found the cap a few feet away and kicked it with his other foot, sending it bouncing across the soil like a rock skipping on a river. He was so thirsty. And he hated his father for wasting the water for no reason.

Rusty sat on his backside in the sun and dropped his head. Tears welled up behind his eyelids, but he blinked them away. He found a leaf and rolled it between his fingers. And as much as he knew he shouldn't, he began to feel sorry for himself.

"What are you doing now?" Bo asked. He was in the row of plants next to the one Rusty was in.

"Nothing." Rusty kept his head down and tore the edges of the leaf away. He pulled it apart until he was left holding only the stem, tossing the small bits of green into the sky. They fell in his lap as the wind died out again. He eventually flicked the stem away too.

"Do you want dad to come out here again?" Bo said as he approached. "It's only going to be worse next time, you know."

"I can't do it, Bo. I can't do this. I'm not strong enough."

Bo sat down next to Rusty, their knees touching. "What are you talking about?"

Rusty held his arms out. "This. I'm not strong like you. My hands are all tore up and I'm out of water. I'm too weak. I'm not a man like you."

"You think my hands don't hurt too? They do."

"But they ain't all tore up like mine."

"Not anymore they ain't. But they used to be."

Rusty turned and faced his brother. "Really?"

"Of course. I was just like you when I was your age. I've just been doing it longer than you, so my hands have gotten used to it, that's all." Bo turned his palms up and showed Rusty the scars.

Rusty stared at the scars and was reminded of the stories Bo told him — about how the blood used to drip onto the plants when his calluses opened; about how the sweat from his forehead would fall into the wounds and make his cuts sting as if they were on fire; about how Bo once drank his own urine when he was out of water but was still thirsty. Rusty sometimes forgot that Bo had been through it all before him and knew what it was like. He liked it when Bo told him stories in bed about what he'd been through, although it could only happen if and when their father passed out drunk. Bo's stories made Rusty realize that what Bo went through was so much worse than anything he'd ever know, simply because Bo had to do it all on his own; Rusty always had Bo there with him, always had Bo's wisdom and advice and protection. Bo had to learn it all on his own; he had to learn the hard way. Rusty regretted ever feeling bad for himself. Bo never did.

One of Lenny's rules was that there was no talking when in bed. But when he passed out he wouldn't know, and Rusty and Bo would sometimes be up all night when that happened, just talking. Ruby would stay up sometimes too, but she wouldn't make it very long. She would crawl in bed with Rusty, and they'd cuddle in the bottom bunk while Bo told stories from the top until Ruby fell asleep on Rusty's chest. The bottom bunk felt safe in those moments. It was as if the wooden frame above Rusty's head was a shield, and nothing dangerous or evil could penetrate it. It was like Rusty's own invisibility cloak; he couldn't do magic, though. Their late-night talks were Rusty's favorite times. He felt like a kid then, and those were the moments when he found himself wishing for a better life, wondering if he'd ever find happiness outside the armor of the bottom bunk. They hadn't had one of those talks in quite a few weeks now.

"Don't worry," Bo said, "you'll become a man someday too."

"You think so?"

"I did." Bo smiled.

Rusty nodded.

"I even got hair down there," Bo said. "Wanna see?"

Rusty laughed and pushed his brother away from him as he leaned in. Bo laughed too while he pretended to unzip his pants and whip out his member. Rusty was glad to have his brother around to make him laugh.

"Wait here," Bo said, then he stood up. He wiped the dirt off his pants and started back toward the row of tobacco plants he'd been working on.

Rusty didn't respond. He just watched his brother, wondering what he was doing, admiring his strength. Looking at him, Rusty reconsidered whether he thought Bo was a man or not; maybe he was one already, after all.

Bo bent over and picked something off the ground, then came back toward Rusty. "Here, take it."

Rusty looked at the outstretched arm of his brother and saw a plastic bottle dangling before him, water sloshing underneath where the label should have been. Bo, as usual, had saved more than half of his water.

"That's yours."

"You can have it."

"No, I can't. It's yours."

"Just take it." Bo said. He shoved the bottle into Rusty's hands, forcing him to take it.

"Are you sure?"

Bo nodded.

Somehow, the water inside Bo's bottle still felt cold in Rusty's hands, despite the heat of the day, and his mouth began to salivate. He felt guilty for accepting Bo's water since he'd be left with nothing if he got thirsty later, but Rusty's mouth was really dry; he could hardly even swallow. With one final glance at his brother to make sure it was okay, Rusty unscrewed the cap with his good hand and poured the water into his mouth without touching his lips to the rim. Although he knew it couldn't have been, the water felt as cold as ice on his tongue, like it'd just come from the Arctic. His teeth screamed at him when the cold hit them, the cavities in his molars untreated. Rusty swallowed hard and let the ice water lather his throat until it was smooth again. He guzzled until there was only a small sip left, then he handed the bottle back to Bo and exhaled. He felt so much better.

Bo took the bottle from Rusty and threw back the final sip, then screwed the cap back on and took off toward his row of plants. He turned back to Rusty and smiled. Then, without saying anything, he got back to work.

Rusty felt replenished, his muscles stronger and looser, his mood not as gloomy. Bo had a way to make him see the positive in every situation, even if finding a positive seemed impossible. Rusty admired Bo for that. He didn't know how he'd ever be able to repay him for everything he'd done for him, but he wanted to try, even if that meant starting out small. Rusty crouched down and grabbed the duct taped handle of the hoe, brushed the sand dust off, then stood back up and jammed the edge of the blade into a mound of soil. He was going to prove his worth to Bo, even if that meant he had to ignore the pain in his hand.

Just as Rusty was starting to gather some momentum in his work, the screen door on the porch of the trailer smashed against the post again, temporarily paralyzing him. All the water he just ingested left his body in a cold sweat, and the little hairs on the back of his neck stood on end. Rusty clutched onto the duct tape and looked toward the trailer. He hoped his father wasn't still mad at him, although there was hardly ever a time when that was the case.

Instead of seeing his father on the porch, Rusty saw Ruby, and she was running toward him and Bo. It sounded as if she were crying, but Rusty couldn't tell for certain through her high-pitched screaming. A shiver of horror ran through Rusty's body when her voice hit his ears. Something was wrong, and he feared the worst. He couldn't get himself to believe it to be true, though. Ruby was too young. He knew it must have been something their father did, but he didn't want to imagine the possibilities. Rusty dropped the hoe and ran to where Bo was, closer to the trailer and to Ruby.

Ruby approached, still running, and definitely crying. She didn't stop until she ran into the outstretched arms of Bo, who caught her and wrapped his arms around her petite frame like a blanket. It was only a moment later when Ruby pulled away, looked up, and Rusty saw her face up close.

He threw his hands over his mouth and gasped.

CHAPTER THREE

Open cuts and bloody abrasions covered Ruby's face with dots. Her skin was pinker that it usually was, her eyes wetter than they should have ever been. If Rusty didn't know any better, he might have thought the cuts were boils that had split, like his calluses. But Rusty knew better. He knew his sister's face wasn't like that earlier, and he knew immediately where they came from. There was only one person in the world who would have done that to such a sweet little girl like Ruby.

"What happened?" Rusty asked. His voice was shaky, frantic. He could feel the anger building within himself.

Ruby didn't say anything. She stood there, her hands dangling at her sides, tears streaming down her face, and sniffed. For as bad as her face must have hurt, she was stronger than Rusty thought. He felt like a wimp for reacting the way he did when their father poured his beer over his hand earlier.

"Did dad do this to you?" Bo asked. His face was red with boiling blood, and Rusty could tell he was trying to hold it back. Rusty caught a glimpse of Bo's hand as it slid downward and came to rest on his bent knee, shaking as if it were cold. Rusty thought he could feel the heat as it oozed from Bo's grime encrusted pores.

Ruby nodded. Bo dropped both knees into the soil and held Ruby in his arms. She lay against him and cried while Bo smoothed her braided hair with the stroke of his hand. Rusty thought he heard a sniffle come from Bo, but he brushed it away. There was no way. Rusty had never seen Bo cry before.

Rusty stood off to the side by himself with his good hand shoved deep into his pocket, feeling the trapped particles of sand scraping against his fingertips. He didn't know what to do. He looked toward the trailer and expected to find his father on the porch, drunk and hideous and cowardly, but he didn't. Something felt off.

When everything fell quiet around him, Rusty heard the clanking of porcelain coming from inside the trailer. Then he thought he heard a glass shatter. The kitchen was on the other side of the exterior wall closest to him, just past the screened in porch, and Rusty expected Lenny to burst through it at any moment. He waited for his father to explode through the screen like a tormented bull, steam emanating from his flared nostrils. Rusty felt like a Torero holding the red flag, but he wanted to be a Matador. Now more than ever before.

Time crawled. The misery stood still. Rusty stared at the dirt. Once the sniffles and tears subsided completely, Ruby pushed herself away from Bo, using the side of her hand to dry her cheeks. Rusty looked at her again, good this time, and surveyed the damage even further. There was some discoloring on her forehead already, just above her left eye, where a bruise was starting to form. There was an egg on the opposite side of her face, and her lip was bloodied. There was a sprinkle of crusted blood in her nose too, but that could have been from an unrelated nosebleed — she got those from time to time. Either way, Ruby was beaten up pretty good, and it made Rusty so angry. He dug his fingernails into his palm on his good hand and tightly clenched his jaw.

Lenny deserved to be punished for what he did. Ruby's just a girl.

"What did dad do?" Rusty said. He was surprised at the calmness and deepness of his voice. It sounded like he was a man already — controlled and confident, maybe even strong. It surprised him. Bo and Ruby seemed to notice too, because they both turned and faced him at the same time, and Rusty felt uncomfortable that all eyes were on him. "How many times?"

Ruby held up three fingers, keeping her thumb and pinky down below. Her lip quivered. Bo turned away, unable to look. Something happened inside Rusty's body that he'd never felt before. It caused his muscles to tense and his hands to tremble. Sweat beaded on his back and neck. His belly churned so hard he thought he'd shriek. He felt as if he were on the verge of exploding.

"Why?" Bo asked once he turned back around. He was still crouched. His hands were balled into fists near his boots.

"He was hungry," Ruby said. Even in spite of her injuries, her voice was as soft as a feather. She spoke with a gentle Kentucky accent, which, over the years, became as thick and heavy as everyone else in the family. The innocence in her voice made what Lenny did to her even more difficult for Rusty to imagine. She was a child, harmless. Innocent.

"He hit you because he was hungry?" Bo asked.

"...because I couldn't make him a sandwich."

Bo looked to Rusty and made a face. Rusty wasn't sure what it was supposed to mean.

"What do you mean you couldn't?" Bo said.

Ruby looked between Rusty and Bo, and she started to cry again. It was harder than it had been before, more like weeping, and she threw herself back into Bo's arms. Bo held and rocked her as if she were his own daughter, swaying to music that only he could hear. In many ways, he looked after her like she was his daughter — Rusty saw it. If it wasn't for Bo protecting her, there's no telling what Lenny might have do to her. Bo was the only father she ever had. Rusty too.

Across the field, the screen porch thrashed open and captured Rusty's attention again. He snapped his head toward the sound, anger still ratcheting through his veins. Lenny walked out onto the porch with a new beer in his hand and a burning cigarette in his mouth. Rusty knew it was homemade — he could smell the freshness of the tobacco that the rolled up ones his father sometimes bought didn't offer. Rusty could recognize that natural smell anywhere.

Lenny stepped out onto the top step and whipped something over the railing, toward the open patch of lawn. Rusty couldn't tell what it was from a distance, but it flew across the sky like a skeet disc. It spun like a record as the wind took ahold of it, then it began its descent just as quickly. The object shattered and exploded into a cloud of dust when it crashed into the surface.

Lenny slurred a drunken obscenity then slammed the door and went back inside. Even after he disappeared again, his voice still echoed through the field, sending vibrations rushing through Rusty's boots, reminding him of the squishiness that molded his toes.

Rusty looked at Bo, who was covering Ruby's ears as their father's voice rumbled through the rows of tobacco plants. Bo was trying his best to shelter Ruby for as long he could, but Rusty couldn't help but feel it was all for naught. Ruby, by now, had heard worse things come out of Lenny's mouth. They all had.

As the echo faded and the field was left in silence, Rusty peered across to the other side, past the strip of grass where there weren't any plants, and out toward the second trailer. The trailer was on a separate flat on the same lot, and a single plum tree separated the two. The plums were just starting to ripen, turning from a soft red to a deep purple. From where Rusty stood, they looked as small as grapes. On the other side of the plum tree was the trailer their mother lived in, along with their grandpa. Rusty always thought the arrangement was strange, but he liked that he could see them both every day, even if it was just a wave. Lenny wouldn't let him or Bo or Ruby go over there much. Lenny seemed to have a major distaste for their mother, although Rusty didn't fully understand why.

Bo's voice broke Rusty's concentration. "Let's go."

Rusty faced his brother and was surprised to see Ruby standing alone, a few feet away. "Go where?"

"To the shed."

The sandpaper regrew inside of Rusty's throat and he found it difficult to breathe normally. "For what?" he said, gasping for air. "Dad will kill us if he finds out we went in there."

"Not if we kill him first."

Bo's words smashed Rusty in the chest, nearly sucking the rest of his wind. Rusty wasn't sure if Bo was being serious or not, but the look in his eye told Rusty to listen. Bo's eyes were glassed over and dark and drowning with passion. Even though he knew it was only his imagination playing tricks on him, Rusty swore he could see little flames burning inside Bo's pupils. Rusty was warm too, and his hand started to ache again. The piece of t-shirt wrapped around his callus didn't seem to be helping as much as he hoped it would.

"Dad hit Ruby because she wouldn't make him a sandwich," Bo said, in such a calm voice it was frightening. "Ruby's only six-years-old. She doesn't know how to make a sandwich. Dad won't even show her how to use a knife."

Rusty thought about it and nodded. He'd never seen Ruby make a sandwich before or use a knife to cut one in two, although he wondered if the two were even related. But he didn't dare question Bo, not right now, not when he was like this. Bo, it appeared, was serious about what he said before. He wanted to kill their father.

"He crossed the line this time, Rusty. It can't go on anymore."

Rusty tried to swallow the puddle of saliva filling his mouth, but he couldn't — his throat was too dry. Instead, he waited back while Bo took Ruby by the hand and led her toward the shed, then he spat into one of the plants. He took a peek over his shoulder at the trailer one more time, just to make sure, and when he saw the coast was clear, he hurried to catch up. Together, the three of them walked toward the shed in unison, their backs facing their father's trailer, the pain of the years of abuse filling their heads.

As they approached the shed, Rusty knew his brother was right. They had to stop their father before things got any worse. They had to stop Lenny before it was too late.

Rusty was scared.

CHAPTER FOUR

The shed was unlocked. There was an old padlock on the outside of it, but it wasn't secured. The locking mechanism was rusted by all the years in the frigid ice and rain, and countless hours in the baking summer heat. Even the rounded parts looked sharp. Bo tore the lock from the door and threw it to the ground, discarding it like trash. Then he swung the door open and stepped inside, slipping into the darkness. Ruby went second. Rusty trailed.

It took Rusty's eyes a moment to adjust to the darkness of the shed. There were no lights inside. Lenny only came out here during the day when the sun was at its brightest through the one window on the far side, and now, Rusty understood why that was. Rusty and Ruby and Bo stood in a line next to one another, filling the entire length of the shed with their shoulders. Once Rusty's vision was clear, he took a look around. It was his first time inside his father's shed. His belly twisted with butterflies. He wondered where the door to Narnia was.

There was a chest-high table on wheels in the center of the shed that was probably only waist-high for his father. The floors were rotted and felt waterlogged under Rusty's feet, made worse by the similar feeling he had inside his boots. He wiggled his toes around to keep them fresh, but his socks dug deeper in the pits of his toes when he did, actually making it worse. Rusty cringed at the thought of the hangnail on his big toe getting infected like his thumb did. He dodged a bullet once, and he questioned whether he'd be able to do it twice. He'd never been that lucky.

Rusty took a step toward the table and peeked at the top. On the table was a familiar leafy plant that smelled of dirt, and some chopped up tobacco that resembled shaved wood chips. Next to the loose tobacco was a white five-gallon bucket that was filled halfway with something of similar consistency as water. Except it wasn't water. Even the water he and Bo were given didn't look that bad. The liquid inside the bucket was tinted green and had bubbles foaming on the surface. It smelled radioactive, a likely combination of pesticides and ammonia. Rusty couldn't help but wonder if it was from another planet. Whatever it was, it made those plants he and Bo tended to grow like fungi on spoiled cheese.

Rusty sensed Ruby's presence behind him, felt her move close to him, as if she were afraid. Bo was fumbling around in the far corner, looking for something Rusty wasn't privy to. Rusty stepped away from the table and put his arm around Ruby's shoulder, pulling in her toward his belly, getting a whiff of cinnamon from her hair. He always found her hair to smell that way, which was odd, since he'd never heard of or seen cinnamon shampoo. Then he thought that maybe the cinnamon he smelled was because of her hair color — the shade of red was like cinnamon. If the scent of someone's hair had to do with the color of it, Rusty wondered what his would smell like. Chocolate was his first instinct — hopeful, perhaps — but he couldn't think of anything else brown that smelled good; he could only think of the nastiest of them all. He hoped he didn't smell like that. He felt a tickle on his nose.

Bo moved from the corner and made his way further along the perimeter of the shed, his boots squelching as they sunk into the floorboards. Rusty didn't ask what he was looking for, although he was curious. Bo looked comfortable as he dug around the perimeter of the shed without hesitation, his hands and feet making noises that seemed to be in sync. Based on the way he moved, Rusty wondered if Bo had been inside the shed before — he didn't act the least bit afraid of getting caught.

Bo's foot crashed into something, toppling it over. He stopped, stood up straight, and took a step backward when it hit the floor, staring down at it as if it were a monster. The object was hidden from Rusty's view, but Bo's reaction scared him.

What if it was a monster?

Then Rusty heard it.

Heavy liquid sloshed as air pushed it outward. Plastic rattled against the floor as the liquid poured out, the volume intensifying as air bubbles pressed against it. The sound was familiar. Rusty closed his eyes and thought about it, trying to remember where he'd heard it before. It didn't take long. The memory rushed back as if it were surfing the wave of the spilled liquid. It overtook him, buckling his knees, causing his calves to tighten. It was the memory of the first time his father hit him.

Rusty was just a boy. Bo was working in the field and Ruby was still asleep in the back bedroom. Lenny locked himself in the bathroom and told Rusty he needed some privacy. He did that often. It was almost noon and Rusty still hadn't been fed, and his belly kept making strange gurgling noises. Rusty found the cereal in the cabinet and retrieved a bowl without incident, but Lenny thrashed open the bathroom door and scared Rusty. The gallon of milk slipped from his grip and crashed against the floor of the trailer, just as he was about to pour it into the bowl. Rusty stood frozen in fear while Lenny cussed him out.

Rusty remembered not being able to move, too frightened of his father to even bend over and pick up the spill. Rusty's shoulders hunched as Lenny pressed two fingers into the back of his neck and forced him onto his knees. It took three smacks of his head against the linoleum for Rusty to finally open his mouth, and when he did, Lenny forced him to clean up the milk with his tongue.

Rusty vomited twice as he licked the floor. There were dust mites and rat turds under the stove that made him gag every time he inhaled. Between those smells and the taste of the milk and the blood from his forehead and the vomit-stained linoleum, Rusty tried and fought but lost, and he blacked out. When he awoke later on, Lenny sat at the kitchen table with a fresh light and a six-pack of empty cans next to him. He was calmer then, with less rage, but no less mean. He forced Rusty to strip off his shirt and use it as a mop for the now warm and spoiled milk. It mostly worked.

Rusty vomited a handful more times that day as the smell of the spoiled milk bled through his shirt and soiled his skin. Lenny forced him to wear the shirt for the rest of the day because he said it would teach Rusty a lesson. Rusty never did know what the lesson was that day, unless it was to never touch the milk. If that was the case it worked, because Rusty hadn't picked up a gallon jug since that day, and he had no plans to do so anytime soon. The next morning, Bo took Rusty's shirt outside with him and buried it behind the trailer. Rusty could smell the spoiled milk on himself for days after, and it took weeks for him to even look at his father again. He joined Bo in the field later that summer, and they'd been at it every day since.

The memory of the first time made Rusty shiver with chills. He could never forget his first time.

Rusty tensed further as he thought of a fallen gallon of milk and what might happen if Lenny found out. But then he realized where they were and didn't think there'd be a gallon of milk in the shed, and so his mind wandered off into a different direction instead.

What if it was the substance that was inside the bucket? What happened if it got on them?

He thought about his thumb and cringed.

Rusty pulled Ruby closer to his chest and squeezed her tighter, just in case the spilled liquid made contact with mold or some of the furry fungus that lined the walls and caused it to grow into an alien. Rusty believed such things could happen.

Bo bent over and disappeared from sight, making Rusty tense even more. But then Bo reappeared, looking like himself and not an alien, and dropped something on the wheeled table. It rolled toward Rusty and Ruby slightly, which startled Rusty and made him stumble backward a couple steps.

"Ruby, come here," Bo said.

Rusty felt Ruby stiffen. He held her close.

"Hurry up. Before dad finds us out here."

Rusty knew his brother was right about that. If Lenny found them out here, they'd be dead. All of them. He didn't want to, but Rusty released Ruby and pushed her toward Bo. Ruby only resisted for a second before walking around the table and approaching Bo, her steps small and slow. Her neck was craned and her face looked at the floor as if she were readying herself to be scolded.

Rusty clenched his teeth in anger. Ruby was too young to be afraid of others already, and she never had a reason to be afraid of him or Bo. Lenny had scarred her.

Bo ripped off another piece of his shirt — this time from the back, after twisting it around to the front so he could grip it — and made it into a ball in the palm of his hand. Even though Bo was standing in front of the window and blocking most of the light, Rusty could see Bo's shirt had been torn to the bottom of his ribcage. Before long, if this kept up, Bo would be shirtless.

Bo popped the cap off the jug he kicked over and put it on the table. Rusty hadn't noticed what it was until now, still afraid of its possible alien origin. His eyes widened. Bo picked up the jug by its handle and tipped it overhand. The balled up shirt soaked up the liquid like an old sponge and whatever else was left dripped through Bo's fingers and onto the rot beneath his feet. Bo crouched to Ruby's level and applied the wet shirt to the cuts on her face. Ruby let him.

"What's that?" Rusty asked. The liquid in the jug was clear, kind of like what he thought water was supposed to look like. The brown stuff he and Bo drank was hardly clean enough to be considered water, although technically it was. He was sure now that the liquid Bo was applying to Ruby's face wasn't harmful — or otherwise Bo wouldn't be doing it — but he was still curious what it was. Bo is one person that would never hurt Ruby, no matter what.

"Water," Bo said, keeping his eyes on what he was doing. His concentration was sharp, as if he were performing surgery.

The sandpaper returned in Rusty's throat again, trying to suffocate him. He'd forgotten how thirsty he still was, and the mention of the fresh water made him crave it even more. He wasn't sure if he misheard Bo or if he was having a mirage, but Rusty felt as if he were surrounded by water. He saw himself swimming in the river, letting the water fill up his cheeks as he swam, felt his hair dampen. The callus on his hand began to sting from the pressure of the current of the river that pressed against it.

"Can I have some?" Rusty asked as he shook out of his daze. He used his good hand to check himself. He was still dry — the makeshift handkerchief too. It was just a daydream.

"Some of what?" Bo said.

"The water."

Bo didn't respond right away. He kept at his surgical precision until Ruby protested she had enough. When he finished, he wrung out the wad of shirt and let the water saturate the wooden floor even more than it already was. He jammed the clump of material into the back pocket of his jeans and said, "All right," then he pushed the jug toward Rusty.

Rusty stepped forward and reached for the jug. He hesitated for a moment as he looked at it, remembering how long it'd been since he picked one up. He thought again about what the consequences might be if he messed up again, but decided it was worth it. His throat was so parched it hurt.

Rusty's good hand was his off-hand, and the jug was heavier than he expected. His fingers wrapped around the handle and squeezed the plastic as hard as he could, but his muscles were tired and weak. The jug began to fall from his grip at once, the handle so slippery it could've been greased, and he used his bad hand to try to catch it. Rusty writhed in pain as the jug hit the softest part of his damaged palm and crashed to the floor beneath him. The callus burned like his hand was melting, and for a second Rusty thought it might actually be. He wrapped his good hand around his wrist and tried to squeeze to put an end to the throbbing, but it didn't help. His hand burned hotter and his fingers shook. If he wasn't so dehydrated he would have cried.

"Pick it up!" Bo cried. "Hurry, before it's all gone. That's the last jug."

Rusty heard his frantic brother and wanted to do as he said, but he couldn't. He closed his eyes and pulled his hand to his chest, cradling it with his good one. He dug his teeth into his lip and bit down. A taste of tin touched his tongue, and he knew that meant he'd gone too far. Even so, the pain of it was nothing compared to his hand.

"Why didn't you pick it up?" Bo asked as he stood in front of Rusty, breathing heavier than normal. His voice was low, and Rusty knew he was angry. Even with the light at his back, Rusty could see Bo's face had reddened. Rusty's eyes met the jug, which was now back on the table, and noticed more than half of the water was gone.

"Sorry." Rusty clutched onto his hand and kept it still.

Bo seemed to understand. He nodded and left it at that without saying anything. It was as if he knew the pain Rusty was experiencing, as if he'd been through it himself. Rusty knew he had. Bo grabbed the jug of water with two hands and held it above Rusty's face. Rusty smiled at his brother and leaned his head back, allowing Bo to pour small amounts of water into his mouth like it were a funnel.

Rusty coughed and choked at first, the water pouring directly into his throat, but he eventually got the hang of it. He raised the back of his tongue so it would trap the water inside his mouth like it was a dam. When he was ready, he closed the dam and let the water rain down his throat like a waterfall. His body felt invigorated each time he did it.

Once Rusty's stomach was full and Ruby had a turn, Bo finished the jug off. There wasn't much left for him, maybe a half of a glass worth. Rusty felt guilty knowing he'd taken it mostly for himself — including the rest of Bo's bottle that he offered earlier — but Bo didn't seem bothered. Bo tossed the empty jug to the side and pulled Rusty and Ruby into a quiet embrace. Rusty's stomach felt full, maybe too much so. He felt bloated as if he were a balloon. He wondered what would happen if he popped.

Even though Bo's skin was warm against his own, Rusty didn't care. While he was still overheating himself, Bo's touch made it all go away — all the emotional pain, all the physical pain, all the bad memories. Even his hand stopped aching for a time. Rusty hung on when Bo tried to pull away, but he was eventually overpowered — his good hand wasn't strong enough.

Bo crouched to Ruby's level and looked into her eyes. Rusty stood back, wishing Bo would look at him in the same way, though acknowledging Ruby needed it more than he did. Even so, he couldn't help that he still wanted it.

"I'm sorry what dad did to you," Bo said to Ruby. "But I promise he'll never hurt you again." Bo looked up at Rusty and they locked eyes briefly. "He'll never hurt any of us again."

Ruby's lip started to quiver again. Rusty felt a pinch in his throat too. He wondered what Bo was feeling.

Rusty didn't know what his brother meant by what he said exactly, but he liked the sound of it. The idea of Lenny never hurting him again was refreshing, a relief, like music to his ears. He could only hope it was true.

The three of them embraced again, harder this time, and held it for a while longer. Ruby cried. The softness of her whimpers were hard for Rusty to hear — they made him sad. He felt so bad for her, like he let her down, like he should have been there to protect her from their father. He suspected Bo felt the same way, although he doubted Bo would ever admit it — Bo didn't outwardly show sadness very often, even though Rusty knew he had to have it in him. Rusty certainly had plenty of it.

Rusty tried to stop his own tears from falling, but it wasn't as easy as he hoped. The pinching in his throat worsened the harder he tried to fight off the tears. He held his breath while he fought with the knot that formed in his chest, but that wasn't much use. He eventually gave in and cried along with Ruby, though in silence. He hoped Bo wouldn't think less of him for giving in, for losing the battle within himself — he wanted Bo to think he was becoming a man, too, just like him.

When Ruby stopped whimpering and Rusty's own silent tears stopped, silence overtook the shed. Rusty heard one more sniffle, which definitely wasn't from him and was too deep to have come from Ruby, which meant one thing — it came from Bo. And while this wasn't the first time Rusty had heard his brother cry — the first time was in the field earlier — he still hadn't ever seen it. That was because Bo was almost a man, and men don't cry. Rusty used his shoulder to wipe his cheeks dry so no one would notice.

CHAPTER FIVE

There was a glimmer in Bo's eyes that sent angst shivering through Rusty's body. There was something about them, something dark, something almost evil. It was as if Bo were possessed by a demon. Maybe Lucifer. There was a coldness that surrounded Rusty and overtook him like a tidal wave. His chest became heavy, his breaths rapid. There was an emotionless, blank expression on Bo's face. The look meant something, something bad, and it frightened Rusty.

Ruby stepped out of the shed and back into the sunlight, leaving Bo and Rusty alone inside. The air was thinner with only two people occupying the space, but Rusty felt small. Something was up.

Bo's eyes shifted upward, directly over Rusty's head and in the direction of the door frame. Whatever was there, Bo was staring at it, his eyes unmoving, as if the demon inside him was trying to escape. Rusty desperately wanted his brother to snap out of whatever it was he was entrenched in, but he was too afraid to say anything. If he did, he feared whatever it was inside Bo might try to come after him instead, that it might overtake his soul and use his body as a costume and force him to perform evil. He worried he'd be turned into someone wicked, someone just like his father. Maybe that was why Lenny was like he was. Maybe Lenny was possessed by an evil spirit that was forcing him to treat Rusty and Bo and Ruby the way he did. That would explain it, if nothing else.

Out of fear of what might happen to him, Rusty stood very still. He avoided looking into his brother's eyes and tried to make himself invisible. He wished he was on the bottom bunk right now, where he'd be safe from the evil surrounding him. He wondered again where the hidden door was inside the shed and hoped he'd find it soon so he could escape to a new world before it was too late. He'd dreamed many nights about what might be on the other side.

"What dad did to me is one thing," Bo said, "and what he did to you, well, it sucks. But at least you and me can defend ourselves. Maybe not now, but someday. Someday we'll be just as big as he is, maybe even bigger. We can make him pay. But, Ruby..."

Rusty snuck a glance at Bo's eyes to see what was happening, and that's when he noticed Bo was no longer staring above Rusty's head. His head was turned and he was looking at the ground, his neck tilted, like someone experiencing deep emotional pain. He seemed to be agonizing over what to say next. Rusty bit his tongue to stop the lump that was growing in his throat from getting any bigger. He still wasn't sure where Bo was going with this, but he somehow felt pained too. Rusty had a feeling Bo was thinking about trying it again.

"But, Ruby," Bo continued, "she can't defend herself. She's just a girl. She'll always be a girl. Girls can't stand up to dad. Look what happened to mom."

Rusty considered that, nodding. He thought Bo might be right.

Bo looked up. "It's time," he said, with a calm resolve. "I think it's really time this time. It's gone on for too long."

A loud thump in Rusty's chest made his torso hurt. A kaleidoscope of butterflies flew blindly in his belly, each set of sputtering wings making him feel more nauseated than the one before. He wanted to say something, but the dryness of his throat put up a barricade that couldn't be penetrated. Even if he did say something, he wasn't convinced it would even matter. Bo, it seemed, had already made up his mind.

"Ruby," Bo yelled, startling Rusty. "Come in here."

Ruby popped her head inside the shed. The sun shone at her back, making the soft red covering on her head look almost orange. The abrasions on her face were darkened. Rusty smelled the cinnamon again.

"Ruby, I need you to stay in this shed for a while, all right? Close the door and put one of them shovels in between the door handles. Don't come out until me or Rusty comes and gets you, okay? Don't open the door for nobody, you hear?"

Ruby nodded without asking any questions. Rusty had plenty, but he didn't ask any either.

Bo found an empty five-gallon bucket in the corner and carried it toward the door. Rusty shuffled his feet and moved out of the way, unsure of what Bo was doing with it. Bo flipped the bucket over and dropped it on the floorboard, right in the center of the doorway. The plastic didn't clank when it hit the wood like Rusty expected it might, which was probably because the wood was so rotten and soft. The sound was more of a squelch, like a boot stepping onto a patch of soggy grass the day after a rainstorm.

Rusty held his breath, hoping Bo wouldn't fall right through the floor.

For the first time, Rusty saw what Bo was staring at earlier. Bo's outstretched arms reached for it, the tips of his toes providing the extra boost he needed, and wrapped his hands around it. There were two u-shaped hooks, both rusted, that were screwed into the wood above the door frame, each insulated with rubber for extra grip. The shotgun between them had a long black barrel with some corroded brown near the pump and a faded stock. The grip was worn so badly that the once glossy finish had turned matte. The brown had vanished almost entirely and had turned the same color as the barrel. Rusty could tell the shotgun had been used with regularity at one time or another.

Bo stepped down from the bucket, carefully cradling the shotgun in his palms as if it were a newborn baby. Rusty had never shot a gun before, never held one, but he knew all about them. When he was younger, before Lenny sent him out in the field with Bo, Rusty used to watch gun shows on TV with Lenny. While Lenny seemed to lack interest in most things, guns were different; guns were his passion. Rusty knew there were some guns hidden in the trailer and accessible by only the key that Lenny kept in the hip pocket of his jeans, but he'd never seen one up close before. The shotgun Bo held was an older pump-action style, twelve gauge, with two side-by-side barrels. The chambers were, in Rusty's estimation, three or three and a half inches.

"Let me see that," Rusty said, awed, reaching for the weapon.

Bo pulled it away and snapped his eyes in Rusty's direction. "What are you, stupid? That's how you get your hand blown off."

Rusty backed away and sank his shoulders. Bo turned his back to Rusty and held the shotgun into the sun. Rusty tried to look over Bo's shoulder to get a glimpse at the action, but by the time he heard the clank of the steel snap shut, it was too late.

"There's one shell left," Bo said, facing Rusty. "And I don't see any others lying around."

"What does that mean?"

Bo took his time answering the question. He looked between Rusty and Ruby as if being sure to take in their faces one last time. When it was Rusty's turn to capture his big brother's attention, he stared back. Bo's eyes were the same as they were before — overtaken by something evil, ignited flames bringing the moisture in the shed near a boil — although he no longer looked possessed. He looked in control.

That was even scarier.

There were two other occasions when Bo toyed with the idea of killing their father. The first time was after their mom left. That was many moons ago, so far in the past that it hardly even registered in Rusty's memory — some memories were stronger than others, he knew. She ran out one night, battered and bruised — just like Ruby now — and never came back. Their grandpa took her in. Bo brought up the idea of killing their father then, it being the first time he'd seen his mother being abused. But he was only eleven at the time, Rusty seven, so they didn't go through with it. They didn't even know how to execute it.

The second time was last Christmas. Lenny bought himself a new .22 and keg of Budweiser, but there were no gifts for the Rusty or Bo or Ruby. Bo always insisted to Rusty that it didn't bother him, that he didn't want gifts anyway. Rusty said he'd agreed, but he didn't really; he just didn't want Bo to think he was selfish. The look on Ruby's face that morning, when Lenny tapped the keg by seven o'clock and was passed out drunk before noon, was crushing. While she kept telling Rusty and Bo that she wasn't sad, the puddles of tears streaming down her face told a different story. She cried herself to sleep that afternoon while Rusty and Bo stood outside the door and listened. Rusty remembered how sick to his stomach he'd felt, how angry. The first time they actually tried to kill their father came after that.

Bo found some rat poison in the cupboard and mixed some of the powder into their father's open can, but it didn't work. Lenny was violently ill that night and covered the bathroom with vomit and regurgitated beer, but he was still alive. Thankfully, Lenny wasn't suspicious, assuming it to be a stomach bug — one was going around at school, so it made sense that he could have gotten it from Rusty or Bo. Even still, both Rusty and Bo were too scared to try it again. If their father ever found out what really happened, Rusty doubted they'd still be here. And if they were successful, in hindsight, the prospect of the three of them — Rusty, Bo, and Ruby — being separated by the state was enough to make them drop the idea fast.

Until now.

This time felt different. Rusty was sure of it. While he and Bo did try it one time before, the detached expression on Bo's face told him this time it was real. This time, without question, would be more than an attempt. It had to work or they wouldn't be around much longer. It was a matter of life or death.

"What it means," Bo finally said, his voice gritty, "is we only have one shot. And we can't miss."

CHAPTER SIX

As they stepped out of the darkness of the shed and into the brightness of the afternoon, Rusty felt the wind lick his hand. The sudden chill on the callus reminded him how much it still ached, so he pressed it to his chest again — it seemed to help when he did.

Bo gave Ruby instructions on how to secure the shed from the inside as Rusty stood with his back to the voices. He looked out over the field, past the tobacco plants and short mounds of uneven soil, and focused on the trailer. A light breeze shook the door on the screen porch slightly, the echo of the banging wood reaching Rusty's ears as if he were standing in front of it. The sound was too familiar, too repetitious, too eerie. It reminded him of the sound an unoccupied wooden swing made as it hung from shagged ropes, swinging back and forth like a pendulum, just prior to a storm hitting. The softness of the banging wood sent only bad memories running through Rusty's mind. The banging, it seemed, was usually accompanied by an angry outburst from Lenny.

A hand on Rusty's shoulder brought him back, startling him. He gasped, cowering slightly, the wrath of an intoxicated Lenny still on the forefront of his mind. He turned to find Bo standing close, one hand wrapped around the barrel of the shotgun, the other scrunched and pulled in tight as if he'd touched a hot stovetop. Rusty sucked in a breath of warm air and let the heaviness cleanse him of his worry.

"You okay?" Bo asked.

Rusty nodded, maybe too quickly, and tried to shake it off. He didn't want to admit he was afraid of their father, although he thought Bo still was too. But he didn't want to talk about it.

"Good. Let's go then."

Bo repositioned the shotgun in his hand and grabbed onto it with the other. It swung with his swaying arms as he brushed past Rusty, an unavoidable trail of pungent body odor catching Rusty's nose as he did. The weapon looked like an anchor in Bo's arms, as if it might pull him to the ground at any second. But the look on Bo's face told Rusty it wouldn't. Bo still had that same look in his eyes — the look of determination — although they were now squinted. His lips were pursed and his jaw was clenched. Bo was ready to go through with it.

Rusty knew there was no turning back, no talking his brother out of this, so he didn't bother to even try. Instead, he ran to catch up with Bo before he got too far ahead. His boots felt heavier than usual, which he assumed was because of the extra weight he was carrying between his toes. It was as if the soles were filled with concrete that was just beginning to harden. The heaviness made his quads ache.

The sun was rapidly starting to fade behind the trailer. Rusty hadn't realized how late in the afternoon it'd become already. Time frequently passed him by without him noticing. Every day was more or less the same. The angle of the sun's descent mirrored off the trailer's metal roof, creating a reflection that looked like glass. Rusty peered to his left and found the plum tree casting a shadow around itself as if it were a force field. Beyond that was the other trailer, whiter than their own, which had vinyl panels that were covered with forest green moss and algae. The second trailer looked closer than it actually was, and Rusty knew it was just his mind playing tricks on him. It was wishful thinking on his part. If something went wrong inside

Lenny's trailer, it would be their only chance for survival — reaching the other one. Rusty couldn't help but worry that his boots might weigh him down if they had to make a run for it. He wasn't sure if he was fast enough to outrun Lenny, even without them.

"Are you sure about this?" Rusty asked, wrapping his thin, chapped fingers around Bo's shoulder. The coarseness of Bo's grimy t-shirt rubbed against Rusty's imperfections and gave him a chill.

Bo stopped. He stood in place, an ear pointed upward as if trying to hear something in the distance. Then he turned, slowly, angrily, and glared at Rusty, unblinking. Rusty could only stare back for a moment before he was overpowered by the ferociousness of his brother's determination before he looked elsewhere and blinked away the sting in his eyes.

"It's time," Bo said. "You know it, and I know it. It's gone on for too long."

The way in which Bo said it — his words were like stones, landing hard, making Rusty pay close attention — made it clear there was no changing his mind. As much as Rusty hoped Bo might back out, he knew now there was nothing he could say to stop him.

"Listen," Bo said, "if you want out, just say so. You don't have to go through with it if you don't want. You can go wait in the shed with Ruby. But I'm doing it with or without you."

Rusty thought hard about the proposition. Bo was giving him an out, giving him a chance to change his mind. Rusty studied Bo's face, searching for untruths, for a signal that Bo was only testing him, challenging his loyalty. Rusty found none. Bo's eyes were widened slightly, his face scrunched so the skin wrinkled in the center, and he was waiting patiently for a decision.

"Really?"

Bo nodded. "Really."

A loud sigh crept out from somewhere deep inside Rusty's belly, and he felt a wave of relief rush over him. He hadn't realized how uptight he'd been about it until now.

"Go wait with Ruby. Same rules apply. Don't come out until I come and get you." Bo didn't wait for a response. He turned back toward the trailer and started in that direction.

Although he didn't say anything, Rusty could see the change in Bo. Some of the intensity had fallen off and some of the passion he had faded from his eyes. He wasn't quite as energetic as he was before. Deflated. It wasn't sadness that overtook Bo, but instead, something worse. Something much worse. Bo looked hurt. He had the same look that a fostered child might have. Betrayal. Abandonment. Not so deep down, Rusty knew that feeling — he knew that look. It's the same way he felt when he woke up and learned their mother left. It's the same way he still felt every time he looked past the plum tree at the trailer she now called home.

A strong gust of wind brushed against Rusty's face and forced him to turn away. With his wounded hand, he shielded his eyes from the flying tobacco soil and kept his nose down. Somewhere in the distance, Rusty imagined a bed sheet fluttering on a clothesline, making a parachute of cotton and polyester; an old truck screaming, its tires screeching; the engines of an airplane humming, the passengers inside enjoying sparkling cocktails and warm meals as the plane glided through the clouds; jubilant children laughing as they played in the street. They were all happy thoughts, but they all made Rusty sad. He'd never get to know what any of those experiences were like.

Unless something changed.

As the wind passed, the noises and visions subsided. Rusty looked up. The first thing he saw was the faraway trailer, the plum tree blurry in the foreground. Rusty got those feelings again — the abandonment, the loneliness, the fear — and had to look away. He was ashamed of himself for letting Bo go at this alone.

Bo was still moving toward the trailer, the wind not slowing him down at all, the determination pushing him forward. The shotgun was cradled in both of his hands still, though his grip was undoubtedly tighter now. Rusty saw the gun sag once the wind passed. Bo was only feet from the porch.

"Wait!" Rusty yelled out. He repeated it, louder, when Bo didn't stop right away, then he ran up to him.

Bo slowed but didn't stop. "You can't talk me out of it. I've made up my mind."

"I know." Rusty's breaths were sharp, his thighs aching.

"Then what do you want?" Bo seemed near frustration.

"I'm coming with you."

Bo stopped fully now and turned to face Rusty. "You don't have to. You can stay behind."

"I know, but I don't want to. I want to help."

A glimmer that resembled a smile took over Bo's face. He allowed himself to smirk and didn't fight the widening of his lips. But he was all business. He licked his lips and the smirk was gone, and the intensity in his eyes returned. Rusty's heart told him not to let his brother go in there alone, and he knew at this moment that he made the right decision by listening to his intuition. It was time for Rusty to show Bo how much of man he was. It was time to end this.

"Okay then, let's go."

So they did. Rusty climbed the stairs first. At the top, he pinched the frame of the door and pulled it open, holding it for

Bo, the splintering wood jagged in his hand. Then he pulled it shut behind them both with a cautiousness that would ensure Lenny wouldn't hear. Together, they stepped inside the trailer.

CHAPTER SEVEN

They found their father asleep in the recliner. The top of his mostly bald head was pointing at them, taunting them, the incline of the chair almost parallel to the floor. There were two empty Bud's on the table next to him, another in his lap, the remote still in his hand. A midday game show rerun was celebrating victory on the television across the room. Rusty recognized the host's voice from all those days he spent inside when he was little. Before he was a man.

There was a stale warmth that filled the room, rising above Rusty's head as if it were a raincloud. It felt musty, heavy like the dampness of a basement in his lungs, and Rusty's throat suddenly tickled with the drip of his nasal. He swallowed hard.

For as much as he hated the work in the field, he would've given anything to be back outside where the air was fresh and the space was open. Being inside the trailer, even at night to sleep, always made him feel claustrophobic. It was as if the burden of Lenny's weight was suffocating him.

Lenny's breaths were slow and deep, his snores soft. His mouth fell open, and even though Rusty stood ten or so feet behind him, he could smell the beer on his breath. It was constant, never subsiding, so much so that Rusty sometimes could taste it himself. But that would be the best taste he'd ever get, because he promised himself he'd never take a swig of the stuff, not ever, not after the way Lenny treated him and Bo and Ruby. And their mother. Especially their mother. Rusty hated what Lenny did to her. It was his fault she left. It was his fault Rusty felt the way he did — so empty.

The anger returned. Then the hatred, the pity, the animosity. And the burning need for revenge. Lenny deserved to be hurt, too, like the rest of them.

The smell of burnt toast filled the kitchen as Rusty and Bo walked through it. Rusty knew Bo smelled it too, because his nose wiggled and his upper lip curled to cover his flared nostrils. The odor was strong, covering up the smell of the booze. On the counter, Rusty spotted the source of the burning. There was a paper plate next to the toaster, which had three or four slices of bread stacked on top of one another — it was hard to tell, each piece stuck together with hard, blackened crust. The slice on the top reminded Rusty of charcoal, and the pieces together looked like something that would be flammable. It was a wonder Ruby didn't burn the trailer to the ground, although part of Rusty wished she had; it would have saved him and Bo a lot of trouble.

Bo nudged Rusty's shoulder with his own and put a finger over his lips. Rusty nodded, understanding, knowing each step closer to their father would only increase the risk. His eyes shot to the gun, which was trembling along with Bo's hands. There were beads of sweat floating on the tops, and Rusty could only guess the bottoms were even wetter. Bo's shoulder rose as he wiped his brow on what remained of his shredded t-shirt.

When they were only a few feet from the chair, they stopped. Bo did first, then Rusty, and neither spoke. There was a thumping in Rusty's ears that made his head ache, a throbbing that gave his calluses a heartbeat of their own. Rusty felt something he'd never felt before. It was an intense rush, an urge to scream.

He got a good look at his father from up close. The stench of booze was stronger than Rusty had ever remembered before, but for some reason, it didn't bother him as much. It passed through him as if it were blood through veins, Rusty hardened to the poison. Lenny's stubble was overgrown, his neck looking more like a patch of burnt grass than skin. What hair remained on his head was oily and unwashed, and the yellow stains underneath his arms looked like urine.

Bo raised the shotgun and pointed it at their father. He struggled to steady it, the barrel shaking as if it were thunder. Despite the pounding in his chest, Rusty felt in control of himself. He felt confident, at ease, almost excited with anticipation. He was eager for his nightmare to be over, for all of their nightmares to be over.

Rusty stood still for a long few seconds, his eyes locked on his father as he slept, waiting. Lenny mumbled something gibberish under his breath as he dreamed. Rusty hoped it was his meeting with Lucifer. There was a squeak next to him — Rusty thought it might be Bo's finger gliding onto the trigger — but no shot followed. Rusty waited for it, anxious, but the barrel remained unfired, quivering only inches from their dad's temple.

Bo's face was pale when Rusty finally looked over. The blood drained from it as if it were a leaky faucet, and Rusty feared Bo might faint. He nudged Bo with his eyes, motioning to the trigger and to Lenny's unconscious body in front of them. Bo only stood in obvious fear, frozen, as if stuck in ice.

Rusty couldn't understand what was happening. While Bo had been so determined and so insistent just minutes before, he seemed unable to go through with it. Maybe it was too real for him, knowing this time would be different. But then Rusty wondered why he felt differently, why he now wanted it more than Bo did, and why that made no sense.

Until it did.

Bo had the shotgun, which meant he had their father's life in his hands; he was the one who'd have to make the final decision. Rusty didn't. But there he stood, still frozen, still unresponsive, still looking so uncertain. And Rusty felt differently.

So Rusty followed his instincts. While he was usually the one to back away and give in to his fear in situations far less intense than this, something was different. He felt cold, emotionless, almost as if the consequences didn't even matter. He knew he had to do something. He reached for the gun and wrapped his fingers around it, prying the weapon from Bo's lifeless grasp.

Rusty was going to have to be the man.

The gun was heavier than he expected it to be, but it felt right in his hands. It felt natural. The stock fell to his waist and his deltoids tensed, but he quickly gathered control of the weapon. Upon repositioning the barrel so it was nearly resting against the peeling skin on the top of Lenny's head, Rusty's hand slipped. He lost control of the gun, just for a moment, and it slid forward an inch. When it did, the muzzle pressed against Lenny's skull.

That's all it took.

From the chair, Lenny groaned and shifted his weight around, stopping only when he seemed to sense an unwelcomed presence behind him. His arm rose above his head and his fingers squeezed the muzzle as if he were trying to crush a can. His body spun, cuss words slurring off his tongue until he was looking Rusty straight in the eye. Lenny said something to him, but Rusty was too paralyzed with fear to comprehend what it was. An evil scowl overtook Lenny's face. Rage burned in his eyes like white-hot coals. His teeth gritted as if he were experiencing a great deal of pain. Lenny pushed the muzzle aside and jumped to his feet, both hands full of curled fingers with talon-like nails. He leaped toward Rusty, hurling obscenities through clenched teeth.

Rusty closed his eyes and screamed.

***

Ruby was alone in the dark. The only sound was that of the softened wood under her feet, each of her small steps squelching out more of the filth as she paced. The shed felt cold in the darkness. A sweater of goose pimples covered her bare arms. Rubbing them away only seemed to make it worse, and they'd come back with friends.

Ruby didn't fully understand what was going on. Her face was hot to the touch, the open gashes tender, and there was a slight tremble in her hands from where her fingertips still ached from burning them on the toaster. She was confused. She couldn't understand why her daddy put his hands on her. It was the first time it happened, and it came without warning.

Her daddy said he needed some privacy, went into the bathroom, and locked the door. He told Ruby to make a grilled cheese sandwich for him for when he was done, so she tried. She never learned how to make one before, but she found some yellow cheese and a loaf of brown bread in the fridge, and so she thought she could figure it out. The bread quickly turned black inside the toaster, and the trailer filled up with smoke as the cheese melted against the toaster's grates. Ruby tried to pull one of the slices of toast out of the toaster just as her daddy came rushing out of the bathroom wearing just a tank top. That was how she burned her fingertips — on the metal of the toaster. Not long after, her daddy made her face hurt too, using the back of his hand.

Thinking about the hurt made her want to cry again, but she feared the pain of her tears passing through the gashes on her face would sting, so she fought it. The outside of her longest finger was wet, having wiped away so many tears already. Her skin was beginning to prune like it did if she spent too long in the bathtub.

A lot of time had passed since her brothers left her behind, and it was making her antsy. Between the heavy gusts of wind that pounded against the side of the shed, Ruby heard her brother's talking about something, but it was much too quiet for her to understand. She'd pressed an ear up against the door of the shed, the shovel between the handles sticking her, and tried to eavesdrop on the conversation, but it offered no help.

All Ruby could do was wait. Wait until Bo or Rusty came to get her, because that's what the rules were. She understood and agreed to it, but she was also afraid of the dark. She was afraid of the strange noises she heard at night — the creaking of the trailer; the howling of the wildlife outside her window; the loud hum the refrigerator would make every time her daddy opened it. She was scared of it all. All the creepy noises seemed to lessen during the day, some even disappearing completely, but they always returned during the night. For that, she hated nighttime, was scared of it, and was afraid to be in the dark by herself. She hoped her brothers would come get her soon.

On the other side of the shed, there was a sound. It was shallow at first, soft, inaudible, then rapidly grew in both intensity and volume. It grew to be piercing, sharp, and loud enough to make Ruby's ears pop, even from inside the shed. The goose pimples on her skin rose even taller. The usually invisible blonde hairs on her arms stood on end as if they were tiny inverted nails. She closed her eyes and listened. She was breathing heavily.

The sound was a voice. A boy's voice. But there were no words. Just the piercing, blood-curdling noise that sounded like a scream. And the voice, it seemed, was far away. It didn't echo through the sky like it might if it were free of interference. The scream was muffled instead, which made it feel heavier on Ruby's ears, as if ricocheting off the walls of the shed.

Ruby thought she recognized the voice, but she couldn't be sure. It sounded like Rusty, but that seemed off. Something didn't make sense.

In the moment, Ruby did the only thing that felt right. She fought with the shovel. She pulled on it frantically, twisting and jerking it until it slipped from the grasp of the door handles. It clanked against the wall as she tossed it to the side.

Outside, Rusty was still screaming — it was definitely Rusty now, she could tell. There was some other yelling too, maybe from her daddy or Bo, and lots of noise coming from inside her daddy's trailer. Using all of her strength, Ruby pressed her shoulder up against the shed's doors and pushed. As she did and the doors swung open, a big gust of wind spat in her face, licking her gashes with a cold tongue.

When she stepped out, the screaming stopped. It was as if someone was watching her, testing her, waiting to see if she would follow the rules or not. Her insides twisted as panic crept in. Her legs started to tremble.

Ruby thought of Bo and his firm instructions — that she wasn't to leave the shed under any circumstances until he or Rusty came to get her — and she felt guilty for disobeying him. But Bo didn't say anything about screaming or what to do if he or Rusty was hurt, so Ruby had to make a choice. Waiting for her brothers didn't seem like the right thing to do anymore.

Ruby looked across the field as far as she could see, her eyes squinting through the setting sun, and thought of her mama. Ruby didn't get a chance to see her very often, and she missed her every day. Things were different once, but that was a long time ago. Still, Ruby knew her mama would know what to do and would be able to help — she was still her mama, after all.

Before Ruby could take a step, there was another sound that came from inside the trailer. It was like an explosion — loud and booming and rattling. Ruby gasped when she heard it, turning toward the trailer to see what it was. But she saw nothing — no fire, no broken windows, nobody running away from the trailer in fright. She waited for five seconds, then ten, then five more. By the time she made up her mind to go get help, her legs had already started running. It was as if they already knew something the rest of her didn't. She listened to what they were telling her.

Tears streamed down her face as she ran, singeing her cuts as she feared they would, and she shouted. She shouted out for her mama, for her grandpa, for anyone who'd listen. Something was wrong inside her daddy's trailer, she could feel it, and she needed help.

CHAPTER EIGHT

A single gunshot roared through the sky, rocking the earth as if it were quaking. To Earl Travis, it brought back memories of the war. None of them were pleasant. The gunshot was heavy and unmistakable, exploding like a cannon on the battlefield, rattling the loose nails that were supposed to keep the floorboards attached to the base of the trailer.

Earl was at the sink in the kitchen when it happened. His hands were wet as he dropped to the floor like a sinking torpedo and wrapped his arms around his skull. The top of his right ear was missing, forming a crescent that tickled his forearm. The missing chunk of flesh was laying somewhere in a field in Vietnam.

Earl's body shook as images of his wounded brothers flashed through his mind — the voices screaming, the bloodstained grass, the toasted bodies. He held his breath until the noises stopped, until his world stopped spinning. Even though it was so long ago, it still felt so fresh and real, like Earl was right back there again, facing it all over. He swore he could feel the burnt grass in between his fingers sometimes, or smell the gunpowder when he stepped outside after a rainstorm. The bits of shrapnel in his back still stung when he sat just right.

Behind him, Earl felt someone's presence lurking. He could taste her decade-old perfume and feel the floorboards shift under his knees as she approached. A thick cough rattled Earl's eardrums. She was above him now, standing on her tiptoes, looking out over the field through the window. Earl wanted her to go away.

"Did you hear that?" the woman asked with a smoker's rasp. It was his wife, Beverly. "What was it?"

Earl stayed on the floor for another moment while the images and sounds of his youth starting crawling back into their hiding spots in his brain. They only came back during times like these, but when they did, they were as authentic as being there in the flesh. The horror was experienced all over again. Outside, Earl thought there'd be another gunshot, another explosion, but it never came.

Slowly, timidly, Earl pushed himself to his feet, using the countertop as a crutch, and splashed some water on his face. The faucet was still running full blast.

"What do you think it was?" Beverly asked again. She was looking in the direction of his son's trailer, her mouth gaped. She didn't even bother to ask if Earl was okay anymore.

Earl shook himself off. "It was a gunshot. A shotgun."

"How can you be so sure?"

"Just trust me, okay? I'd recognize a gunshot anywhere."

Beverly nodded.

She was thirty years younger than Earl and half as smart, but Earl kept her around for the sake of the kids — that's what he told himself; the truth was, he was fearful of being alone. And if not being alone meant he had to spend his remaining years with the woman he no longer cared much for, then so be it. At least he wouldn't die a lonely soul. Beverly was married to his son once upon a time, but that was long ago. Circumstances had changed a lot since then.

"I wonder what Lenny's up to this time," Beverly said. "Probably shooting squirrels again."

Earl groaned, disagreeing. That shot didn't sound like it came from outside.

"Oh my God!" Beverly shrieked, jumping. She cupped her mouth and brushed past Earl, nudging him with her shoulder.

"What? What's wrong?"

Beverly was already gone. She was outside on the steps before Earl saw it. He joined her on the porch to get a better look.

It was an unusual, but welcome sight. The kids weren't usually allowed over to visit unless Lenny escorted them himself, but not today. Ruby was by herself, though, running as fast as Earl had ever seen her run before, shouting something inaudible. It wasn't until she passed the plum tree and got closer to the trailer that Earl noticed the streams of tears running down her cheeks.

He stiffened.

Ruby's face was flushed and puffy, and was covered with red blotches that looked like blisters. Even more unusual, the boys were nowhere to be seen. Beverly shrieked again, and Earl cringed. Something was terribly wrong.

***

Ruby's legs burned like fire as she ran, the wind against her face stinging like dry ice. There was a heaviness in her chest that frightened her, but she kept running — she had no other choice. She ran as fast and as hard as she could, and she told herself she wouldn't stop running until she found help. She wouldn't stop running until she made it to her mama.

Out in the flat, the trailer her mama and grandpa shared was nearing, growing larger against the backdrop of the forest as she moved toward it. Ruby yelled out when she was close enough to be heard, her legs still pumping, her throat cold. The screen porch flung open as her mama stepped out onto the deck with a hand over her mouth as if she'd seen what happened firsthand. Ruby didn't stop running until she leaped into her mama's arms at the base of the stairs.

Her mama smelled of ash and rice, even though she tried to mask it with a double layer of perfume. Ruby hadn't seen her mama in weeks, but she hugged her like it had only been yesterday. Her hair was coarse and dirty, her clothes torn and stained with grease. Despite how badly her daddy tried to keep her away, Ruby still loved her mama more than anything in the world; she didn't care about all those other things.

"What's wrong, baby?" her mama asked as they separated from an embrace.

Ruby stood at the base of the steps, tears covering her cheeks, a split in her lip, and tried not to cry.

"What happened to your face?"

Ruby shook her head.

"It's okay, you can tell me." Her hand pulled away from her mouth as she spoke, showing off a handful of gaps where teeth used to be. There was one black tooth on the top, pointed on the edge and sharp, which looked like it might fall out any day now. It had been that way for as long as Ruby could remember.

Ruby shifted her eyes and met her grandpa's, who joined her mama on the porch. His eyes bulged and his mouth was open a crack, and he was staring at her like she was from another planet. Her grandpa had all of his teeth, although he took them out and put them in a cup of water at night. But at least they were white.

"How did you get those cuts?" her grandpa asked. He sounded angry. He descended the stairs without much grace and stood over her, his breath hot. "Did your daddy do that?"

Ruby didn't want to tell them what happened. It wasn't because she didn't want her daddy to get in trouble, because she didn't mind if he did. But instead, she was afraid of what he might do to her once he found out she was snitching. Her daddy always found out, no matter what. She remembered Rusty getting a nosebleed one time after he tried to tell their grandpa what their daddy did. Her daddy found out about it and brought Rusty into his bedroom to have a talk, and the next thing Ruby knew, Rusty's nose was crooked and bleeding. He didn't want to talk about it — Bo never wanted to talk about what happened to him either — but Ruby found it uncomfortable, even as a little girl. As far as she knew, Rusty never had a nosebleed before that, and she couldn't remember one since.

"Where are your brothers?" her mama asked.

Her grandpa was still hovering over her, air tracing the abrasions on her face with his finger. Ruby ignored it.

"In daddy's trailer."

"Why aren't they working in the field?"

Ruby shrugged. She looked away so she wouldn't have to lie to her mama's face.

"Ruby, baby, look at me." She used her longest finger to gently turn Ruby's face toward her. "Why are your brothers in the trailer?"

Tears welled up in Ruby's exhausted eyes and started to fall down her face again. It burned a little, but Ruby hurt inside too much to notice. She didn't want to tell, but she knew she had to. "Something happened, Mama."

"What, baby? What happened?" Her mama placed her hands on Ruby's shoulders and looked her straight in the eye. Ruby thought her hands felt cold at first, but then she realized it was just perspiration.

"Something bad."

"How bad? Tell me."

"Really bad."

CHAPTER NINE

Ruby told them what she knew. She told them about the gun Bo and Rusty found in the shed, about what Bo told her, about hearing Rusty scream, about hearing a loud boom. What she didn't tell them, though, was how loud Rusty's scream was, and how scary it sounded. She didn't tell them because she feared Rusty might have been shot with that gun.

Her grandpa disappeared into the trailer like he was in a hurry, leaving Ruby and her mama alone outside. Her mama walked around in a circle with a hand cupped over her mouth again, mumbling something Ruby couldn't understand. There was a faded gold chain around her neck with a cross hanging from it, and she rubbed the cross in between two of her fingers. Ruby always thought the necklace was pretty, but never knew what it was for.

Within minutes, her grandpa appeared back in the doorway wearing the same blue jeans he wore before. They were worn so often they'd turned almost gray, and there were holes down the legs and had faded patches on the knees that looked like permanent dirt marks. He wore the same type of shirt her daddy wore all the time, except her grandpa's didn't have yellow stains under the arms and didn't smell like beer. It was more stretched out in the front, though, from where her grandpa's belly was big.

In his hands was a heavy gun. It looked similar to the one Bo and Rusty had found in the shed, except this one was significantly shorter and had a long handle in the front. Ruby hadn't seen a gun like that before.

"What are you gunna do, Earl?" her mama said.
"I'm gunna find out what happened."
"Well, you don't need that thing to find out. Leave the M3."
"I ain't goin' in there unarmed. The last time I was unarmed my face nearly got blown straight off."
"That was fifty years ago."
"So what?"
Ruby stood still and watched as her mama turned away, apparently not having anything further to say to her grandpa.
"You girls go in the house now," her grandpa said. "Don't want nobody gettin' hurt."
Ruby felt an arm around her shoulder. It was bony and frail, and she knew it was her mama's. It didn't always feel that way — her mama had lost a lot of weight in the last couple of years for some reason; Ruby wondered if her mama was sick or something. She was led up the stairs and onto the porch, where she and her mama pushed further into the trailer. The porch was screened in just like her daddy's was, and the heavy door banged off the frame in the same way as it closed. Something pattered underneath the porch.

Inside the trailer, Ruby pulled out the step stool from its spot next to the refrigerator and unfolded it in front of the sink, then she climbed to the top and watched out the window. Her grandpa headed straight toward her daddy's trailer, the gun with the two handles dangling on his hip. The sun reflected off the steel roof in the distance and shone directly into her eyes, leading to an uncomfortable warming sensation that distorted her vision. She held up a hand to shield her eyes, but it was too late; she'd already lost sight her grandpa as he disappeared into the shadow of the plum tree.

***

The smell of blood was pungent and overbearing, still fresh. Rusty's stomach churned, his guts twisting like a corkscrew, threatening to force him to retch again. It happened once already, shortly after the shotgun went off, the stains on his shirt an unwelcomed reminder.

The body was already gone. The way the shell entered in through the Adam's apple and exited out the back of the neck caused a lot of spewing blood, but, luckily, it also meant it ended quickly. The body only staggered for a moment before succumbing to the loss of blood and inability to breathe. He backpedaled a few steps, stumbling, tripped over his own ankles and fell with a thud to the rug. Rusty didn't move closer to the body when it fell, but he knew by the sounds — the way his head smacked against the floor as if it were a sack of sand; the way the blood squelched as it pooled underneath the body almost immediately; by the gurgling that bubbled in the hole in his throat, then stopped — that he was dead.

Rusty wasn't sure what happened, exactly — how the shotgun went off, or what happened afterward. He remembered screaming as his father dug his fingers into his neck, his nails tearing into the flesh as if it were as soft as marshmallow. Rusty clenched his eyes shut and tightened his neck, then the gun went off.

After the body dropped, Rusty blacked out. When he came to, he sat on the cold tile with his back pressed against a section of wall that extended beyond the rest. There was vomit on the collar of his shirt and more crusted in the crevices between his lips. His philtrum was dry and caked with mucus, and the acidity was rancid. He was unsure how long he was out.

When he stood and went to take a closer look at the body, it was gone. The area rug where the body laid was gone too, as was the blood that puddled. The air still smelled like blood, though, and Rusty wondered if it would stay that way forever. He wondered again how long he'd been out.

A knock at the door startled him. His heart leaped, nearly toppling him onto his side. A deep man's voice yelled out through the screen on the porch, followed by the banging of wood against wood. Before Rusty knew it, he was no longer alone in his father's trailer. The room warmed, and the taste of heat kissed Rusty's crusty lips. He turned and faced his grandpa.

***

With his M3 clutched in his hand, its magazine loaded and ready to strike, Earl pushed his way into his son's trailer. His heart fluttered like it used to way back when. He heard some commotion in the kitchen after he yelled out for the boys, but neither one answered or came to the door. Earl was starting to suspect he was about to run into some trouble. In some ways, he relished the adrenaline rush.

"What's going on in here?" he asked when he entered the kitchen, finding only Rusty.

Rusty sat with his back against the wall, glassy-eyed, his arms dangling lazily at his sides as if they were bloodless. He tried to swallow, but it looked painful, his face scrunching. His t-shirt was stained with bile, and his face was as pale as the clouds on a sunlit day. Earl sniffed, capturing the scent of burnt metal and sulfur. He knew that smell. A metallic taste appeared on the tip of his tongue, which he licked away. He knew it was just in his mind, just more memories, but he could have sworn it was real.

Earl let the M3 dangle in his hand, the magazine whacking against his knee as it swung. The weapon was more than fifty years old and didn't need to be registered, which was good, because Earl wasn't supposed to have it. He'd taken it with him when he was discharged from the Army, feeling he deserved it for giving some of himself to the cause. It hadn't been fired since then, but only because Earl hadn't had a need to.

"Is that blood?" he asked, motioning to Rusty. Aside from the bile stains on his shirt, there were also dark splotches of red. Earl took a few steps closer, the M3 swinging like a pendulum, and saw more on Rusty's neck and face. Earl thought it looked like splatter.

On the opposite side of the room, past the sofa and through the notch in the wall that wasn't there when Lenny first bought the trailer, a door squeaked. Earl's fingers clenched around the grip of the M3 and tensed. He balled his free hand into a fist and held it waist-high as if he were preparing to toss a grenade at the sound. He held his position, his eyes locked and unblinking, until someone appeared in the doorway.

"Grandpa, what are you doing here?" It was Bo.

Some of the tension released from Earl's fingers, the M3 dropping back into a lazy pendulum. The bottom half of Bo's t-shirt was missing, an uneven tear crossing over his navel. What was left was covered in dark spots of reddish black, just like on Rusty.

"Why are you both covered in blood?"

Bo looked down at his shirt as if it were news to him. Rusty stood and averted his eyes, keeping them straight ahead. One of his hands was wrapped up in a cloth, and the other was pressed against the wall behind him as if he needed it to help his balance.

"I heard a shot," Earl said. "And now you're both covered with blood. What happened?"

Bo shuffled his feet and leaned his back against the same door frame he came in through. His chest rose rapidly as he breathed fast. It was faster than normal breathing, more labored, as if he'd just done aerobics.

"Where's your father?"

"Went into town," Bo said without hesitation, almost as if he'd rehearsed the line.

Earl took another step forward and peeked out the window. Lenny's rusted pickup was resting idly in the drive. "Where'd the blood come from?"

"Elk."

"Too early for elk."

Bo folded his arms over his chest and shrugged.

"What'd you do with it?"

"Got rid of it."

Earl shifted his eyes to Rusty, whose head was pointed downward and was staring at his feet. Earl wasn't the smartest man in the world, but it would've taken an idiot to think Bo wasn't lying. Earl knew he was. "Is that so?"

Earl held his position and slowly scanned the trailer, looking for the unknown. The television was switched off. There was a heavy blanket draped over the arm of Lenny's chair, the television remote resting on the table next to it. The kitchen smelled of char. Everything was orderly, maybe too much so, which intrigued Earl to investigate further. He took a few more steps forward.

When he crept past the chair, he noticed the area rug that was usually in front of Lenny's chair was missing. It was the color of mud with red swirls stitched into the fabric, and it was hard to miss. But it was gone. There was what looked like a water stain where the rug used to lay, but the red swirls and muddy upholstery were missing.

Earl could taste blood on his tongue again. And he could feel some on his hands, sticky like adhesive. He found Bo's eyes and said, "Why don't you boys head on over to my trailer? Your sister is worried sick about you."

Bo motioned to Rusty, who pushed past Earl, keeping his head down, and walked out through the screen porch, the wooden door bouncing on its frame. Bo held back a moment, took his time, and followed. Earl met his gaze and held it, the both of them at a stalemate that was bound to end badly. Their relationship had already been fragile for quite some time, although Earl couldn't remember where the tension between them originated from. Earl knew Bo was lying, and Bo knew Earl knew he was lying. But no more words were exchanged between them. Bo joined his brother outside the trailer.

Earl backpedaled and moved his gaze to the screen porch. Bo was saying something to Rusty in secret, which Rusty responded to with a nod. The boys took off toward Earl's trailer, their backs facing him, their feet lifting heavy work boots. The sun was near the horizon behind a canopy of trees in the distance, the dark woods preparing to awaken.

Earl held his gaze, the M3 unmoving on his hip, and watched them go. He licked his lips and got a mouthful of blood.

CHAPTER TEN

Rusty didn't realize he was covered with his father's blood. Distracted by the lingering taste in his mouth and smell of stomach contents on his shirt, he somehow missed it. Everything was hazy.

Not being dragged down by squelching boots or rotting toes, Bo walked faster than he. Rusty tried to hurry to keep up, but his feet felt like cement. The wrap on his hand was like a wrung sponge, still slightly wet and smelling of decay, but it was working, because the pain underneath was dulling.

It was a struggle to see their grandpa's trailer in the distance because of the increasing darkness, but Rusty knew the general direction in which they were headed. The air was still warm, but not as humid, and the temperature was starting to drop.

Darkness brought a cooler air that usually rejuvenated Rusty, but it only lasted until the darkness gave way to sunshine again the following day. Except, on this next day, Rusty knew, things were going to be different. He and Bo and Ruby would wake up to a new sun and fresh hope, maybe even a new life. He and Bo wouldn't be forced to spend their days in the tobacco field, baking in the sun, trying to ration their water. They'd be given clean water and three full meals every day and fresh clothes. They wouldn't be forced to snack on scarabs or June bugs if they got hungry after lunch, and they wouldn't have to beg for more to eat at supper. Yes, things would definitely be different from now on, Rusty told himself, because as far as he knew, Lenny was dead. His father, after all the years of physical abuse and neglect and emotional torment, was gone. And Rusty felt happier about that than he knew he probably should.

The trailer wasn't much further once they passed the plum tree. Bo was still ahead of Rusty, the distance between them growing. By the time Rusty finally caught up, Bo was sitting at the base of the plum tree, hidden by overgrown limbs that hung down like arms. When directly underneath the tree, Rusty looked up and caught his breath, feeling tiny compared to its wide girth. The top of the tree soared far above the tops of the trailers. Many of the tree's limbs were out of Rusty's reach, leaving hearts and Luisas and ovals of red and purple unplucked and hanging close to the branches. Many plums were missing from the limbs closest to the ground, but they'd grow back. They always did.

Rusty expected Bo to get up once he approached, but he didn't. He sat on one of the roots that rose above the ground with his hands on his knees and a blade of grass in his mouth. He spun the blade from one side of his mouth to the other with an ease that resembled perfection.

"Here," Bo said, tapping on the flat ground next to the root underneath him, "come sit."

Rusty was exhausted — both physically and emotionally — and knew he shouldn't. Sitting down and resting his aching feet was all he wanted to do, but he knew he might not have the strength to get up again if he did. So he stayed standing instead, not even using the trunk of the tree as a crutch. Darkness crept through the leaves.

"Fine," Bo said, "I'll stand too." And so he did. He pushed himself to his feet with a grace that made Rusty jealous. Bo seemed to be handling himself so much better, and Rusty didn't know how much strength he had left. He wasn't sure he could even make it to their grandpa's trailer before succumbing to the exhaustion. He was parched again.

"Let's just go," Rusty said. "We're almost there."

"We can't go to the trailer."

"Why not? Grandpa said we could."

"Didn't you see grandpa's face? He knows we're lying about dad."

"About what?" Rusty was still cloudy on what exactly happened.

Bo rolled his eyes and made a clicking sound with his tongue. "Don't joke, Rusty. You know exactly what I'm talking about."

Rusty didn't, but he didn't have the energy to argue about it either. Instead, he nodded.

"It's only a matter of time before grandpa notices dad's truck is still out front, then he'll know something is up."

This, Rusty did agree with. And he also thought he knew where Bo was headed with this, and he didn't like it one bit.

"So, we can't go to the trailer. Not tonight."

A moth landed on Rusty's shoulder, its weight so heavy he thought he might tip over. He stepped toward the trunk of the plum tree and leaned his hip against it. "Where are we going to go?"

"We'll hang out close by. We can set up camp off to the east." Bo pointed out past the tree line that formed a perimeter around the two properties. "That way we can see both trailers, watch what's going on. We can sneak into dad's trailer tomorrow and grab some food and new clothes and stuff."

Rusty looked toward their grandpa's trailer. He knew Ruby was inside with their mom, and he wanted it badly too. He also wanted supper and fresh water and a warm bath. But he thought Bo might be right — it actually sounded like a good idea. Their grandpa was Lenny's dad, and if he found out what really happened inside that trailer, well, Rusty wasn't sure what he might do. He wished he knew what happened himself, so to make a better judgment of the situation. All he had was Bo's word.

Rusty shifted his attention back to Bo, who was hardly noticeable with the darkness as his backdrop. His eyes shone when he blinked, deep and penetrating, convincing. Rusty knew he had to trust his brother's judgment on this one.

"What about supper?" Rusty asked. "I'm starving. I'm not sure I can wait until morning to eat."

Bo looked around, as if in deep thought. It only took a few seconds before he looked up and stood on the tips of his toes, reaching high above his head. A cool breeze brushed over Rusty and made him shiver, but he was still able to catch the plum that Bo tossed to him.

"Here," Bo said, "have one of these." He pulled at some of the lower branches until he had two handfuls of almost ripe plums. "And we'll save these for later."

Rusty couldn't argue with that.

Just then, a faint but familiar bang rustled through the sky. Rusty and Bo both stepped out of the shadow of the plum tree and looked toward their father's trailer. Their grandpa was on the steps of the porch, a gun in each hand. His military-grade machine gun was in his left, still dangling by his knee, and a shotgun hung in his right. Even from a distance, Rusty could tell it was their father's shotgun, the same shotgun that went off inside the trailer. The wooden door stopped bouncing off the frame once their grandpa stepped onto the dirt.

Rusty dipped behind the tree again, a pattering in his chest jolting him awake. His fingers dug into the plum in his hand, forcing juice to trickle down his fingers and wrist, just like the pus had earlier.

"Shit," Bo whispered. "He found it."

"Bev!" Their grandpa's voice was distant but clear.

"Rusty, we have to go now."

Rusty was frozen, his head spinning.

"Bev, get those boys out here. Them and me gotta' have a little talk!"

"Rusty," Bo said, two handfuls of plums still intact, two unblinking eyes desperate. "We have to go. Come on."

Rusty shook off his fear and ignored the hunger and the pain. The sound of their grandpa's voice was getting closer, but it was still far enough away. They had time if they moved. But, as Bo said, they had to go now.

Rusty followed Bo into the openness, only the darkness providing them with cover. Rusty's hands were empty now, having discarded the squished plum in the tall grass. The juice on his hands felt sticky and wet, but the smell of it made his mouth salivate. He wanted nothing more than to take a bite out of one of those plums and let the juices refill his body with some of the sugars he sweated out, but he'd have to wait. Once they reached the shelter of the woods, he told himself, that would be his reward.

They slithered like snakes in a field of tall grass, keeping their backs hunched and their feet moving. Their grandpa still hollered to their mom fairly consistently, which allowed Rusty and Bo to pump their legs even harder and run faster without fear of being heard. By the time they reached the edge of the forest, their grandpa was almost to the plum tree. Rusty knelt beside Bo, head down, his heart pumping so fast he thought he might pass out, and watched what their grandpa's next move would be.

Their grandpa vanished into the blackness of the plum tree's shadow, only to reappear on the other side a moment later. It was almost completely dark now, but the illuminated porch light on the trailer helped Rusty to locate their grandpa's reemergence. He kept walking toward the trailer, both guns swinging, his voice cracking as he hollered for their mother.

Rusty thought of Ruby and how she was doing, and if she was going to be okay during the night. He feared for her safety every night she'd been alive, and as strange as it seemed, he thought tonight might be the most worrisome of them all — he didn't know why he felt that way, but he did. And while he thought about that, while he wondered if he was ever going to see his baby sister again, he started to doubt if he and Bo were doing the right thing. Whatever happened inside the trailer was bad, and everyone seemed to know it except for him. He had so many questions that he thought Bo could answer, but he knew they'd have to wait until morning, like everything else. Tonight would be about survival, about finding a way, about making it until tomorrow. All the questions he had, all the uncertainties, would have to wait.

Bo nudged Rusty with an elbow and whispered, "Come on."

Rusty nodded and followed Bo the rest of the way, a bright white crescent moon lighting up the sky overhead. They slinked their way into the forest, slipping behind the trees and directly into the throat of the wilderness. They'd made it this far without being seen, which was something to be proud of. But, on the other hand, he also knew with certainty that tonight was going to test him like never before. He knew, one way or another, he was going to find out if he had what it took to become a man. The problem was, with all the pain and physical limitations holding him back, he wasn't sure he was up to it.

CHAPTER ELEVEN

Earl's shoulders were beginning to ache from carrying two heavy guns across the field. The shotgun he found was hidden under the bunk beds in one of the bedrooms down the hall, haphazardly, the bed skirt ruffled and scrunched up in one place only. Earl found it in a matter of minutes, and knew immediately that it hadn't been used to poach an elk. The dead giveaway was the blood on the barrel. The shotgun, Earl knew now, shot something at close range, and even a clever hunter wouldn't be able to get that close to an animal that size. Not ever. Earl knew he was looking for a human body. For Lenny's body. For his son's body.

The yellow glow of the light above the screen porch shone dimly from the fixture, forming a passageway that extended out a few feet in front of his trailer. A thin moon bowed behind the tops of the trees, leaving Earl to rely solely on the porch light to find his way home. It wasn't far between the two trailers, but it was a challenge in the darkness of dusk that was quickly becoming opaque.

Earl passed through the invisible property line that he knew existed ten or fifteen yards beyond the plum tree and crossed onto his portion. It wasn't his land, but the arrangement made it feel that way — he had free reign to do whatever he wanted. The arrangement seemed to work for everybody for their own reasons, although Earl's were dark. Lenny didn't know nearly as much as he thought he did.

It wasn't long after Earl passed through the unmarked property line that he stepped into the passageway of light, grasping his fingers around the butts of the guns as they both started to slip from his grip. He pushed up the porch steps, swung open the door on the screen porch, and made his way inside the trailer.

Beverly sat alone at the kitchen table, chewing on her nails until they bled, waiting for him. She didn't get to her feet when Earl walked in, and Earl didn't expect her to — that phase of their relationship had long since passed; Earl was just happy if they went a day without yelling at one another. Earl tossed the shotgun on the table in front of her, the stock heavy and a faded shade of brown, slamming into it like a gavel. Beverly leaped when it dropped.

"Didn't you hear me calling you?" Earl said, his eyes on her.

"No."

"I told you to bring them boys front and center. Where they at?"

"I ain't seen them."

Earl left the shotgun on the table and walked out of the kitchen. Beverly didn't follow him. He moved from room to room, checking each for the children. In the living room, the television was off and the sofa and recliner were empty. The blankets draped over each were unwrinkled and appeared to be unmoved, and the recliner was resting still. Earl moved out.

Opening the bedroom door, the bed Earl and Beverly shared remained unmade, the pillows and blankets tangled in a heap. A heavy, checkered comforter sat on the floor at the foot of the bed. A basket of dirty laundry was next to the door, the overbearing smell of a combination of seawater and chlorine wafting from it. Earl tossed the M3 on the bed and stepped back into the hall, shutting the door behind him.

The other bedroom was dark. Earl sensed a presence in the room, felt the heat of a body that wasn't his, recognized the sound of a child sleeping. He crept deeper into the bedroom, sliding alongside the bed that was larger than the one he and Beverly shared, and leaned in close. Ruby was in the center of the bed, alone, squeezing a pillow against her chest, soft breaths moving in and out of her nose. Earl smelled her hair, her skin, felt her breath on his face. Lilies and roses bloomed in his nostrils, sending rare cheerful thoughts rushing through him. He smiled. Ruby was here, and he was happy to have her. He was always glad when she visited.

Earl crouched down next to the bed, lowered his hand to Ruby's face, and felt the heat against his fingers, felt the pain in his own chest. The cuts were deep. There would be scars left behind if Ruby wasn't careful, and Earl feared she would grow up never loving herself the way she deserved to, having been marked by Lenny as if she were an object. Lenny was a monster, one in which Earl helped to shape, and Earl was ashamed of that.

He gritted his teeth and choked back tears, forced himself to look away. He couldn't help but wonder if it was all his fault in some way, as if there were something he could have done to stop it. Worse, he knew the answer, and it made him sick. He could have stopped Lenny a long time ago.

Earl shook it off. There was nothing he could do about it now. Everyone went through hard times in their lives, and this was no different. He tried to convince himself of that, but even he couldn't be persuaded by the propaganda. He could lie to other people, but he couldn't hide the truth from himself. No one could — that was the irony of it. He could go through life covering up the truth and telling falsehoods, and people would believe it. But he could never escape himself, no matter how hard he tried. He was partially responsible for what happened to Ruby, and he'd have to live with that until he was in the grave.

Once Earl regained control of himself and remembered what he was looking for, he became angry, but not at himself. Not this time. He needed to have a talk with those boys, yet they were nowhere to be found. They had some explaining to do, and Earl wasn't going to let them off the hook. They had to answer for what it is they'd done.

Tiptoeing, Earl backtracked out of the bedroom and shut the door, then stormed back into the kitchen. The shotgun was still on the table, and Beverly still chewed on her fingers as if she were starved. Earl stood in front of her, glaring, until she acknowledged him.

When she looked up, he said, "Where are they?"

"I told you. I ain't seen them."

"Did they come here?"

"No, I told you."

"Well, I told them to. Where'd they go?"

"How am I supposed to know?"

"You're their mother, ain't you?"

Beverly looked away and jammed another finger into her mouth. She said nothing. Earl kept staring at her with discontentment. He felt his skin warming as his blood pressure began to rise — Beverly had a way of doing that to him.

"See the blood?" Earl asked, nudging his head toward the barrel of the shotgun. "Bo told me they shot an elk."

Beverly turned her eyes toward Earl and blinked, the tint of her widened pupils disappearing only for a moment. She swallowed hard and looked away again, and dropped her nubby hands into her lap. Earl knew that look.

"I'm calling Clete," he said, then he took a step toward the corded rotary that hung on the wall.

"Wait!" Beverly leaped to her feet, suddenly attentive. Earl took the phone off the jack and held it in his hand, one finger poking into the plastic two. "So, you have seen them?"

"No, Earl. I told you I ain't."

"Then, what?"

Beverly stepped toward Earl and placed a soft hand on his forearm. Her skin was dry and chapped, but otherwise, the warmth was surprisingly pleasant. Beverly didn't touch him much anymore, and it took him by surprise. He looked into her eyes and saw a wetness forming behind them. Her reaction didn't do much for him anymore emotionally, not like it used to, but he could tell by looking at her now that she was telling the truth.

"Please. They're my sons."

Earl thought about it for a moment, then sighed. He hung up the receiver and looked deep into the dark brown of Beverly's eyes. He didn't have many feelings for the woman anymore, but she was still his wife. And as much as he knew what those boys did was wrong, he thought it might be in his best interest to let Beverly have this one. So he did. Wherever the boys ran off to, they couldn't have gone far. They're just kids.

"Okay, but if they don't show up by morning, I'm calling Cletus."

***

Even through the slits that were her eyes, tears fell like rain down Ruby's cheeks. She kept her eyes clenched, refusing to wipe away the tears as they tickled her skin, trying her hardest not to let herself sniffle aloud. She tried to hear what was being said on the other side of the door.

Ruby loved her grandpa because that's what she thought she was supposed to do, but there was something about him that made her uncomfortable. He treated her differently than he did her brothers. Maybe it was the heaviness that rose along with his voice as he spoke to her mama, or perhaps it was the way he towered over everyone like he was a statue. His breath got extra warm when he was angry, his shoulders stood even straighter than they usually were. He never laid a hand on Ruby or even threatened to — he was nothing like her daddy in that way. But sometimes, in those rare situations when Ruby would be alone with him in the trailer, she wished they weren't. She didn't know why she felt that way, but she did. She never told anyone about it.

The name Cletus was familiar to her. She'd heard her grandpa use it once or twice before, but as far as she could remember, she'd never met anyone with that name. It wasn't a common name, she knew, and she doubted more than one person shared that name in a small town like Plum Springs. She didn't think she could forget someone with a name like that.

Ruby missed her brothers. She gathered that they were all right, that nothing bad happened to either of them inside of her daddy's trailer, which she was thankful for. But she also gathered that something, possibly bad, happened to her daddy. She thought back to the scream she heard from earlier and tried to picture what may have happened inside the trailer. She had no idea. At the time, she was sure the scream came from Rusty, but that didn't make sense anymore. The scream, she assumed now, must have come from her daddy.

Still with the mist tickling her lashes, Ruby turned onto her side and buried her face into a pillow, the warm air surrounding her face like a heater, the smell of her grandpa's aftershave still billowing in the empty space next to her. He made her uncomfortable when he touched her face, but she was feeling better now that he was gone, less tense. Her cheeks were throbbing.

She really missed her brothers.

The three of them shared the bed whenever they stayed over, and she thought she could smell them both on the sheets, even though she knew she was alone. She placed an open hand on one of the other pillows to make sure, and the emptiness of it made her sad. She hadn't spent a night away from her brothers. Not ever.

Ruby felt alone.

She longed for the warmth of Bo's strong hands as they stroked her hair until she fell asleep. She craved the comfort of Rusty's whispers when only she and he were awake late into the night. She missed the way they'd all curl up together when it was cold, and the way they'd all spread out with only their toes touching when it was too hot. But most of all, as Ruby lay by herself with only the pillows and happy memories to keep her company, she wished they'd be here when she woke up in the morning. Not only because she needed them and missed them, but also because her grandpa was going to ask her what happened in the trailer, and she didn't know anything. And she also knew her grandpa wouldn't like to hear that.

CHAPTER TWELVE

It wasn't long before the sounds of the caliginous forest started to frighten Rusty. It began with the ruffling of nearby leaves, followed by the pattering of small feet and a hushed squeal that sounded muffled. A slapping noise surrounded them, resembling more of a squeaking sneaker than a nocturnal beast. But then the slapping stopped and the flapping of tiny wings began — hundreds of them, colonized — moving closer to where Rusty and Bo were walking, close enough so Rusty could feel the chill on his skin as the wings passed by.

Rusty screamed and dropped to the ground, covering his head with his arms as if they were being bombed. To Rusty, it felt that way. It felt like they were being attacked by the small winged creatures, surrounded and forced into surrender like prisoners. Rusty kept his arms over his head and twisted his torso violently as if trying to keep away wasps or black flies. He thought of the giant horse fly that tormented him earlier, and he wondered if it rounded up its winged friends to help finish the job.

Rusty's throat burned as he shrieked, the high-pitched echo of his voice bouncing off the oaks that suffocated him. The branches were thick and full of leaves, and they hung over him as if they were dripping wax. What was visible of the crescent above was dull behind the thickened limbs, the oaks dimming it as if they were one big lamp shade.

As quickly as the attack of the night creatures came, it passed. The flapping of the wings subsided, fading into the deep blackness of the forest, leaving only a trail of echoed squeals behind. Rusty was still on the ground, his chest now pressed into the leaves, a sharp rock causing a dull pain in his belly. He breathed in heavily and a cloud of sand filled up his nostrils, making him cough. There were particles of dirt and twigs and small stones making indents into his good hand, while his bad hand still ached. He tried to pull the stones out without it hurting — they were in deep — not realizing he'd fallen so hard in the first place.

He sensed Bo was near him, but he didn't know where or how close. His vision was mostly black. Rusty pushed himself to the sitting position, the collar of his boot pulling as his feet became untangled underneath him. There was a dampness in the back of his pants that made him squirm.

"Are you okay?" It was Bo.

Rusty felt the warmth of Bo's stale breath on his face as he hovered over him, its odor strikingly pungent. A noticeable trace of sweat hit his nose. "What was that?" he asked when he stood, the moisture in his boots squelching as he wriggled his toes.

"Bats, I think."

"Bats!"

"Don't worry, they ain't gunna hurt you."

Rusty smoothed his shirt and straightened his back, then remembered Bo couldn't see him. "I know that. I ain't scared." He hoped Bo couldn't tell he was lying.

"Good. Then let's go."

Rusty followed Bo out into a clearing.

There was a gap between the trees where the light from the moon crept through, giving Rusty's eyes a chance to adjust. The trees went on for miles, stretching to the edge of the earth and extending up toward the stars, close enough to touch them. Rusty wished he could climb to the tops of one of the trees to see just how close he could get to the top of the world. He always wondered if the heavens were beyond the stars, or if one had to pass through the galaxy first. Or if the heavens even existed at all, or it was just a fictional place that grownups made up to help them feel better about their own lives. All at once, the stars blew and the tops of the tallest trees began to sway. Being as small as he was in comparison, Rusty didn't feel it, but he saw it. To him, on the ground, the night was still.

On the other side of the clearing, the biggest oak tree of them all sat unmoving, the wind above not strong enough to have an effect on it. Like with the plum tree in between the two trailers, its roots rose above the ground and formed a row of cubbyholes. The roots stretched out like welcoming arms as if it were a wise man offering a bed, and its wisdom. On the base of the trunk where the roots were raised were small caves, each one wide and deep enough to hold a child. Bo was already climbing into one, disappearing as the cave swallowed him whole.

From somewhere deep inside the forest, a wolf began to howl. Rusty didn't know much about wolves, but, to him, it sounded hungry. He did know that wolves traveled in packs, so one howl meant others would likely follow, and one hungry wolf meant there'd be others, too. Small dots crawled out from underneath his skin and covered his body with bumps at the thought of it.

More leaves ruffled at his back. Big, strong wings flapped far above his head. An angry owl hooted. Rusty felt green eyes staring at him, yellow ones penetrating his skin with a malice that only the forest could offer. He imagined his own blood dripping from the canines of a black bear, staining the floor beneath a dark, murderous red. He pictured his dead body lying face down on a bed of moss, his limbs and muscles and bones being torn apart by rabid bobcats or coyotes. In his mind, he saw the horse fly laughing, making a mockery of Rusty's mutilated body with all of its forest friends. His mind kept playing tricks on him, and it was working. He was getting scared again.

Panicked, Rusty scurried across the clearing, sticks cracking under his boots as if they were fractured bones — maybe that's what his would sound like when they were snapped in two. He felt unsafe standing alone, as if being in the open was a means of offering himself up as sacrifice. He hesitated as he leaned over a cubbyhole at the base of the tree, smelling the bark, but only slightly. He climbed over the edge and his tired fingers wrapped around the root, the unevenness of it similar to the bark that lined the trunk. The cave wasn't as deep as it looked, covering only up to his knees as he stood. But when he lay on his back and pulled his knees toward his chest, the roots covered him completely, wrapping itself around him like a cocoon.

As his breathing slowed, Rusty felt safer being out of the clearing. But he was still fully aware that, if found, his defense against an attack was limited. With hardly anywhere to move, even rolling onto his side would be difficult. If it came down to it, he wondered if playing dead would be his best chance. Pretending or not, without some luck, Rusty knew his cave could easily become his coffin tonight. He held his injured hand close to his chest, hoping the hungry wolves wouldn't smell the blood underneath the wrap and come looking for him. He didn't want to be supper tonight.

In the hole next to him, Bo was chewing on something, snapping as he bit, reminiscent of the sound it made when biting into an apple. "Incoming," Bo said, his voice calm and steady, not at all scared.

Rusty was envious of how strong Bo was, of how much of a man he was. It was yet another reminder of how far Rusty still had to go.

Out of nowhere, something oval and soft and squishy fell from the sky and landed on Rusty's forehead. The impact wasn't painful, but a sticky, wet residue remained on his face once the object rolled away. Rusty sat up, feeling for the object that had slipped between his legs. When he did, a second object flew at him, this one landing on his belly.

"What's this?" Rusty asked, grabbing the first item, rubbing a finger over the spherical surface. He pulled it toward his nose and took a whiff. The object felt leathery in his hand, but he didn't recognize the smell at first.

"Supper," Bo said, his mouth full of whatever it was.

Rusty leaned forward and took another whiff. It smelled like dirt, but there was something sweet about it, too. He closed his fingers around it until it flexed, then he squeezed until a cold liquid swam in between his fingers and ran onto his chest. He brought his hand to his face again, this time sticking his tongue out and licking the substance. A bitter tang rushed through the tip of his tongue, the tartness forcing one eye closed. But instantly, he craved more. Rusty bit into the soft part of the object, sucking out the juice and flipping the skin around inside his mouth.

By now, Rusty knew he was chewing on a plum, and it was delicious. He remembered when Bo grabbed two handfuls before they rushed into the forest, and he was reminded how hungry he was as he chewed. Rusty scoffed the first one down without tasting it, then he lay on his back and ate the second more slowly, enjoying the flavor. He closed his eyes and savored it. He used his front teeth to peel away the skin, chewing it until it disintegrated in his mouth. He meticulously undressed the plum until only the squishy part was left, then he peeled away those layers until only the core remained in the palm of his hand. He licked his lips and sucked his fingertips and discarded the core, then he crossed his arms over his belly.

He smiled, satisfied, for he knew if this was the last meal he'd ever have, he could accept it, knowing he enjoyed it.

CHAPTER THIRTEEN

Morning came and the boys still hadn't arrived. Earl felt like Beverly might have pulled a fast one on him, as if she knew what they were up to and gave them a head start on running. He was fuming about it, and he couldn't put it past Beverly to do something like that — she'd choose her kids over him a hundred times out of a hundred.

He twirled the rubber coil around his fingertips, squeezing until his fingers were purple. His throat was scratchy and the joints in his knees were aching from standing, but he kept his eyes on Beverly. Her hands were crossed and resting on top of the kitchen table, her foot tapping repetitively on the linoleum underneath. She tried and failed to remove more of her fingernails with her teeth.

"Where are they?" Earl asked.

Beverly stayed quiet.

"Where are those boys of yours, Bev? I know you know."

"I don't know, Earl."

Earl let the coil unwind around his fingers. It took only a few seconds for the tingling to stop and for the color to return to normal. Except for the bruise that was implanted into the skin underneath the nail on his index finger — that was permanently discolored. He eyed the shotgun that sat idly on the kitchen table still, the blood on the barrel dried, the red faded to pink. He thought about his son, wondering if he suffered, debating whether or not he actually cared. And he thought about those boys and what drove them to do what they did. He thought he knew.

"I'm calling Cletus."

Beverly spun in her chair and faced him, but said nothing. She begged him with her eyes, pinching them together until tears fell. But Earl wasn't going to fall for it this time. Whether or not Beverly knew where those boys were didn't matter anymore. The sun was awake now, which meant Earl had waited long enough. He did what he promised he would.

He reached for the rotary and began to dial the number. The coiled cord hung at his waist, brushing up against his belly if he stood in the right spot. When the call connected and the ringing sounded through the earpiece, Earl pressed his back against the wall and faced Beverly. She still had desperation in her eyes, but she knew better than to speak her mind; Earl's decision was final. She shoved a finger in her mouth.

"Cletus? It's Earl. Listen, we've got a problem here."

"What is it?" Cletus said between chesty hacks.

"It's Lenny — something's happened. And I think those boys are responsible."

***

When Rusty opened his eyes, he was surprised to be alive. The sounds of the night had faded and were replaced by innocent chirping from morning birds and crickets. A monarch landed on the edge of Rusty's cubbyhole and sat, watching him, its antennae humming. The black lines against the orange backdrop of its wings were split, giving the appearance of broken glass. Rusty sat up and leaned in for a closer look, startling the wonderful creature. It spread its wings and flew off, the orange and black and white forming a brilliant kaleidoscope in the sky. Rusty watched it go, amazed at how quiet and peaceful the forest seemed.

His neck was stiff. He tried to twist his head from side to side, but couldn't, the muscles too taut from lying uncomfortably in the cubbyhole overnight. He hadn't noticed the discomfort initially.

When Rusty looked down at his fingers, which were stuck together as if glued, he gasped. Blood covered the palm on his good hand, seeping in between his fingers and staining parts of the tips. The tips of his fingers on his bad hand were stained too, and there were some bloody spots on the outside of the wrap. His hands trembled as he studied them, turning them over and back, the muscles tensing in his neck causing a stabbing pain. A shallow hum developed in his throat and crept from his mouth, making a sound that he never heard before. Panic was setting in, he could sense it, but he didn't understand why his hands weren't in pain. He thought maybe he was in shock.

"What's wrong?" Bo said, popping his head out of his cave and peeking over the edge of the root, his eyes wide.

Rusty held up his hands higher and tried to speak, but couldn't. His entire body was beginning to convulse as he wondered what happened and where the blood was coming from. He didn't feel pain.

Bo locked his gaze on Rusty's bloodied hands and kept them there, motionless, for a short time. His face stayed neutral, his lips touching, his eyes resting normally. After a few seconds, Bo's lips parted and he smiled, small indents forming caves on his cheeks. His head disappeared back into his cubbyhole, which was followed by laughter. Bo howled uncontrollably, sharp intakes of breath breaking it up only occasionally. There was a slapping sound of skin hitting skin, and Rusty knew Bo was slapping his knee — he did that when he laughed really hard, but it'd been quite a while since that happened.

Rusty was frozen where he sat. While his hands bled and his chest tightened, he couldn't understand why Bo wasn't helping him. When the laughter subsided, Bo's head reappeared over the edge of the root. His face was flushed with a deep shade of red and his teeth were showing through his open mouth. As much as Rusty liked to see his brother laughing and smiling, he found it to be entirely distasteful at the time. But at the same time, the laughter helped to ease some of whatever was intruding Rusty's body, as the knot in his chest loosened and the bulge in his throat softened.

"Why are you laughing?" Rusty said when he was finally able to speak again.

"You." Bo's laughter started back up again.

"Why? Don't you see my hands?" Rusty held them up as high as he could, stretching until his neck hurt.

Bo laughed harder. His head bobbed below and above the edge of the root as if he were surrounded by water, waves forming as the water crashed against the shore. It went on for a couple minutes like that, and Rusty grew frustrated. He lowered his hands and crossed his arms, feeling as if Bo played a trick on him.

"Smell your fingers," Bo said, struggling to find a break in the laughter.

Rusty hesitated, but he did it. He brought his bloodied hands to his nose and inhaled, then he felt his face go flush.

"I'm the same way," Bo said, holding his hands over his head so Rusty could see. By now, Rusty already felt embarrassed, having looked down and recognized the red on his shirt was much darker than the shade on his hands —

almost purple. He recognized the sweetness of the dried plum juice on his hands. Bo lost it again. He howled louder than before, sending a nearby hummingbird scurrying from the treetops and booming echoes through the forest. When he snorted, Rusty finally let go of his embarrassment and laughed too. It was okay to laugh at yourself sometimes, and so he did. Along with Bo, Rusty laughed long and loud until his belly hurt and he could hardly breathe. Eventually, the pain in his neck disappeared too, which allowed him to laugh even harder. It was the first time he and Bo laughed together like that in forever, and Rusty didn't stop until he peed himself.

CHAPTER FOURTEEN

The mood changed when they got to the edge of the forest. There was an eerie silence that surrounded the two trailers, creating an aura of mystery. There was no wind or signs of wildlife or nature sounds. Only silence. Dark, heavy silence. While the sun was out earlier, it was now hidden behind faded, ominous gray clouds that showed up out of nowhere. It was still warm — Rusty's neck was drenched from the humidity — but the air smelled like rain.

As Rusty crouched next to Bo, looking out over the empty field, he felt the swamp in his boots. Even without wriggling his toes, he could tell his boots had gotten even heavier than they were before. The moisture seeped into the slits in the material, making the soles of his feet feel like loofahs. Between the dampness of the air and the moisture in his socks, his boots were like anchors on his feet.

Rusty breathed heavily, his chest tight over where his lungs were. The laughter that he shared with Bo was now only a fading memory, and all he could feel was the fungus growing in his boots, along with the wetness around his groin. While he survived the night on two plums, he was hungry again. His belly was eating at itself, his guts contracting each time he took a breath.

Rusty couldn't see their father's entire trailer, but he could see their grandpa's. There was no movement in or around it, which he found to be strange. Usually, their grandpa was outside already, shooting at squirrels or digging shallow drainage ditches or setting up traps to catch coyotes or using a metal detector to hunt for buried treasure. He usually spent his mornings outside until it got too hot — Rusty was always envious that he could go inside whenever he wanted.

Rusty closed his eyes and listened hard for Ruby's pretend voice that she'd use when playing with her dolls. He couldn't hear it. Maybe he and Bo were too far away to hear, even though he knew the bedroom window would be open — it was always open, since the frame was warped and wouldn't close completely.

Nearby, Bo appeared to be in deep thought. His neck was dipped low, his shoulders hunched, and he was counting something on his fingers. Rusty watched him for a moment and tried to guess what it was, but nothing made sense to him.

"What do we do now?" Rusty said. His knees were getting tired from crouching, so he dropped them to the ground and knelt in the dew.

"I figure we have two options." Bo switched his eyes from their father's trailer to their grandpa's. "We can stay close to the trees, then make a run for the trailer." He pointed in the direction he was looking, making an arrow in the sky with his fingers. "Or we can make a run for the plum tree, then straight back to the trailer from there."

Rusty thought about both options and wasn't sure he liked either one. To him, cutting across the field diagonally would be the quickest route, but there must have been a reason why Bo didn't suggest it, so he didn't suggest it either.

"What do you think?" Bo asked, looking at him.

At first, Rusty didn't like being put on the spot — his belly twisted. But then he thought about it and recognized that Bo was offering him the chance to make a choice, that Bo was giving him a chance to be a man. He liked that. He liked being given that kind of power. He puffed his chest out, ignoring the pee in his pants, and said, "Let's go the tree."

Bo nodded but didn't say anything. He seemed to be satisfied with the decision, as if he made it himself. Rusty wanted to smile, but he fought it.

"Are you ready?" Bo said, taking one final glance between the two trailers. "It looks like the coast is clear."

Rusty nodded. He waited for Bo to step out into the open first before following. Rusty did just as Bo did, running with his neck and back leaning forward, head down. His legs were pumping hard, but the cement in his boots was weighing him down, causing him to trail back behind Bo. As he ran, the humidity blowing through his hair like an oscillating fan, Rusty remembered a movie he saw with his dad when he was little. There was a scene where two men in dark suits ran away from a helicopter, keeping their bodies low. That's what Bo looked like from behind — one of those men running away from the aircraft — and Rusty thought it was badass. Knowing he looked the same, Rusty felt his lips widen into a grin, giving him a sudden burst of energy. The cement blocks in his boots started to splinter, his feet breaking through it as if they were jackhammers, his legs vibrating, and he picked up speed. Never feeling more like a man, he ran as hard and as fast as he ever had in his life, his muscles burning, until he reached the plum tree. He was only a step behind Bo when he got there.

Continuing to follow his brother's lead, Rusty held out his arm, using the tree's trunk against his good hand to stop his momentum. His palm began to sting as he spun himself around, the coarseness of the tree's covering cutting into him. Rusty squeezed in next to Bo, their backs against the trunk, facing their father's trailer. Rusty tried to catch his breath. But before he could, Bo took off running again.

Rusty's head fell in exasperation, his lungs pinching, his breath wheezing as he inhaled. He needed a few seconds to recover, his burst of energy burned off just as quickly as it came. Only he didn't have a few seconds. He knew if he didn't start running now, he might not ever catch up to Bo again. Without looking over his shoulder, he pushed off the plum tree and kept moving.

By the time he approached the trailer, Rusty's feet were barely off the ground. The toes of his boots scrapped the ground with each step, his ankles rolling slightly in the grass, his body lumbering toward the finish line. He imagined this is what it was like to run a marathon, and he wondered how anyone could make it to the end, or why they'd even want to try. Rusty made it up the stairs and pulled open the porch door, then collapsed into his father's trailer. The last thing he heard before succumbing to the blackness was the sound of wood pounding against wood, followed by a quiet buzzing that could have been his horse fly friend, back for more.

***

Something cold and wet rushed over Rusty's face, startling him awake. He coughed and choked and spat onto the floor as he rolled onto his side. His chest was still heavy and his heart pounded like a drum. His ears rang. Everything was trembling. Rusty tried to sit up, but the muscles in his arms and shoulders were weak. His hand slipped out from underneath him and his chest slammed against the floor. It didn't hurt, but the surprise snatched away his breath for a moment. Underneath his chest was a puddle, whatever it was wet and soaking his shirt and cooling his skin.

"Rusty?" Bo's voice was barely audible, blurred from Rusty's haze. "Rusty, you in there?"

Rusty felt something on his shoulder, but he was too weak to reach for it. Struggling, he rolled onto his back and breathed in hard, only to wince in pain as the air stung his lungs. When he found the strength to open his eyes, he saw that Bo stood over him with a metal bucket dangling from one hand, and something white and plastic in the other.

"What happened?" Rusty asked once he came to, still on his back, his eyes pointed toward the heavens.

Bo's forehead was wet, the droplets of sweat gleaming off a reflection of glass to his right. He wiped it with his wrist and appeared to exhale as color crept back into his face. "You had an attack," he said, leaning forward. "Take this." He pushed the mysterious plastic object toward Rusty, his hand mostly steady.

Rusty's vision was blurred still, but after he blinked a few times, the fogginess subsided. There was a metallic cartridge sticking out from the top of the white plastic casing with some sort of pharmaceutical label on it that Rusty was unable to read. As the seconds passed and Bo's wobbly hand approached Rusty's face with his thumb resting on the top of the cartridge, Rusty recognized the object. He tried to raise his arm and take it from his brother, but his muscles fought him. Instead, he forced his jaw open and let Bo slide the base of the plastic object into his mouth. The combination of wet plastic and cool filtered air hit his lips and brushed over his tongue.

Bo pumped the top of the cartridge twice, then a third time, and Rusty's mouth filled up with cold mist. He pinched his lips closed and breathed in the mist, which provided his chest with instant relief. A chill ran through Rusty's body and he felt alive, like he could breathe again. His lungs were clear when he took another deep breath and sank further into the hardwood beneath his back.

Within minutes, Rusty sat up and spread his legs out and pushed them away from his body, beginning to feel almost like himself again. He wasn't sure how long he'd been out. "What happened?"

"You had an asthma attack. You fell as soon as you stepped into the trailer."

Rusty thought about it and tried to recall, but drew a blank. "How long?"

"Only a minute or two."

Rusty nodded, relieved. He and Bo still had a job to do.

"Take this," Bo said, handing Rusty the inhaler. Rusty took it and slipped it in his pocket. The cartridge was heavy, nearly full.

Bo helped Rusty to his feet and led him into the kitchen. His balance was rocky at first, his center of gravity uneven, but he gathered his footing not long after stepping into the kitchen and leaning against the still filthy counter. Flies were enjoying the same stack of blackened toast as well as the blood, which emitted a strong coppery odor along with a metallic taste in the air. His stomach churned as he thought about what happened the day before, bile forming in his throat. Rusty knew their father was dead from a shotgun wound to the neck, but didn't know what exactly happened, or where the body was.

Rusty insisted to Bo that he was feeling better, which was the truth, and Bo took him at his word. Bo left him alone and found a backpack in the pantry across the kitchen. He began to fill it up with canned food and matches and other supplies from the pantry. Rusty crossed the room and went toward their bedroom, which opened across the hall from the other bedroom, as Bo began removing empty beer cans from the trash and filling them up under the faucet.

Lenny's bedroom door was closed and probably locked, because it always was. Rusty and Bo and Ruby weren't allowed in there, and none of them cared to know what was on the other side of the door. The last time Rusty was in there was the previous winter, and that was to be punished because he missed a spot on the porch steps when putting down salt to cover the ice, and Lenny slipped. Lenny swung the heavy leather belt with all his might against Rusty's bare skin. Rusty's cheeks stung for weeks afterward. Even six months later, Rusty could feel the welts across his backside if he ran his finger across it a certain way.

Inside the bedroom he and Bo and Ruby shared, Rusty slid open the closet door and grabbed the backpack he brought to school. He unzipped it. Ruby's bed was tight against the far wall, while the bunk beds he and Bo shared were on the opposite end, blocking the only window. Rusty slid open the drawers to the wooden bureau that stood as tall as he and started piling in spare clothes for him and Bo. He grabbed dirty t-shirts and ripped jeans and socks with holes in the heels until the bag was full. He shoved one fresh pair of underwear for each of them into his pockets and backtracked out of the bedroom. Bo was calling his name when he hit the hallway.

"What?" Rusty said as he entered the kitchen, fighting with the zipper on his backpack to climb over the hill at the peak. Bo's bag was full too, and he was crouched behind the counter, his back against a cabinet door.

"Get down!" Bo said, waving his hand toward the floor.

Rusty dropped to his knees. "What's wrong?" His airwaves were still clear, but his heart was thumping hard again.

"We're in trouble. We have to sneak out the back."

"Why? What's wrong?"
"Don't get up, but he's here, over at grandpa's."
"Who?"
Bo gritted his teeth. "Cletus."

CHAPTER FIFTEEN

Leaving a hushed Beverly inside, Earl stepped out of the trailer and waited on the porch for Cletus to pull up. The silence at his back was so quiet it was deafening, but it told him more than words ever could. Beverly, he knew, was distraught about what was happening. It must be her worst nightmare.

Rain began to fall. Earl wrapped his fingers around the splintered wood at the base of the screen, using his weathered hands to support his weight. He looked past the tightly woven squares of metal wires and let a light mist brush against his face without wiping it clean.

Outside, balding tires rumbled over gravel, stones popping as Cletus's car approached. The strip of lights on the roof flashed once, the swirls of red and blue shining brightest from the grill. The wiper blades were gliding along the glass like squeegees, the silicon squeaking as they touched over a dry spot. Earl stepped out of the porch and into the rain, his shoulders taking the brunt of it.

Sheriff Cletus parked his squad car next to Earl's truck and joined Earl in the elements. The brim of his hat went all the way around, the oak brown clashing with the softness of his uniform, creating a juxtaposition that was pleasant on the eyes. Earl felt a warmness in his presence, but he knew it wouldn't last, not after what he was about to tell him.

"How you doin', Clete?" Earl said, shaking Cletus's hand. His grasp was as solid as stone, as it always was. If Sheriff Cletus had a last name, no one knew what it was. Details like that didn't matter much in Plum Springs, so everyone just called him Cletus. It didn't halt Earl's curiosity from time to time, though.

"Just fine." The sheriff spat something brown onto the dirt of the driveway, muddying a puddle. He wiped the corner of his mouth with the side of his hand and flicked away the leftovers. "Are you going to tell me what's going on?"

Droplets of rain hung from the brim of Cletus's hat as if they were diamonds, but he paid no attention to them. The green of his eyes shone like opals through the crown of the water diamonds, their uniqueness mesmerizing Earl for a second. When he caught himself staring, he jammed his hands into his pockets and looked up, trying to find something else to concentrate on. Everything above was covered in a blanket of somber gray, patches of white absent. One particular cloud was darkening as it crept over the canopy of trees and rolled toward the trailer. It seemed to be moving fast, and Earl didn't much like the look of it. He guessed it would be mere minutes before they'd be in the heart of the storm.

"Can we step inside?" Earl said. "That way we can get out of the rain. And the boys' sister is in her bedroom. I think she might know a thing or two about what's going on."

"Fine," Cletus said, and he followed Earl into the trailer.

**

Ruby sat on the edge of the bed, her feet suspended above the floor as if she were hovering. She'd been awake for a while but afraid to leave the bedroom — she'd heard her mama and grandpa arguing again. Ruby's sadness pressed in on her even more, knowing now that her brothers were still missing. The bed sheets were only ruffled where she slept, as near to the edge of the mattress as possible. She hoped by saving them a spot next to her, they might come and take it.

But she was wrong.

Outside, a car door closed. The sound came from somewhere on the opposite end of the trailer, away from where the bedrooms were. Ruby got up and went over to the window to try and get a peek. There was an opening at the bottom of the window frame where it wouldn't close all the way, so she put an ear toward it and listened. The air felt muggy against her cheek, which was splashed with rain drops. The cuts stung.

As she listened, she thought she could hear two men talking, but the conversation was drowned out by the pattering of rain against the steel roof of the trailer. The voices quickly turned to silence, and the quiet in the trailer turned to anything but.

Ruby's mama said something aloud, which was followed by two different male voices, the first one Ruby recognized as her grandpa's. The second voice was deeper than her grandpa's, and scarier, and Ruby's belly began to twist. The thud of heavy boots and lighter ones pounded against the floor, sending the trailer rattling beneath Ruby's feet. The thuds got louder and louder as the boots came closer, starting at one end of the hallway and ending up at the other. A third set of feet accompanied them, Ruby could tell, although they were much softer than the two. Even though Ruby knew the three sets of feet were just outside the bedroom door now, a gentle knock on the door still startled her, making her jump.

"Ruby?" It was her mama's voice. "Are you in there? Are you awake?"

She didn't know why, but Ruby hurried back to the bed and slid under the covers. Even though she was already hot, she pulled the blankets up close to her chin and clenched her eyes shut.

The bedroom door squeaked open, and Ruby could sense the presence of other people right away. The room felt smaller, the walls closer, the temperature rising. The gentlest pair of feet approached the bed and someone sat on the edge of it. Ruby kept her eyes closed as her mama stroked her hair, the lavender on her skin subtle, but still recognizable. Ruby felt her mama's weight lean over her as she placed a soothing hand on Ruby's knee and began to hum into her ear in a tone just above a whisper.

"Ruby, baby, wake up."

Ruby held out for another moment, fully enjoying the intimacy from her mother that she missed so much.

"Ruby-Sue?"

When her mama stopped caressing her hair and lifted her hand from Ruby's knee, Ruby gave in. She slowly opened her eyes and pretended to yawn, although she didn't know if she fooled anyone or not. Her mama smiled at her.

"Hi, baby."

"Hi, Mama."

"Your grandpa would like to talk to you about what happened with your brothers yesterday. Will that be okay?"

Ruby felt her throat tighten.

"You remember Sheriff Cletus, don't you?"

Ruby sat up and looked past her mama and at the two men standing in the doorway. A man wearing a police uniform and a big hat stood on one side of the door, while her grandpa stood on the other. Sheriff Cletus was the one wearing the heavy boots she heard, the ones on his feet as black as midnight. Ruby looked back to her mama and nodded, although she didn't recognize the sheriff. But the name she heard her grandpa say the day before made sense now.

"Good, they'd like to have a few words with you."

Ruby swallowed hard and massaged her throat with the base of her tongue. She really wanted to see her brothers. "I'm hungry."

Her mama smiled at her again, her pointed teeth showing. "Sure, baby. Come out into the kitchen and I'll make you some cereal. We can talk there."

Her mama tossed the blankets to the side and helped Ruby out of bed, smiling patiently while Ruby pretended to stretch. Ruby's grandpa and the sheriff left the bedroom and started down the hall, their boots clanking against the floor again. Ruby and her mama eventually followed.

Ruby was set up at the kitchen table with a bowl of cereal and a tall glass of milk. There was a gun on the table like the one Bo and Rusty found the day before, but her grandpa told her to push it to the side while she ate. That's what she did. Her mama sat in the chair next to her and folded her hands on her lap while Ruby spooned some cereal into her mouth. The little circles didn't have much flavor, but compared to what she was used to, the unflavored circles were like a delicacy.

Her grandpa and the sheriff stood quietly while Ruby ate, the tiny circles crunching between her teeth. Her grandpa had a hand on his hip and was leaning his bum against the counter, fidgeting with his hands. The sheriff stood with his arms crossed and chewed on his lower lip while water dripped from his hat, slowing forming a ring of puddles around him on the tile. Their backs were facing the window over the sink, which Ruby had a good view of. Even though the sky was dark, she could make out her daddy's trailer in the distance, on the other side of the plum tree.

Eventually, once Ruby emptied the bowl, her grandpa cleared his throat and said, "Can we talk now?"

Ruby nodded and took a long sip of cold milk.

"Let's begin with how you got those cuts on your face," Sheriff Cletus said.

Ruby touched the cuts with her the tips of her fingers. They started to hurt again when she did.

"Was it your daddy?" the sheriff asked.

Even the sound of his name made tears well up. Ruby looked past the two men and tried not to cry. Outside, the rain was starting to come down hard. Ruby locked her eyes on a drip that dangled over the edge of the roof. She knew she had to tell the truth — which was what her daddy did to her, and about the scream she heard from the trailer. Besides that, she didn't know what happened to her daddy or her brothers.

Just as Ruby shifted her eyes from the window back to the sheriff, something across the field caught her attention. She looked back at it and tried not to gawk, but it was hard not to. She felt her mama's eyes on her, and she knew the others' were too. Her chest tightened as she held her breath. When she realized what it was out in the field, she began to cry, unable to stop the tears from falling.

But it wasn't because she was sad at what she was seeing — she just wanted to make sure no one else looked out the window and saw her brothers scurrying toward the forest, as she did.

CHAPTER SIXTEEN

The rain stung Rusty's face, the wind fierce through his hair, as he followed Bo back toward the forest. The knot in his lower back twisted as he ran, hunched, the backpack of linens pulling him down. Bo was a few yards ahead of him, tin cans clanking against one another from inside the sack on his back.

The dark clouds went on for miles, rain all but certain for much of the day. Sheriff Cletus was inside their grandpa's trailer with the rest of them, the metal roof shielding them from the elements. His police car was now hidden, gone from sight. Rusty was jealous they were all staying dry — Sheriff Cletus, grandpa, mom, and Ruby — and he didn't understand why he and Bo weren't. Once they made it back to the forest, he told himself, he'd ask Bo.

This was all Bo's idea — to hide out in the forest without any shelter or food or dry clothes — and Rusty still hadn't figured out what the point of it was. One night was one thing, but he had the sense Bo was planning on staying in the forest for a while. Rusty was beginning to think that maybe Bo planned to stay in the forest forever.

Rusty needed to know what happened to their father. His memory was still foggy, his only recollection of the scene inside the trailer from the day before was the same that it had been. Images of his dad's desperation flooded Rusty's mind — first, his dad's hands covering his throat as red liquid covered his fingers and ran down his chest like wet paint; then his eyes and how wide they were, and how large his pupils became; then how his mouth opened as if he tried to speak, but no words came out, only gurgles. Rusty heard the thud of his father's body hitting the floor, felt the vibration under his feet as if it were happening again.

His belly retched as he saw the color fade from his father's face until his body stopped seizing and became lifeless. Rusty remembered sitting in the corner and breathing heavily, hyperventilating, and vomiting on himself as his father lay dead in front of him, Bo somewhere else. He passed out sometime shortly thereafter and didn't remember coming to until his grandpa showed up later.

Rusty felt the warmth of the gunpowder on his fingertips, the heaviness of the shotgun resting in his hands. He looked down as he ran, expecting to see the bloodied shotgun taunting him, but found emptiness. The wrap on his bad hand was beginning to separate, the tie loosening from the moisture.

Bo leaped into the underbrush at the edge of the forest, his entire body disappearing as if swallowed by the overgrowth. Rusty was still behind and slowing, his wind all but lost. With one final push that offered up everything he had left to give, Rusty took a big step and dove toward the spot where Bo landed, his arms spread out wide as if they were wings. He felt as if he were flying as he coasted through the rain in slow motion, his body hovering over the ground like a saucer. He closed his eyes and took in the smells of the dampness of the grass and the mud that was drowning it. Then he could taste them both on his lips as he landed chest first in the underbrush.

***

When they got back to the clearing, both Rusty and Bo were covered in brown muck and dripping wet. Rusty was miserable, the clothes on his back soaked, the dry clothes in his pack no longer dry. The bandage around his hand had fallen off completely, leaving the open callus free to attract infection. A stream of water leaked from his backpack onto his calves and into his boots, giving the fungi an even better breeding ground in between his toes.

"What do we do now?" Rusty said, raising his voice so Bo could hear him over the rain as it smacked against the leaves like a thousand whips.

"We make shelter."

"How?"

Bo was already gone, disappearing deeper into the forest, the pack of supplies from the kitchen still strapped to his back. Rusty stood in the rain and wondered what he should do. He felt helpless. He was on the verge of tears, the frustration from everything they'd gone through reaching its boiling point. He stiffened his jaw to try to fight the tears away, but thought better of it and allowed himself to cry while his face was already wet. He thought he felt better after a while.

Not long after he disappeared, Bo reemerged in the clearing. He was dragging a broken tree limb behind him as if it were effortless, one hand wrapped around the trunk where it'd been split.

"Check this out," Bo said. "There are a ton of these in a pile just through those bushes." He let go of the branch and let it fall at Rusty's feet.

The branch was thinned out at the base and missing some strips of bark, the insides of the tree visible and a shade lighter than the outside. Rusty tried to count the rings, but quickly lost his place. To him, it looked as if the bark was peeled away like the skin of a plum, and there were tiny gashes that he thought could be from a knife blade.

"Look at this," Bo said, crouching. There were clusters of extra leaves on top of the leaves that were already there, tied together with rope made from the bark. "It looks like someone made this."

Rusty knelt beside the clumps of leaves and admired the arrangement. Rain continued to pour down on them, soaking through their packs. Rusty began to shiver. Smaller branches of leaves were tied together in trios, which were then tied into the gaps on the main branch where leaves were missing. It was as if a real-life Indian tribe lived in the forest, reclaimed their land, and made shelter out of the resources. Rusty was amazed, yet a bit worried at the same time. If an Indian tribe was really roaming around these parts, they'd be really angry if he and Bo stole their supplies.

But before Rusty had a chance to protest, Bo got back to his feet and said, "Come on, grab an end. Help me stand it up."

Rusty helped him move the limb over to the massive tree roots they slept in the night before. The ground was slippery, the footing difficult. Rusty's bad hand dangled near his hip. He bit his tongue as he held the base of the limb in place while Bo pushed the top, wanting to say something to his brother, but also liking the idea of being shielded from the rain like everyone else. He continued to bite his tongue while he helped Bo retrieve a second limb, then a third, fighting against the rain and mud and wind, which seemed to be picking up. Together, Rusty and Bo stacked the three limbs in a row and leaned them against the trunk of the massive oak. The limbs weren't standing vertically, but they were close. The bases sunk into the mud, which helped keep them in place.

More tears fell from the clouds at a rapid pace, crashing against the tops of the newly-formed rain shield above Rusty's head, pouring over the sides and leaving the space underneath drier but muddy. The line of limbs looked more like palm trees than oak trees, but fuller and wider, like an umbrella. But Rusty knew they couldn't be palm trees since those were found mostly on the coast, and the map in the drawer in the kitchen of his father's trailer told him the coast was at least a few inches away. But even that didn't make sense. Regardless, whatever type of tree it was, it was keeping most of the rain away, so he was happy. He tried not to worry about what the Indians might think.

"It's working," Rusty said, holding his good hand out, expecting to catch a puddle, but not.

"Cool, right?"

"Where do you think they came from?"

Bo had his hands on his hips and shifted his eyes around, as if looking for something — his thoughts, maybe. "I don't know. Maybe it was a gift from God."

Rusty turned to look at his brother as the wind howled outside the umbrellas. "God can do that?"

"God can do whatever he wants. He's God."

Rusty nodded, but he didn't understand. He still thought the Indians might be responsible. "What do we do now?"

Bo stayed quiet for a while, moving his hands from his hips and interlocking them behind his back, his body swaying to the rhythm of the wind. "Whatever we want."

Bo unstrapped the pack from his back and tossed it against the trunk of the oak. He unzipped the bag and reached his hands inside, pulling out two partially crushed Budweiser cans that were missing the tabs. He handed one to Rusty. Bo must have recognized Rusty's apprehension, because he smiled. "It's okay. It's just water."

Rusty held his ground for a bit, staring at the red square on the can until he imagined his father's face in the fancy emblem that looked out of place. Rusty saw his father tormenting him, standing over his body as he lay injured in the field, pouring warm beer on his injured hand. He saw Bo sitting on the edge of their bed, shirtless, refusing to cry as their father whopped him from behind. Leather snapped. Crushed aluminum pinged his ears. Rusty's own screams bellowed in his mind.

He saw Ruby. He saw her ginger curls and rosy cheeks. He smelled the cinnamon in her hair. He saw her tight smile and her crooked teeth. He heard her laugh. He heard her cry. Then he heard her scream, and he saw the cuts on her face that looked like they came from a pocketknife. He saw blood.

Rusty saw the shotgun, felt its weight in his hands, felt his finger wrap around the trigger, remembered how cold it was. Something happened inside his belly that made him want to throw fists. His throat tightened with anger.

The stink of the can hit Rusty's nose as Bo pushed it toward him, urging him to take it. Rusty thought he might be sick. All he could think about was his father and how much he hated him. After all of those years of physical violence and neglect and intimidation, it was finally over. But something was missing — something still felt off. There was a sense of closure that he felt he needed, yet he didn't have.

"Tomorrow," Rusty said, loosening his fists, "can we go see dad's body?"

"For what?"

"I just want to see it."

Bo didn't reply.

Rusty continued to stare at the can in Bo's hand, which now rested by his hip. Nearly every bad memory Rusty had involved one of these cans, and he was getting angrier the longer he looked at it. "Well? Can we?"

Bo brought the other can to his lips and took a sip. The contents filled up his cheeks until they were fat, but he didn't swallow for a while. When he finally did, gulping loudly, he simply said, "Okay."

Rusty nodded. He shifted his eyes away from the can and looked back up. Something hanging from a low branch across the clearing caught his attention. Curious, he took a step forward and squinted, but he couldn't make out what it was through the elements. The wind was blowing hard now, and the raindrops were flying sideways like tiny missiles. Brown and black leaves flew in a funnel through Rusty's line of sight.

"What's that?" he said.

"What's what?"

Rusty pointed to the hanging object. "That."

Bo moved next to him and followed the direction of his outstretched arm. When he spotted the object, he said he didn't know what it was.

Rusty felt up for an adventure. He grabbed the beer can from Bo and chugged it, still smelling some lingering booze, but not tasting it. Then he slid out from under the cover of the makeshift umbrella and stepped back into the rain, the wind tearing into him as if he were insignificant.

CHAPTER SEVENTEEN

Earl's only weapon was an umbrella, although Sheriff Cletus was carrying. The rain formed a waterfall around the brim of Cletus's hat while he stood outside the umbrella, the brown of his uniform turning black from the rain that flew in at an angle. He stood motionless while Earl fumbled with the handle of the door of Lenny's truck.

"Well?" Cletus said.

"It's locked."

"Break a window."

"With what?"

Cletus made a sound that resembled a sigh, but it could have been thunder roaring in the distance. "Stand back," he said, unholstering his Glock.

Earl did. He kept the umbrella high over his head and held on tight. There were three quick pops, one right after the other, which left Earl's ears ringing. He scrunched his eyes and turned away, shielding his face from any residual debris that may have bounced in his direction. Glass shattered and fell to the ground, some of it splashing as it landed in the puddle beneath the truck, other pieces noiseless as they fell onto the soft cushion of the driver's seat. Earl stuck a finger in his ear and shook it, trying to fight off the demons that returned each time a gunshot went off. The physical flashbacks came and went, but the screaming voices of his platoon mates were constantly with him, terrorizing his thoughts.

When Earl turned back, Cletus holstered his weapon and crossed his arms, as if nothing had happened. "How about now?" he said, his voice steady and soft, strangely calm.

The ringing in Earl's ears eventually subsided, and that's when he approached the truck. He handed the umbrella to Cletus, who took it but didn't stand under it, holding it the wrong way, choosing instead to let water pool inside the parasol. Earl leaned into the mostly glassless window, being careful to avoid any shards that remained around the rubber of the weather stripping, and pulled the knob that undid the lock.

The cabin of the truck was warm, but the engine was ice cold. Earl hadn't seen Lenny take his trip into town yet this week, which meant there'd be another day or two before anyone would wonder where he was. Earl found a rag stained with oil on the dash, specs of blue underneath the black only barely visible. He took it and made it into a ball in his hand, then he used the rag to brush away the broken glass from the bench. He stepped up into the truck and sat on the cushioned seat, his knees aching, and put his hands on the steering wheel and tried to put himself into his son's shoes. Glass crunched underneath his feet.

He felt underneath the seat, slid a fingernail around the loose rubber of the shifter, and jammed his hand behind his back where the cushion of the bench met the backrest. He found nothing in either place. The sun visor on the passenger's side was missing, but the one near Earl's forehead wasn't. Rusted metal made a crease in the visor that looked like it hadn't moved in years, the indentation creating a permanent scar. It reminded him of Ruby.

Earl sighed.

He reached up and flipped the visor down, revealing a photo, its color faded and dull, with thick dust streaked across the ink. It didn't take him long to recognize who was in the photo. It was a woman, nude, lying on her back on top of a checkered bedspread that Earl recognized as his own from many years ago. The woman's breasts were full and shaped like perfect watermelons, the pink in the centers so soft they could have been candies. One of her hands was covering the area between her legs, but not well enough to include all of the fuzz, the brown so light it was almost ginger. The woman's other arm was outstretched and out of the frame as if reaching for the photographer, begging to be pleasured. The woman looked barely old enough to be legal in the photo, but the smirk on her face told Earl she was enjoying being a star.

The woman was Beverly, long before she was his wife.

A fit of jealousy ran through Earl as if he were a younger man. His son enjoyed Beverly during her best years, and raised those children with her, who were, at best, only occasionally tolerable. Those boys, especially. Ruby-Sue was different, though; Ruby-Sue was special to him in a way that few people knew, that few people would ever understand.

The damage Lenny did to Beverly's body was irreversible, the lines on her stomach and around her thighs a sour point for Earl. Her breasts now were nothing like the ones of her late teenage years in the photo, the children having sucked the life out them. Her imperfections were the reason why Earl only got close to her when the lights were out, of if he was desperate for a release. That way, without her noticing, he could avoid those areas on her body that made him resent his son, and those children.

"Got something?" Cletus said, unmoving, unfazed by the water that continued to pour over the brim of his hat.

Earl tore the photo from the visor, the rust of the metal binder clip slicing away a corner. As he thought about the photo and about Beverly as a younger woman, there was some movement around his prostate that sent a trickle of blood rushing through his hips. A small bulge formed against his thigh that he hadn't experienced in quite some time without the assistance of a pharmaceutical. He knew Beverly was wrong about him — he wasn't dysfunctional, she just wasn't stimulating enough in her old age. This was proof.

"Nothing here," Earl said, pocketing what remained of the photo. He snuck a glance over his shoulder and noticed Cletus staring in, but he said nothing.

The final place to check was the glove compartment. Inside, Earl found what he was looking for. There was a small key ring with two brass keys dangling from it, each about the same size. The keys could have been for anything, but it wasn't beyond Lenny to hide them somewhere where the children couldn't find them. And it made sense they were together. He grabbed the key ring and spun around to show it to Cletus.

"Got it."

"About time," Cletus said, then he took off for Lenny's trailer, stomping through the mud, leaving the umbrella on the dirt, spinning on its ferrule.

***

Inside the trailer, Cletus dropped his dripping hat on the kitchen table and took off down the hallway, puddles of rain spreading over the wooden surface. Earl stayed in the kitchen and used one hand to brush the water from what reminded of his hair, adjusting his belt with the other. A splash landed on the curvature of his ear where the flesh was missing, forcing him to wipe it away, reminding him of its ugly presence. He didn't like to touch or look at it, but sometimes it happened, and the memories were all too real when it did.

Sheriff Cletus waited outside Lenny's bedroom door when Earl found him, his arms crossed, his posture perfect. His face was unshaven, a light shadow of black blanketing his neck and face. The bushiness of his eyebrows gave the impression of experience, as if he'd seen just about everything there was to see.

Much of the sheriff's past was a mystery, and that's the way he liked it; that's the way most of the people in Plum Springs liked it. Earl remembered when Cletus showed up as a scrawny patrol officer two and a half, maybe three decades before. Even then, Earl wasn't certain of his age. He always thought he and Lenny were of the same generation, but now, Cletus looked much older, his imperfections more succinctly defined. Maybe it was the line of work he was in that prematurely aged him, or maybe it was something else. Maybe it was the sleepiness of the town, or maybe there was something in his past that wore on him over the years. Earl understood that. Everyone had secrets. And nobody talked about them.

"Is this it?" Cletus asked as Earl approached.

With one of the keys separated from the key ring, Earl nodded. He tried the key in the door. It worked, the lock clicking as it disengaged. They pushed inside. Lenny's bedroom was ordinary, nothing unusual. The only sound was that of a humming ceiling fan, surprisingly spinning. It smelled a bit like sweat but was otherwise neutral. The bed was unmade. The tri-fold closet was ajar. A window was cracked.

But none of that mattered.

What Earl and Cletus were looking for was in Lenny's safe. They found it under the bed. Cletus spotted it and Earl dropped to his knees and yanked it out. It was gray and compact and lightweight, with two plastic snaps on the edges and a keyhole in the center. Cletus hovered over Earl's shoulder as he fit the second key into the lock, his shadow making Earl uncomfortable. There was a rugged odor coming from Cletus, which made it worse.

The key fit perfectly, and when Earl twisted his wrist, a short cylinder popped up from underneath the keyhole. With the key still in the cylinder, more than half of it gone beneath the surface, Earl popped open the snaps with his thumbs. The lid slid open and revealed a white security envelope, still sealed and with no writing on the outside. It was the only item in the safe.

"Is that it?" Cletus asked with a spike in his voice. It hovered around excitement, but Earl knew that couldn't be right — Cletus never got excited about anything.

"Must be." Earl handed the envelope to Cletus, who pocketed it. Earl closed the lid and slid the safe back under the bed. He worked his way to his feet, the joints in his knees screaming, and faced Cletus. He spun the key ring around his finger and waited for the pain of his years to pass. It seemed as if it took longer to subside with each passing day.

"I'll take care of this in the morning," Cletus said. "I've got a guy."

Earl nodded. He felt confident in Cletus's ability to get it done, and was relieved that it was out of his hands. "What do we do now?" Earl asked the question, even though he already knew the answer.

"Let's go find Lenny."

Earl knew Cletus was right. Lenny had to be around the trailer somewhere, and it would only be a matter of time before his body would start to decompose. When it did, the rot would start to infiltrate the trailer, and someone might notice. He also knew when he and Cletus were done with Lenny, they were going after the boys next.

CHAPTER EIGHTEEN

The day grew late. The rain stopped, but the clouds were still dark and dreary, as if they could open up again at any moment. Ruby saw a burst lightning flash over the trees in the distance, but it seemed distant. She didn't mind lighting — she liked the brightness of it, actually — but thunder scared her. Thankfully, she hadn't heard thunder in hours.

Ruby's mama was asleep on the couch in the living room, the inaudible chatter of the television helping her nap. She'd been asleep for a while. Ruby was bored, left to entertain herself. The chair that faced the window was becoming uncomfortable underneath her bottom, a cracked hunk of plastic sticking her thigh like a dagger. A gurgling sound rumbled inside her belly.

All of Ruby's toys were at home in her daddy's trailer. She usually carried around a rag doll she called Lucy, but she didn't expect to stay the night. Lucy's hair was made of yarn that was the color of ginger, like Ruby's. She wore a pair of purple overalls with one strap loose, the button having popped off long ago. Lucy was like the book about a lonesome teddy bear that Ruby saw once in that way, and that's why she was special. Ruby would keep Lucy close, rubbing away at the edge of her denim overalls until she fell asleep at night. She was especially protective of Lucy when her daddy would drink too many cans and get angry. He once tore Lucy from her hands, just because, and threw her against the closet door for no reason. One of Lucy's button eyes broke off that day, so only one of them remained. Ruby never understood why her daddy did that to Lucy. She struggled to understand many of the things her daddy did.

If it wasn't for her grandpa and the sheriff, Ruby would go over to her daddy's trailer and find Lucy. She knew exactly where Lucy was hidden, her broken eye lying face down underneath the lone pillow on her bed so her daddy wouldn't find her. Only she and Rusty knew where Lucy was kept, and that was because Ruby told Rusty everything. Besides Lucy, Rusty was her best friend. She missed him and Bo both so much.

She looked out the window in the kitchen and saw her grandpa and Sheriff Cletus walking back and forth between her daddy's shed and trailer. Part of her wanted to go in the other room and find something to watch on the television while her mama slept, but another part of her wouldn't let her. By staying in the kitchen, she hoped to catch another glimpse of her brothers. And with what her grandpa told her earlier, she knew she had to warn her brothers if they came by again. Her grandpa was really angry about what happened, about what Rusty and Bo did. She even heard him tell Cletus that he was going to kill them once he found them. Ruby believed him.

Across the field, past the plum tree and through the dense fog that frequently came after a rainstorm, there was some activity near the shed again. Ruby squinted to see better, the movement in the distance not much more than a blurred speck. The shed door opened and stayed ajar as the speck disappeared inside, leaving a spiral funnel of fog where the speck once stood. Ruby got up from her seat and made her way toward the sink, her thighs tingling as the blood rushed through her legs and down to her toes. The step stool was still there, leaning against the cabinet, its hinges slick with grease. The grease disappeared when Ruby unfolded the legs, the hard plastic at the base making a platform for her to stand on.

The shed was larger outside the window now, but no clearer. The window was open a crack at the bottom, and Ruby smelled the calm after the rainstorm. She listed hard, trying to find out what was going on across the field in her daddy's shed, but the distance was too far. Whatever other noises there were outside, if any, were drowned out by water splashing in puddles as it fell from the roof of the trailer. Inside, laughter roared from the television set in the other room, and Ruby's mama snored.

Ruby sunk, her muscles deflating as she blew out warm air. The cereal from the morning tasted good, but her belly was already grumbling again. She wanted to eat something, but the reminder of the blackened toast she tried to make for her daddy made her face ache. The cuts were still hot when she touched her cheeks. Until her mama got up, Ruby would have to wait to eat; she didn't dare try to cook something again. She could go and try to wake her up, but she feared the pill her mama took would make her angry — Ruby didn't know how alike her mama and daddy were, and her skin was already in too much pain to find out.

Ruby sat on the stool and rested her chin on her fists. Sadness began to creep in. Ruby felt her eyes getting wet, her lashes trying to brush the water away when she blinked. It didn't work, though; her vision was blurring. There was a twisting sensation in her throat that made her lower lip curl. She rubbed two fingers together and imagined Lucy's overalls, imagined the comfort she felt when she held her. The coarseness of the denim against her skin seemed real, the fabric rubbing against the creases of her two fingers that almost lined up. And, in her mind, she felt the spot where the fabric wore away, the blue faded to white, the material quite a bit softer than the rest.

Thinking of Lucy helped. The tears stopped. She almost smiled. Ruby shrugged, pushing her shoulders up, and used her shirt to wipe away the water. She was scared, yes, but she had to be brave. She needed to keep an eye out for her brothers so she could somehow let them know to stay away from the trailer. She wondered if Bo would be proud of her for being strong, like him. He was always the strongest of them all.

When Ruby stood back up and faced the window, the speck returned next to the shed. The sun threatened to break through the clouds. The object near the shed became clear as it shone in the mist, its long legs and round belly forming a shape that resembled her grandpa. A second object appeared from inside the shed, this one covered from head to foot in a brown suit that reminded Ruby of a cocooned caterpillar.

Ruby thought about the circumstances and put the pieces together. Looking harder, squinting, she recognized the objects as people, as men. It was her grandpa and Sheriff Cletus, and they must have been looking for something inside the shed.

Her grandpa had something long in his hand. It looked like a stick that was rounded like the ones Rusty and Bo used in the field, except the one her grandpa had was even longer. The other end was pointed like an arrowhead, whereas the ones Ruby's brothers used were boxy and flattened. Sheriff Cletus was carrying something too. In his hand was something rounded and white, and it appeared to be floating in midair, his hand dangling in a fist a few inches above the object. He bent his knees and put the object on the ground, then faced Ruby's grandpa. It seemed as if they were talking to each other, both men nodding as they faced one another.

Ruby's grandpa took off for the trailer first, the wooden handled object sagging down by his knee, the pointed end resting on his shoulder. Cletus bent down again and reached for something, and that's when Ruby saw the handle swing upwards. He lifted the bucket and stumbled forward as if the weight of it was too much for him to handle, but regained his footing before toppling. Ruby wondered if it was the same bucket Bo found in the shed, the same bucket that made his face scrunch up when he looked at it, the same bucket that smelled like a combination of poison and ammonia. Ruby couldn't fathom what it might be used for.

"What are you looking at?"

Ruby leaped, nearly falling from the stool at her mama's voice. She didn't hear her approach, too distracted by the activity across the field. Her hand snapped at the countertop in front of her, her fingertips wrapping around the laminate like a vice. She just barely kept her balance.

Ruby's grandpa disappeared around the backside of her daddy's trailer when she looked back up, and Sheriff Cletus was close behind. Ruby heard her mama's feet shuffle on the tile and imagined the bottoms of her white socks turning black, just as her own had. Before she knew it, Ruby felt the breath on her neck — the warm, stale, after nap breath that built up in the back of the throat and made the tongue stick to the roof of the mouth — followed by a gentle hand on the small of her back. Ruby quivered at the touch of her mama's fingers penetrating through her shirt and sending a tingling sensation rushing through her skin, as if small legs were crawling all over her. Ruby sunk when her mama wrapped her arm around her waist, her fingers loosening their grip from the edge of the counter where the laminate was still intact. Ruby felt so good being in her mama's arms, so secure.

"What do you see out there?" her mama asked.

Ruby said nothing but kept her eyes on the sheriff as he made a wide loop around her daddy's trailer, leaving the mist in his wake.

"Are you looking for what you saw earlier?" Ruby stiffened, her neck swiveling to look at her mama. Her mama was smiling, that tooth sticking out.

"I saw them too, you know," her mama said. "Your brothers."

"You did? But…"

"I should have said something, right?" her mama joked, half laughing, half not, as if trying to convince herself. Her eyes were glazed over, a haze hovering around the dark color in her pupils like a cloud. Ruby couldn't tell if her mama's eyes were brown or black, although she'd never seen someone with black eyes before.

"Why didn't you tell grandpa? Or Sheriff Cletus?"

Ruby's mama spun her on the step stool until she faced her, taking her hands. Ruby let her mama lead her down from the stool, her toes slipping underneath her as she reached the bottom.

"Ruby, baby, let me tell you a thing or two about your granddaddy." Ruby's mama led her back to the table, where they both sat, facing each other. "Your daddy and your granddaddy are a lot alike, you know."

Ruby shrugged, not really knowing, but taking her mama's word for it.

"But they're also a lot different in many ways, too. You understand?"

Ruby nodded because she thought that's what her mama wanted her to do, even though she didn't.

"You see, your granddaddy loves you kids very much, and your daddy does too. Especially your granddaddy — he loves you very much." Her mama paused, shut her eyes, and turned away for a moment. "It's just...They love you differently. That's all. Your granddaddy doesn't approve much about the way your daddy treats you kids, or me, but he still loves him anyway."

Her mama paused again and bit onto the nail on her thumb as if thinking, trying to find the words that were too painful to say. Ruby sat in place, her hands resting on the table in front of her, wondering what her mama was really trying to say, not understanding.

"Mama?" Ruby said as her mama's mind looked like it was beginning to wander, her eyes pointed upwards as if trying to look inside her brain. "Mama, why do you live with grandpa?"

Ruby's mama's nose whistled as she blew out air. "We've been trying to get you kids to live here with us, you know that? We've filled out the papers and brought them into town to talk to one of them fancy lawyers and everything, but it never seems to work out. What your daddy does out there in them fields...What he has...He's a powerful man."

Ruby's mama stood up quickly, as if shocked with a bolt of electricity. Her voice shook. She shoved her fingers into her mouth and began to chew on them as if they were snacks. The color of the skin on her face started to change from pink to white.

"Mama?"

"Things ain't always what they seem, baby. It's just not that easy sometimes. I don't expect you to understand."

Ruby unfolded her hands and dropped them in her lap, unsure what her mama was thinking, afraid of what she might say next.

"Would you like some milk?" her mama asked, the tremble in her voice not as prevalent. Ruby nodded because she did. She always said yes to a glass of milk. Her mama went to the refrigerator and pulled on the door, her hand shaking as she did. Milk sloshed around in the half-gallon container and she carried it over to the counter, noticeably worsening as her mama poured some of it into a glass she found in the cabinet.

"Here you go, baby."

Ruby took the cup from her mama and brought it to her lips, the coolness of the edge surprising her as it touched.

Her mama put away the milk container and left the room, bringing an abrupt end to the conversation. Keeping her eyes peeled for her brothers in case they came back, Ruby stayed sitting at the table and drank her milk, looking out the window over the sink, wondering what was going to happen next.

***

Later that day, after the clouds and the sun went to sleep, Ruby's grandpa came back. Ruby sat on the carpet in the living room, practicing making bunny ears with the strings of her shoes, the television laughing at her in the background. She still hadn't eaten since breakfast.

When the door to the screen porch clanked, she got up and went to the doorway and watched her grandpa lumber into the kitchen. His shirt was muddied on the front and there was a dark spot in the shape of a horseshoe on his back. There were smears on his cheeks and forehead that made his face darker than it usually was, and the knees of his jeans were dirty. His eyes looked angry and tired, and the way he pressed a hand against his lower back and grunted was like he was in pain.

"Bev," he yelled out, dropping into one of the chairs at the kitchen table, leaning against the back of it. Outside the window, the headlights on Cletus's car lit up and were soon gone as the car backed down the driveway. Gravel spit as his tires rolled in reverse, the sound gradually fading. Ruby's grandpa groaned from the kitchen and called out for Ruby's mama again.

The suction of wet bare feet sticking to the floor came from the hallway, and Ruby's mama appeared in the entryway. Her hair was wet and she'd changed into different clothes, and there were two dots sticking out of her chest. "What is it, Earl?" she said, crossing her arms, covering the dots. "Where have you been all day?"

Ruby's grandpa said nothing as he slouched in the chair, his back barely touching the seat. Ruby's mama walked further into the kitchen and stood over her grandpa, blocking Ruby's view. Ruby stood still for a moment, watching her mama trying to help her grandpa to his feet from behind. Ruby's belly grumbled.

When her mama got her grandpa to his feet, she wrapped her arms around him and gave him a hug, whispering something in his ear. Ruby's grandpa stood with his arms dangling at his sides, his eyes closed, his jawbone flexing underneath his skin. Ruby's mama counted aloud to three and made a grunting sound, lifting Ruby's grandpa's feet off the ground as if he were a small child. The pop of bones snapping and the thud her grandpa made as he hit the floor made Ruby duck back inside the living room and cover her ears.

Ruby buried her face into the cushion on the sofa and held her breath. The smell of dust and mothballs and cigarettes trickled in through her nose and crept into her throat, forcing her to sit up and cough. She heard another groan from the kitchen when she did, followed by a long bout of silence.

Ruby wondered if she just witnessed her mama killing her grandpa, and she panicked at the thought. She clenched her eyes tight and thought about the things she cared about the most. She thought about Bo and about Rusty and about Lucy, and about how much she wanted to see them all again, to hold them all. She squeezed her eyes even tighter and began to rub her two fingers together, imagining there were denim overalls between them.

As she felt her mama's presence enter the room — the increase in heat in the room, the taste of her perfume on Ruby's tongue, the smell of death lingering on the other side of the wall — Ruby rubbed her fingers together as hard as she could, moving them so fast that the skin on the insides of her fingers became hot. Her mama stepped further into the room and moved closer and closer to Ruby as she leaned over the sofa cushion, hovering behind her like a shadow that Ruby couldn't see but knew was there. Ruby gritted her teeth, balled her fingers into fists, and wondered if she was next. And when her mama's cold hand landed on her shoulder blade and squeezed, Ruby got her answer.

She flailed her arms and screamed from the back of her throat.

CHAPTER NINETEEN

By nightfall, the rain stopped. Most of the tree branches with leaves were still wet, some dripping, creating mud puddles in the dirt. The dirt loosened and softened like clay. Rusty and Bo's boots made molded imprints in the soil as they walked back and forth between either side of the clearing. The boot prints were hardening as the mud did, forming deep impressions that could be used as ornaments if extracted properly. Rusty wondered what the forest would look like if it were decorated.

They had a fire going, the wood Bo found in a manmade teepee dry enough to stay lit. Bo found the pile further in the forest, just past where he discovered the strewn umbrella oaks, huddled underneath a weatherproof tarp. The wood was chopped and stacked in a perfect cord, as if it were split by an expert lumberjack. There were no tools around — no ax, no log splitter, no splitting block — that Rusty saw when Bo showed him the pile, which, to him, meant only one thing — it was most definitely the Indian people.

The night air was thick and humid, but Rusty held out his hands over the fire anyway, the flames making his palms sweaty. The sweat stung his callus, the still forming scab not yet fully hardened. The experience reminded him of what he thought roasting marshmallows might be like — he'd never actually done it before — which only made him hungrier. Most of the food Bo had gathered from the trailer was already gone, the manual labor of moving and restacking the wood burning off more energy than they expected. All that remained were two cans of beans, a can of tuna fish, and no can opener. It was the minor details, Rusty learned, that mattered most. It was hard work living in the forest.

"Someone's out here with us," Rusty said, pulling his hands away from the flames as a gust of wind sent them climbing toward his skin.

"What do you mean?" Bo fidgeted with a strip of bark, trying to replicate what was done to the oak branches on a smaller scale.

"Someone had to make all this stuff. And I don't think they're working alone."

"I agree."

"I think it's a tribe."

Bo looked up. "A tribe? Like the Native Americans?"

"Indians, yeah."

"With face paint and spears and moccasins?"

Rusty shrugged. A log snapped at the base of the flames.

"And buckskin dresses and leather satchels and those ridiculous feather hats?"

Rusty dropped his eyes and reached for the leather satchel he found hanging from a tree branch on the other side of the clearing. It had a wide flap that draped over the front and a strap that was worn and tied together with some bark string. Everything about it looked like it came from an Indian — the shade of brown was just dark enough, yet still light enough to show its age; a string of dried berries hung over the edge, resembling beads; a loop on the backside of the satchel seemed wide enough to hold an arrow or two — and considering all the other manmade supplies they found, it all made perfect sense.

"You can't be serious?" Bo said, one dimple showing as he grinned.

Rusty was, but he only shrugged again.

Bo's grin went away, as did the indent on his cheek.

"There's not a tribe out here."

"How do you know?"

"Because there's not. Trust me."

"But, how? Just because you say—"

"It's because Native American's don't have Swiss Army knives."

"They might."

"No, they don't."

Rusty knew Bo was right, though he didn't want to admit it — that was the only thing that didn't make sense. There was a multi-tool in the satchel, and that seemed off.

Maybe the Indians found it somewhere.

"I don't know, I still think there are Indians out here."

Bo said nothing, looking back down to his bark. Rusty looked into the sky, out across the tops of the oaks that were still in the night. The horizon was full of stars and bright lights that disappeared then reappeared, as if winking. A single red light blinked between two white ones as an airplane flew to a better place. The night smelled of burning leaves.

Something howled in the distance. Rusty thought it sounded more like a voice than an animal, but he knew that wasn't possible. But then he thought about the Indian people again, and thought maybe it was, wondering if maybe Bo was wrong this time. The voice was faint, barely recognizable behind the popping and crackling of the flames in the fire pit. It came from somewhere deeper in the forest, much further than he could see. Rusty hoped that meant the tribe was moving west toward the Mississippi, maybe toward the territory Huck Finn said was theirs.

"Can I ask you something?" Rusty said as he shifted himself down the log and away from the heat of the fire.

"Okay." Bo didn't look up.

"Why can't we just go to grandpa's trailer?"

Bo stopped what he was doing and looked up now, meeting Rusty's eyes. "Is that what you want to do?"

"I don't know, but I don't understand why we can't."

"It's like I told you — grandpa knows what we did."

Rusty started to ask Bo what happened again, but he stopped himself before he began. Instead, he said, "But, what if we just explain to him what happened? If we tell him what dad's done—"

Bo dropped the bark and stood up. He made a loop around the fire and sat next to Rusty on the log, their thighs touching when he did. Rusty got a good look at Bo's face and saw how serious he was. It was as if he knew secrets that Rusty didn't. But it also looked like he was about to share those secrets.

"You don't know about grandpa and dad, do you?"

Rusty tensed unexpectedly, his memory ready to seal the secrets Bo was about to tell him.

"They're the same, you know."

"The same how?"

"He knows."

"About what?"

"About what dad's been doing to us."

Rusty shook his head, not wanting to believe it. "No, he would have done something."

"Listen to me, Rusty. I'm telling you — grandpa knows."

Rusty stood, his legs shaking. His heart was starting to beat really fast, and he felt himself getting angry, his insides warming. "No, it can't be true."

Bo stood up too. "It is true."

Rusty shook his head again and kept doing it until he felt Bo's clammy palms clasp around the skin on his forearms.

Something was happening inside of him that was all too familiar. The sense of betrayal started to burrow within his heart, and it reminded him of his mother, of how he always felt when he thought about her. There was no way his grandpa, too, was just like everyone else.

"Rusty, you have to listen to me."

"If grandpa knows, why didn't he —"

"Because he's the same."

"You already said that. What does that mean?"

"It means he doesn't care. He doesn't care about us and he doesn't care about Ruby."

Rusty backed away from Bo, pulling his arms free. He looked Bo square in the face and searched for a lie, but Bo's expression was flat. His eyes were filled with truth. If Bo was lying, he hid it well. Rusty sat back on the log and looked at his hands, at the brown crust that was trying to cover the callus. Any appetite he had before was gone.

"Grandpa did to dad what dad did to us," Bo said, sitting beside Rusty on the log, his voice low. "Like I said, they're the same."

Rusty shook his head again, but this time out of disbelief that grandpa would do that, and not that he could. Grownups were, he began to realize, all the same. "How long have you known?"

"For a while."

Much of Rusty's life started to make sense now. All the times Bo told him there was no other way, all the times he said killing their father was their only chance, all the times he said they had to protect themselves — it all made sense. Rusty was a man now, and he was strong enough to handle this information. Bo must have known that too, or else he wouldn't have told him. Rusty knew now that they made the right decision by doing what they did — they truly had no other option; nobody else was going to help them.

Then it hit him.

Ruby.

Ruby was staying in grandpa's trailer, under the watchful eye of the man who raised their dad to be the way he was. And if grandpa was the same as Lenny, then that probably meant Ruby was in danger. As a man, Rusty knew Ruby wouldn't be able to fight back; he wasn't able to at her age. And she's a girl.

"What about Ruby?" he said, looking up. His chest was bouncing hard, his hands shaking. There was a pinching feeling inside his belly that he didn't recognize. He felt sick. "She's staying with grandpa."

"Not true. She's staying with mom."

"But grandpa's there too."

"Mom will protect her. She's one of us, not one of them. Dad treated her no different than us. She'll know how to protect Ruby."

"She couldn't protect us."

Bo stayed silent for a while, as if he didn't know what to say to that. "Yeah, well, things are different now."

Rusty thought he understood, hoped he did, but he wasn't convinced. Their mom was never there to protect him or Bo from Lenny, so Rusty had no reason to believe she could protect Ruby, either. She'd soon have scars on her face to prove their mom couldn't.

"We have to get her," Rusty said.

"I know we do."

"We have to keep her safe out here with us."

"And we will."

"When?"

"Tomorrow night," Bo said without hesitation. "We'll go get her when the sun goes down."

***

Later that night, once the bright orange flames faded to a glimmer and the moon began to dull, Rusty peeled off his boots. The laces were tight and knotted in doubles, the tongue underneath waterlogged. Pulling the first boot from his foot made a sucking sound that reminded him of walking through mud, and water poured out from it when he flipped it over. The interior of the boot was submerged in water for so long that the liner came unglued from the bottom and was floating freely in the boot as if it were a raft in a river. Rusty covered his nose when the smell hit.

The only explanation was that something had died — a fish or a squirrel or a muskrat. The odor was so strong and powerful and dominating, that was the only thing that made sense. He thought about the infection he had under his thumbnail and what that smelled like, and it was nothing compared to this. The second boot was no better.

"What's that smell?" Bo asked, covering his mouth and nose as he peed into the base of what remained of the fire.

"My boots."

"Check your toes. There might be something growing. It's not supposed to smell like that."

Rusty knew that — he wasn't stupid. He peeled off a damp sock and set it on the log beside him. It made a slapping sound as the wet cotton wrapped itself around the bark like a strip of uncooked bacon. Bo put his member away and backed away from the fire pit. There wasn't much light left that allowed Rusty to see in detail, but he felt something slimy when he ran his finger through the pits of his toes. There was a milky film that stayed on his finger when it emerged, and although unable to confirm it, Rusty placed it to be the source of the odor. He rubbed his finger on his pant leg until his skin felt normal again.

"Make sure you leave your socks off tonight," Bo said, his nose still covered, his voice nasally. "And your boots — flip them over so all the water can drain out. We need to get you some new socks tomorrow."

Rusty did what Bo suggested — he laid out his second sock next to the first and flipped his boots upside down. He knew whatever was growing wouldn't stop until he washed his feet and changed his socks, but he hoped airing his feet out might halt the growth's development at least a little. And the smell — he was hopeful the smell would lessen through the night.

Once Bo zipped up and made his way across the clearing to the wide oak with the exposed roots, Rusty got up. The earth beneath him poked at the soles of his feet, irritating the softest parts of his skin. The soles of his feet were tender initially, the first sticks and small pebbles cutting into him like splintered glass, but he quickly got used to it. When Bo was far enough away, Rusty unzipped his pants and pulled out his member. He began to urinate on the pile of ash, just like Bo had.

"Nice baby penis," Bo said, laughing, as he came back over.

Rusty tried to cover himself, but couldn't, the stream still going strong. "Shut up! Get out of here."

Bo howled with laughter as he bent over and picked up the satchel they found earlier. He held a hand up for Rusty to see, then squeezed his thumb and forefinger close together until they were almost touching. He was still laughing.

"Shut up, I said!" Rusty turned away from Bo, his pee splashing up against the base of the log and back onto the tops of his feet. "It's not that small. It's just cold out here."

Bo laughed harder, holding his belly as he staggered back out into the clearing.

Rusty felt humiliated. He knew his face was flushed.

The stream died out and Rusty flicked away the remaining drops with a few angry whips, determined to prove his brother wrong. He turned his back to the clearing and looked over his shoulder and watched Bo disappear underneath the umbrella oaks. Rusty looked down and held his member in his hand, draping it across his palm as if it were a loose noodle. It didn't even make it halfway across, but he didn't know if that was normal or not. But when he grabbed the tip with his other hand and stretched it, it made it to the other side with ease, and then some. Once in a while, it would get that way by itself without Rusty having to stretch it, but it looked different then. And he felt different when it happened too, so he never seemed to remember to compare it to his hand then. He was always too busy trying other things to see what would happen. Some very strange feelings arose during those times.

With his member put away and his pants zipped, Rusty made his way toward the umbrella oaks and slid into the cubbyhole as quietly as he could, hoping Bo wouldn't say anything to him. Bo, thankfully, wasn't laughing anymore.

Rusty lay on his back and folded his hands over his waist, looking beyond the umbrellas as best he could. There was one star that was brighter than the others, and it seemed to be looking right at him. Rusty closed his eyes and made a wish, wishing for Ruby's safety for one more night. He imagined her alone, afraid, tears streaming down her rosy cheeks, the huge bed swallowing her between the sheets.

Tomorrow he and Bo would rescue her, then they'd all be safe in the woods together, as a family — the way it should be. Although he'd never know what it was like to have a real family — a mom and a dad that loved him and protected him and took care of him — he would try his hardest to give Ruby that chance. And he knew Bo would do the same. Between the two of them, they could give Ruby a chance of having the life they never had, the love they'd never been showered with. And if that meant they had to stay in the forest forever, then so be it. Rusty was resigned to that now. He and Bo could give Ruby a good life in the forest. And maybe, just maybe, they could all find happiness somewhere within the labyrinth of giant oak trees.

Rusty opened his eyes for a second just to make sure the star was still listening, and when it winked at him, he closed his eyes again and kept them that way. Then he unzipped his pants and slid his good hand inside and began to pull on his member, hoping that if he stretched it enough times, it might stay that way permanently.

CHAPTER TWENTY

When the sun came up, Rusty's hand was still in his pants. He felt the shriveled skin bunched up in his palm. It felt like a slinky might, just a lot less. He pulled his hand out and zipped up before Bo noticed. When he turned over, Bo was awake and standing near him, his back and neck hunched as he tried to look at something across the clearing. Rusty sat up.

"What are you doing?"

"Shhh," Bo said, putting a finger to his lips. He kept his eyes looking straight ahead. Rusty noticed he was shaking.

Rusty came fully awake. He slid out from the root as quietly as he could, setting his feet on the cold dirt. The bottoms of his feet were sweaty until now, the coolness of the ground refreshing. The smell coming from his toes didn't seem as potent anymore, either.

With a finger still pressed against his lips, Bo made eye contact with Rusty and pointed out across the clearing with his free hand. Rusty followed it as if it were an arrow, moving his eyes slowly until they found the target. When he did, Rusty froze, his muscles tensing, his toes curling into the dirt like talons. Bo nudged him with his shoulder, turning him, and reiterated that Rusty was to be quiet by pressing his finger even tighter against his lips. Rusty understood.

Across the clearing, near the pit where the fire died out, stood a boy. His back was to them, one hand sorting through Bo's backpack, the other tending to something near his face. From behind, Rusty placed the boy to be around his age — considering his height and build was about the same as his own

— but it was only a guess. The back of the boy's t-shirt was muddied and stained with dark streaks and covered with lots of tiny holes. He wore long pants that were cut off at the knees with white threads hanging down near his calves like thin tentacles. His hair was buzzed close to his scalp. The boy didn't look like an Indian.

Rusty looked behind him and noticed his own backpack was gone too, like Bo's, and he grew angry. He balled his hands into fists and took a step forward, ready to fight for what was his.

"Stop," Bo whispered. "What do you think you're doing?"

"He stole our bags."

"And we stole his trees." Bo pointed above them at the makeshift umbrellas.

Rusty nodded, remembering. "So, what do we do?"

"I don't know."

They both stood in silence and watched the mysterious boy for a while.

Eventually, the boy turned around and faced their direction. He didn't seem to notice them, though, as he moved his attention to Rusty's bag at his feet. The leather satchel they found was wrapped across the boy's chest, worn the way Indiana Jones did. In his free hand was a plum, bright purple and half eaten, and his jaw was rotating in a circle as he chewed it.

"He's eating our food!" Rusty said, the words coming out louder than he planned.

The boy stopped what he was doing and looked up in their direction, his eyes wide like a bug's. Bo snapped his eyes at Rusty, and Rusty clasped his good hand over his mouth.

"Oops," Rusty said, muffled, his hand still cupped over his lips.

"Shit." Bo turned back to the boy. He made his face look angry by scrunching it, then he took a step out into the clearing and yelled, "Hey!"

The boy dropped Rusty's bag in an instant, the plum falling from his mouth like a loose tooth, and took off running. Bo took another step into the clearing and yelled out to the boy again, but the boy kept going, disappearing into the thickest part of the forest until the underbrush swallowed him whole. Rusty could tell by the way Bo's legs were trembling that he had no intention of chasing after the boy — he was just trying to spook him.

When the leaves stopped rustling and the boy's footsteps could no longer be heard, Bo went back underneath the umbrellas and stood in front of Rusty. Rusty saw Bo's heartbeat underneath what remained of his t-shirt.

"He's gone."

Rusty lowered his head. "Sorry."

"Doesn't matter. He's gone now."

Rusty ran after Bo as he backtracked out of the shade and stepped back into the clearing. He leaped over a pile of acorns that weren't there before and landed flat-footed on an exposed root, sending a throbbing pain rushing through his arches. He winced when the pain hit, but limped it away as he continued to chase after Bo.

"Wait," he said, but Bo didn't stop. "Wait a second."

Bo stopped when he got to the fire pit, but didn't turn back to look at Rusty. He was either mad at him for what he did, or he was consciously choosing to ignore him. Rusty wasn't sure which was worse.

Rusty caught up and tossed himself onto the log, next to his socks that were still laid out like strips of meat. His boots were still flipped upside down on the dirt too, the rubber soles stealing all the warmth from the sun as if they were magnets.

"Told you there weren't any Indians out here," Bo finally said as he looked through their backpacks.

"Who was that?" Rusty pulled a foot onto his knee to inspect the damage.

"Don't know."

"Did he take anything?"

"Doesn't look like it."

"Just our food?"

"Not even that," Bo said, standing up straight, holding the two cans of beans in one hand and the can of tuna in the other. "We didn't have any plums left. Just these."

"Where do you think he got it, then?"

"I don't know."

Rusty was surprised at the condition of his feet. Not only were there no slivers of bark or acorns implanted into the bottoms of them, but whatever had been in between his toes last night wasn't as bad as he thought. There was some flaky skin surrounded by a white, creamy liquid, but that was pretty much the extent of it. For once in his life, things weren't as bad as they seemed.

"Do you think he'll come back?" Rusty asked once he put both feet flat on the ground, feeling the coldness again.

Bo worked to strap his pack onto his back. "I don't think so. I guess he just wanted his satchel back."

Rusty wasn't sure why Bo seemed so sure of it, but he was. Whatever the reason, he was happy to believe Bo might be right this time. He usually was.

"Come on," Bo said. "Put your socks and boots back on, and grab your bag."

"Why?"

Bo looped his thumbs through the straps of his pack and shifted his weight onto his heels. "Because we're going back to the trailer so we can get more supplies."

Rusty grabbed his socks. They were completely dry. "Supplies for what?"

"For tonight. We're gunna get Ruby tonight, remember?"

That's right, Rusty thought, pulling a sock over his foot and snapping the elastic band around his ankle. He did remember.

CHAPTER TWENTY-ONE

They made it to the trailer without any trouble. Not even the horse fly found them. The first thing Rusty noticed when they walked into the kitchen was the smell. Bleach and ammonia and something not as strong had been used recently, each of the odors still pungent. The bleach was the strongest, and it sat heavy on his lips when he licked them. His throat burned as if he'd drank some directly from a cup, his lung pinching as he breathed in. The inhaler in his pocket pressed against the flesh of his thigh, reminding him of its presence. He was thankful for the reminder, in case he needed it. He thought he might.

Bo was busy in the kitchen, filling his bag with all that could fit. He put a can opener in first after showing it to Rusty, shaking his head. Rusty went into the living room and stood in the center of the room. The irony hit him, the idea that the living room was meant for families to gather together and create happy memories and joyful times. For him, and for Bo and Ruby and their mom, the living room of the trailer offered nothing but memories, but they were memories of the worst kind. Rusty thought of the whoopings and the yelling and the backhands, and of the broken glass and crushed beer cans and leather belts, and of the bone bruises and the swelling and the all the tears. Between the four of them, there were so many tears. So many nights, so much yelling, so much pain. So many tears.

The living room was where it first happened. Admittedly, Rusty didn't remember what actually went down that night. He was young, still in diapers. Ruby wasn't born yet. His recollection of the events were all based on what Bo told him, which he always took to be the complete truth. Bo's face turned white every time he talked about it, and his hands shook as if his bones were vibrating underneath his skin.

The story was that Bo got up in the night to use the bathroom and overheard it happening from the hallway. There was a light on in the living room, and their mom and dad were in there arguing about something. Bo didn't catch the early part of the conversation, and as a little boy, he didn't understand much of what he did hear. He crept down the hallway and stood where he could see what they were doing, and he stayed there and made himself small while the argument worsened.

Lenny was standing close to their mom, his face so close she surely would've been able to smell the Budweiser on his breath. There was a can in one hand, mom's wrist in the other. He forced her against the window, spinning her head with his hand so she could look over toward grandpa's trailer, even though it was dark. Bo said the plum tree wasn't as tall then, so their grandpa's trailer could be seen from the window. Lenny called their mom nasty names — like whore and bitch and slut — and while Bo didn't know what any of those words meant at the time, the angry way in which Lenny said them made them sound like insults.

Their mom kept saying that Lenny didn't understand, and that if he just let her explain, he might. But Lenny never let her explain — he never let anyone explain — and he threw the back of his hand at her face instead. Their mom eventually slid down the wall and sat on the floor with her hands covering her face, screaming and pleading for Lenny to stop, agony in her voice. But he didn't. Lenny kept swinging and swinging until their mom stopped fighting, then he grabbed her by the collar of her shirt and pulled her onto the porch.

Bo didn't see what happened after that, but he guessed the rest. Lenny came back into sight and grabbed an orange bottle of pills and disappeared onto the porch again, yelling something at their mom that Bo couldn't decipher. When Lenny came back in again, Bo had crept past the edge of the wall, trying to hear, and Lenny saw him. Bo's entire body was already trembling.

"How long you been standin' there?" Lenny said, his forehead shining with sweat, his fingers balled into fists. His face was red with rage, and the thickest vein in his neck stuck out like a tripwire. "What'd you see?"

Bo didn't answer. He didn't know what he was supposed to say or do, so he said nothing. He was stuck in place, his feet like stones, iced to the floor.

Lenny walked over to him and stood close. He bent his back and crouched to Bo's level, looking into his eyes with fury. Bo could smell the beer on his breath, taste the aluminum as it sweated out of Lenny's pores. The browns in Lenny's eyes turned almost black. Small flames behind his pupils made them glow.

"If you say anything to anyone," Lenny sad, moving his lips so close to Bo's ear he could have licked it if he wanted, "you'll be next."

Bo went back to the bedroom and sat on his bed and cried. He believed his dad with all his heart, so he did just what he was told — nothing. He kept what he saw a secret for a long time, until he eventually told Rusty many years later.

Their mom would come back to the trailer every few months, and she and Lenny would make up for a while. Bo would hear loud noises coming from their parents' bedroom during the night — moaning that wasn't scary, wood pounding against the wall like the door on the porch, strange grunting coming from their dad that made Bo feel nauseous — followed by the smell of cigarette smoke that seeped underneath the door frame when the noises stopped. But their mom never stayed for long. The fighting returned during the nights that followed, and she went to stay with their grandpa again for a while. Even when Ruby was born the pattern stayed the same, and eventually their mom stopped coming back at all.

Then Bo and later Rusty took their mom's place in the living room, on the receiving end of Lenny's drunken fits in the night. And now Ruby. Sweet, little, innocent Ruby.

Those were Rusty's memories of the living room. That was what his life was like. It was hard to be happy when he wasn't sure he even knew what happiness was. He was just glad to be alive, although he questioned more than once whether it was worth it or not, wondered what was so great about it. It was a gift, he was once told, but he didn't feel like a fortunate recipient. He was still trying to figure out why some people smiled and others didn't, and what that experience might feel like. All the other kids at his school smiled more often than not.

Rusty turned and left the living room, his cheeks wet with tears. So many tears, even still.

In the bedroom, he dropped his backpack on Ruby's bed and sorted through the clothes he packed the day before. He took out what hadn't yet dried and tossed them in a pile on the floor. He changed his pants and his pee-stained underwear and his muddy shirt, and he went across the hall and washed his hands and feet and cleaned out the mess in between his toes. He found a box of Band-Aids in the secret compartment behind the mirror above the sink and put one over the scab on his palm. What was left of them he took and shoved in his pocket, storing them next to his inhaler for safekeeping.

Back in the bedroom, Rusty changed into a fresh pair of socks and put his boots back on. They squelched again when he slid them over his heels, but it wasn't as bad as before. They were drying out nicely. He filled the empty space in the backpack with clothes for Ruby and started back for the kitchen. He heard Bo calling his name.

Before he left, he stopped in the doorway and took another look around, just to make sure he didn't forget anything. For some reason, he had a premonition that he may not return to the bedroom, or to the trailer, in quite a while, and he was okay with that. The forest was going to be his home now. He'd be safe there.

In the backpack, he had clean clothes for him and Bo, and now Ruby. They didn't need blankets yet and they didn't have the hands to carry any pillows, but they could figure that out later. They had plenty of matches to keep them warm for now. That would be enough. But he still felt like he was forgetting something.

And he was. He remembered when his eyes hit Ruby's pillow.

Stepping over the pile of clothes on the floor, Rusty slid his good hand underneath Ruby's pillow and felt around for the curls. The yarn made contact with the pits of his fingers and stuck there, and Rusty pinched them together and pulled out the doll by its braids.

Lucy looked sad with her one remaining eye barely hanging on, her ginger braids loose. On her overalls, a single white thread looped through the small holes in the center of the button and disappeared somewhere into Lucy's stuffing. Rusty held her close, the overalls crusted with old pencil shavings and a dab of peanut butter that never went away, and thought of his little sister. Ruby loved this doll more than anything in the world, which made it all that much more important that he keep it safe. She was going to need it out there in the forest.

***

Outside and around the back side of the trailer was a crawlspace. There was no basement underneath the trailer and the perimeter of the screen porch was blocked off with woven fencing, so the only access to the plumbing was through the crawlspace. The fit was tight, the hole just barely wide enough for an average grown man to fit his shoulders through. A burly man wouldn't make it. An old one wouldn't take the time to try.

That made it the perfect hiding spot.

Bo went in first. He had a flashlight.

Rusty stood on the grass, his feet feeling brand new in the fresh linen that covered his toes, watching over his shoulder the entire time. Their backpacks were at his feet. Their grandpa's trailer was hardly visible from where Rusty stood, and that made him nervous. Someone could sneak up on them and he wouldn't even see them coming. He tried to think about what he'd say he and Bo were doing if that were to happen.

The sun was bright, the ominous clouds that blanketed the sky the day before long gone, floated away toward the sea. The grass was still wet with a mist from the night, but Rusty hardly noticed; he hadn't been this dry in days. Making a path in the direction he and Bo came from were their boot prints, which made impressions on the grass as if the blades were made of pins, the crushed ones lying down flat. Rusty remembered the feeling of the pin point impression toy he had as a younger boy — the one where he'd press his hand into and it would leave a handprint engrained in the pins — and he wondered if the grass felt it too. The pressure, he remembered, felt like little needles prodding his skin each time he tried it. He remembered how cold the needles were on his skin, how good it felt. He missed being a boy sometimes. Life was simpler then. Being a man was hard.

Once Bo's feet disappeared into the black hole under the trailer, Rusty got down on a knee and peered inside the crawlspace. Aside from the dull path of light Bo shone somewhere deeper inside that gradually faded, blackness was all Rusty could see. He held his breath and went in head first.

His shoulders fit when he pulled them toward his chest, and the dampness of the soil let him slide through easily, as if greased. The land was sloped slightly downward, forming a miniature ravine beneath the trailer that opened up and widened at the bottom. Bo was standing when Rusty got through, his neck craned and his back hunched, but his two feet were flat on the ground. Rusty stood up straighter than his brother, the bottom of the trailer further away from the top of his head than it was Bo's. But he felt more comfortable sitting on one knee, so that's what he did.

Light shone in through the fencing around the porch and lit the space beneath the trailer. Bo flicked his flashlight off and slid it into the pocket on his hip. Rusty scanned the openness, seeing nothing but dirt and stones and chunks of splintered wood, expecting his father's body to be somewhere out in the open.

But it wasn't. There wasn't a body anywhere.

Wooden, steel, and brick support beams were scattered throughout the space, creating legs for the trailer to stand on. With all the legs it had, it's a wonder the trailer didn't just walk away.

"Where is he?" Rusty asked. It was stuffy underneath the trailer, and his chest was tightening. He felt for his inhaler in his pocket.

"I don't know." Bo was sitting now, his fingers busy scratching his head. "He was right over here."

Rusty looked where Bo was pointing, close to one of the wooden legs, and shuffled his way toward it like a crab might.

"I don't get it," Bo said, "I put him right here. I know I did."

Rusty didn't know what to say. He didn't remember taking part in it, if he had. Out of nowhere, something toxic hit his nose and pushed him backward, sending him choking for air. He cupped his nose and mouth with his good hand as if the plague had gone airborne. His lungs were burning.

"What's that smell?" he said, his voice muffled behind his fingers. He thought his stomach might empty right there in his hand.

Bo covered his nose with his shoulder. "It ain't a decomposing body, I can tell you that."

"Then what it is?"

"I don't know, but we should get out of here."

Rusty went first this time, as fast as he could. The incline of the small hill, even in the darkness, was easy to climb. His hands slipped in the damp soil a few times, his chest slamming into the dirt, but he kept on moving. The tunnel led back to the grass and to their bags and to fresh, clean air. Rusty climbed out and pressed his back up against the trailer, pulling his knees up to his chest and breathing in hard. He took a puff from his inhaler and tried to concentrate on breathing out of his nose while the medicine worked its way through his lungs. Perspiration drenched his neck as if he just showered.

A moment later, Bo emerged from the hole and sat beside him with a shade of white covering his face that Rusty hadn't seen before. It almost seemed as if there were a tint of green in it, like he was turning into a leprechaun. Rusty doubted they'd be lucky enough to find a pot of gold.

"I just don't get it," Bo said, his shoulders slouching, his nose wiggling. "I wrapped his body in the rug and dragged him out the back door, then I pushed him into the hole and left him there, behind one of the support beams."

"Are you sure?"

Bo looked at him like he was stupid. "Of course I'm sure."

Rusty looked away. He wondered how Bo was able to do all that by himself, but he didn't question it.

They sat in the quiet. The humming of the engines of a distant airplane was the only sound for quite a while. Then a cricket chirped in the long grass. Then a bee buzzed. Then Bo coughed once.

Rusty sensed Bo was thinking hard, trying to make sense out of everything. He tried too, but he still didn't even remember who pulled the trigger, never mind what happened afterward. But at least he was starting to breathe better, the medicine having loosened the restriction in his airways.

"It doesn't make sense," Bo said, breaking the silence between them, his tone slow and sullen. "There wasn't even any blood down there. The dirt was smooth. No rug. No body. No footprints. There was no sign of anyone being down there. It's impossible."

Rusty looked at him skeptically, wondering if he was feeling all right, wondering if he inhaled too much ammonia or bleach or whatever that smell was underneath the porch. It wasn't possible for a body to just disappear like that.

Bo looked spooked, the skin on his face still a mellow shade of off-white. The green tint had gone away.

"It's like he vanished."

CHAPTER TWENTY-TWO

Earl's back was killing him. Beverly gave him something strong last night which knocked out the pain, something numbing, but it wore off hours ago. It hurt to stand up straight. It hurt to sit. It hurt to breathe. It felt best if he stood near the counter and used his hand as a crutch against it. That way, the tugging and stretching in his muscles would stop. But every slight movement — every time he shuffled his feet or scratched his face or pushed out a little cough — the pain tore through his obliques again, causing the muscles to spasm with fire.

"Bev," he called. "You got any more of them pills?"

Beverly came into the kitchen from the living room, her feet dragging, barely rising above the floor. Her arms swung freely at her sides as if she had no control of them, like she was a puppet. The floorboards shook as she came closer, her entire body weight crashing against the floor with each short step on her heels. She stopped when she got close to Earl and looked up. Her eyes were only half open, sagging on her face. It was as if miniature anchors were attached to her eyelids, pulling her down and trying to drown her.

Beverly opened her mouth and smiled, her eyes rolling behind her anchored eyelids. Her black tooth stuck out as if it didn't belong, even though it'd been that way for decades, gradually decaying more and more as time passed. Earl moved his tongue around the front of his mouth and rubbed it back and forth on the teeth that weren't the originals — he lost his own a few years back after nearly a half-century of neglect and abuse through cigarettes and, a long time ago, the powder. They were smoother than real teeth and more perfectly straight than his ever were, and they worked like they were supposed to. He was glad he didn't have to look in the mirror and see the same mangled mess that Beverly saw every day.

"What's the matter with you?" Earl asked. She looked out of it, loopy.

"Nothing's wrong. I feel great."

"Why are your eyes closed?"

"Hmm?"

Earl tried to stand up straight, but he groaned in pain. "Jesus Christ, Bev. Are there any left?"

"Any what?"

"You know what I'm talking about."

"Lighten up, old man," Beverly said, grinning.

"This is exactly the shit I'm talking about with you —"

"Relax," she said as she slowly bent at the waist and dropped to her knees. "I know what'll cheer you up."

Earl clenched his fingers around the hard edge of the countertop and flexed his jaw. Beverly was a different person when she was high, which is what got them in the situation they were in the first place.

Earl thought about the photo he found in Lenny's truck. It was in his shirt pocket. He thought about the look on Beverly's face, about her posing on the bed and how her eyes were begging for it. She was begging for Lenny in that photo, just like she begged for Earl to touch her that night she ran from Lenny's trailer and into his own after an argument. Just like she did after every time Lenny time hit her, or after every time they had a loud disagreement. She'd pop a pill or two or three and become submissive, and Earl would do whatever he wanted to her, unable to control himself in a moment of ecstasy. He knew it was wrong in so many ways, but she begged for it, begged for him. She pleaded with him to give it to her, to dominate her, to humiliate her. She got it, she took it, and she loved it. They both did.

But that was a long time ago.

Earl didn't want that from her anymore.

He didn't realize his jeans were already unzipped until he looked down. Beverly was elbow-deep in his crotch, feeling around inside as if she didn't know where to find him. The nubs of her fingernails tickled the thinnest patch of skin on his thigh, and her hand eventually moved in between his legs and began to strangle him. Earl flinched, his body unable to stop it. His obliques stiffened when he did, and another jolt of hot lighting crashed through him. His skin was on fire.

"Why aren't you hard?" Beverly asked, rolling her fingers over him, licking her lips in a way that repulsed Earl. "See, I told you something's wrong with you."

"Get out of there." Earl leaned forward as far he could and grabbed Beverly's wrist. A sharp pain tore through his back.

"What's the matter?" She looked up with those same loopy, subservient eyes. "Don't you want it?"

"No." He yanked her arm out of his pants the best he could, pushing through the pain. "You'll cut me open with that thing."

Beverly let go and stood up, almost toppling backward as she moved too fast. "Fine." She turned her back to him and starting for the living room.

"Where are you going? What about those pills?"

"If you don't want what I'm offering, then you're going to have to suffer without them."

***

Later, Beverly sobered up. Earl made his way to the couch and was lying flat on it, his muscles burning. He'd been that way for hours. Beverly came into the living room with a glass of water in one hand and a couple of horse pills in the other. Her hair was damp and tied back, and Earl could smell the generic floral scent he doubted existed naturally in nature. She looked lively and well-rested, like a normal person should.

"How's the pain?" she asked as she kneeled next to the couch, handing Earl one pill at a time.

"Terrible." He took the first pill from her and popped it in his mouth. Then he took the second one and threw that in too, and he washed them both down at once with the water from the glass.

"I'm sorry," Beverly said, her voice soft and sincere.

"And how are you? Feeling better?"

"I'm sorry, Earl. I don't know what happened. It must've been the stress."

"You do realize this is exactly why you're here and your kids are over there, right?"

"Were. They were over there."

"They're still not here, are they?"

"Ruby's here."

"But not the boys."

Beverly shook her head. "No, not the boys."

"Then what's the difference?" Earl tried to sit up, but he couldn't.

"I said I was sorry. I'll try harder."

"If you don't get your shit together before the state—"

"I'll try harder, I said."

Earl only nodded, staying silent.

A long minute passed.

The toilet flushed down the hall.

"So, can we finish the conversation we were having last night?" Beverly asked.

"Sober now?"

Beverly ignored it. "Did you find him?"

Earl tried to sit up again, and this time, he was able to. The pain was already starting to numb. "We found him, yes."

"And?"

"What do you think?"

Beverly looked away and took a moment for herself, sadness overtaking her eyes. Earl let her have it, considering all those two had been through together. There were those times when the booze got the best of Lenny and he did things he regretted, yes, but there were also plenty of good times, too. They were happy once upon a time — Lenny and Beverly. It's just the bad memories that get magnified sometimes, leaving the good ones to die in the abyss of our minds. As Earl sat there watching his wife's wheels spin, he hoped Beverly was reminiscing on some of those good times too.

"So, what's next?" Beverly asked once her moment passed.

Earl could tell her heart was suffering. He almost sympathized with her. "Cletus is meeting with a buddy downtown today to find out what our options are, then we'll go from there."

"Then what?"

"Don't know. We'll find out."

Beverly nodded, then she stood up. "Well, okay then." She brought a hand to her lips and kissed her fingertips, and pressed her fingers against Earl's lips. It had been a while since she'd done that. Earl closed his eyes and let the sweetness of the flowers penetrate his mouth. He could smell the lilacs and jasmines and magnolias, and he could taste the cocoa butter they were camouflaged in. But before he could think to kiss

Beverly's fingers back, they were gone, as were the scents and the tastes. When he opened his eyes, he saw the back of his wife's head and her oversized t-shirt and her dirty sweatpants, then she was gone around the corner.

As Earl sat up further and fought with the pain that still lingered, he was thankful Beverly didn't ask what he and Cletus did with Lenny's body. Even if she did, he wouldn't have told her. He wasn't proud of what happened, but it was something that had to be done. And with it, he just hoped that Lenny, his son, would rest in peace, wherever he was going next. If given a second chance, Earl prayed Lenny would make the best of it.

CHAPTER TWENTY-THREE

"Did you see dad's truck?" Rusty asked. He and Bo were back in the forest with their packs on their backs, the clearing just a few hundred yards further down the trail.

"What about it?"

"The window — did you see it?"

"The glass was broken. I saw it."

"What do you think that's all about?"

"Don't know."

Now that Rusty's socks were dry and his boots weren't as heavy, he was moving faster, feeling lighter. Bo's pack was fuller than his, packed with cans, and it seemed as if Bo was the one who had to catch up now. Rusty had to slow his pace so he and Bo could walk next to each other and talk.

"Are you scared?" Rusty asked. Bo seemed off, still spooked by what happened underneath the porch. He hadn't been himself since that happened.

Bo kept walking but shifted his eyes, locking in with Rusty's. "I'm just a little confused about what's going on. Why, are you?"

Rusty shrugged. He wasn't really, for some reason, but he didn't want to make Bo feel bad about it if he was. Men were allowed to be scared sometimes, weren't they?

Seemingly out of nowhere, Bo stopped and stiffened, as if he saw a monster. Rusty stopped too, but only when Bo's hand went out and made a gate in front of his chest. Rusty scanned the forest for the beast but saw nothing that didn't belong. The trail was still.

"Smell that?" Bo asked, his nostrils flaring.

Rusty raised his nose to the sky and breathed in hard. All he smelled was the fresh forest air and a hint of wet bark from the shaded trees that hadn't dried yet. He doubted that was what Bo was talking about.

"What is it?"

"Smoke. Something's on fire."

Rusty's eyes widened. He couldn't smell the smoke or hear the crackling of the flames, and he certainly couldn't feel the heat from the burning wood. But he believed Bo did, which could only mean one thing — the Indian people had found them.

"Come on," Bo said, grabbing Rusty's sleeve and yanking him off the beaten path.

Bo started to run. He kept his back bent and his head craned forward, and he pushed hanging branches and crawling vines away from his face. He ran like a man on a mission.

Rusty tried to keep up but found himself running into roadblocks with every branch and stump and mound of moss that tried to trip him up — the same ones Bo found no trouble maneuvering around. He eventually caught up to Bo near where the clearing opened up, out of breath and gasping for air. Bo was leaning against the trunk of a huge oak, using its girth as a shield, with only his head out in the open. Rusty leaned up against an adjacent one, its girth just as wide, his lungs pinching.

"What's going on?" Rusty asked once he found some air, his words choppy.

Bo kept his attention on the clearing, motioning with his eyes. "Look."

"Why don't you just tell me?"

"Just look. Trust me."

Rusty sighed. Then he did as Bo said, turning and looking past the trees, out into the clearing.

He gasped at what he saw.

***

Everything Ruby thought she knew was wrong. Over the last day, she overheard more about her life than she ever knew to be true. As it turned out, her mama didn't kill her grandpa and was trying to help him instead. He did something to hurt his back that involved a shovel and the dirt underneath the porch on her daddy's trailer. Whatever it was, Sheriff Cletus helped him do it.

Ruby's mama was taking some medicine she wasn't supposed to, and it made her act strangely, unlike her usual self. She became loopy and looked really tired and smiled a lot. She'd say things that didn't make sense and would giggle while she talked to herself. Ruby's grandpa didn't like it much, and Ruby didn't know what to think.

Even though it wasn't said directly, Ruby knew her daddy was dead. And worse, she knew her brothers did it. Something was going to be happening soon — something that involved her and her brothers and her mama and her grandpa — that involved whatever it was her grandpa and Sheriff Cletus found in her daddy's trailer. Nobody seemed to care much that her daddy was dead. Even though he hit her, Ruby cared. At least a little.

There was something else bothering Ruby too. When her brothers first went missing, her mama and grandpa and Sheriff Cletus were looking for them, trying to rescue them, trying to bring them home. They were talking about them and trying to guess where they went and tried to figure out how to find them.

But now, ever since her grandpa and Cletus went to her daddy's trailer, Bo and Rusty hardly ever came up in conversation at all. It was as if nobody cared anymore, like whatever it was they found in her daddy's trailer was more important than finding her brothers. Nobody spoke to her all day, either. She was scared about what was going to happen to her — and to her brothers, if they were found.

After all Ruby heard, after all she learned about her mama and grandpa and about who they really were, there wasn't much she knew to be true anymore. But if there was one thing she knew for sure, one thing she knew to be true, it was that her brothers loved her. They'd be okay out in the forest, and when the time was right, they'd come for her — she knew deep in her heart they would. And when they did, she'd be ready.

***

The boy was back. It was the same boy Rusty and Bo saw earlier in the day, the same boy with the same torn up t-shirt and pants that were cut off at the knee. He wore the satchel across his chest the same way he had before. The boy sat on the same log Rusty had the night before, with his front facing the edge of the trail where Rusty and Bo stood. The fire pit was burning with huge orange flames.

The boy used a Swiss Army knife on something on his lap. His elbow was bent and the lower portion of his arm rose and fell in rapid succession. From a distance, it could have looked as if he were trying to start a lawnmower or chainsaw by its pull cord, but Rusty knew better than that. He considered the markings he and Bo saw earlier — the way the bark had been shaved from the trees — and figured the boy was carving something. That meant the boy, despite not looking it, was definitely one of the Indian people.

Rusty's heart leaped at the sight of seeing one in person. He felt giddy. The Indian people didn't look like he expected them to, though. The photos of the ones in the books at school wore big feathers on their caps with brown, leathery cover-ups and moccasins without laces. They had their faces painted and carried a bow and arrow and made sounds by hitting their open mouths with a cupped hand while they danced silly dances around an open fire. This boy was nothing like that. He looked like a regular person, like Rusty or Bo. Thinking about it, Rusty felt the excitement fading away. Disappointment crept in. He really thought he'd see one like the ones in the books.

"Follow my lead," Bo said. He took a step outside the shadow of the oak and started toward the boy.

"What are you going to do to him?"

"Just follow my lead."

Bo started tiptoeing toward the boy. Rusty fell in behind him and did the same, although he wasn't feeling anything. He really thought the Indian people dressed the way they did in the books.

"Hey! You!" Bo yelled out when they got closer. He walked flat-footed now with his chest puffed out and his muscles flexed, and Rusty knew Bo was trying to act tough to scare the boy.

The boy dropped whatever he was carving and stood up. The knife blade disappeared inside the red casing in his hand and slipped into the boy's pocket. He looked frozen with fear, his eyes widened and his legs straightened, as if his entire body was stuck in quicksand.

"Wait there," Bo said. "Don't move."

Rusty expected the boy to run like he did before — like the wind. Bo was getting closer to him with Rusty not far behind, but the boy just stood there, not backing down, unmoving. Even from a distance, it was clear Bo soared above the boy. Bo was much taller and filled out his t-shirt a lot more than did the mystery Indian boy. The boy, Rusty realized, looked similar to himself. They had the same body type and the same hair color and the same shaped face. He and the boy couldn't have been born more than a few months apart.

As they approached, it became clear the boy wasn't going to run. Something was different this time. His hands eventually rose in surrender, and he stood in place until Rusty and Bo reached the opposite side of the fire pit. The heat coming from it was sweltering, hotter than theirs. Rusty's hands began to sweat, the adhesive of the Band-Aid softening. The scab on his palm kept his callus from stinging this time.

Bo slid around to the other side of the fire pit and stood face to face with the boy. He had to have six inches on the boy, at least. Bo said, "Who are you and what are you doing here?"

The boy said nothing.

"It was you this morning too, wasn't it?" Bo said.

The boy shifted his weight and lowered his hands, dropping them to his hip, but he stayed silent.

Bo waited him out.

Rusty looked between Bo and the boy, wondering who was going to say something first. They were at a stalemate. The tension was thick.

"Well?" Bo said.

"Well, what?" the boy finally said, his voice cracking.

"He does speak."

"I was here first," the boy said. "Before you two came here and took my stuff, I was here first."

Bo said nothing. He took a step back and looked at Rusty, then back at the boy. "There was no one here when we got here. You took our fire pit."

"It was mine first. Everything here was mine. I made it all."

Bo turned to Rusty again, but Rusty looked away. He knew those umbrellas had to have been made by someone for a reason. He knew they should have let them be.

Bo looked for a distraction. "What's this?" he said, turning back to the boy and pointing to the fire.

Rusty didn't notice before, but there was more than just a fire in the pit. Soaring above the flames was a tin pan without a lid, suspended from thin strips of tree bark that were hung at the point of a manmade teepee. The teepee made a tripod over the fire with three sharpened legs made of sturdy branches meeting in the center at the peak. Each leg was leaning inward just a bit, and all three were tied together at the top with the same bark string that was used on the umbrellas.

Whoever this boy was, Indian or not, Rusty admired how skilled he was. He wondered where he came from and what he was doing out here.

"Boiling water. If you don't boil water out here, you can get really sick."

"Where'd the pan come from?" Bo asked.

"Found it."

Bo pointed to a stick on the ground. The edge was pointed like a javelin. "What's that?"

"I was making a spear."

"For what?"

"Fishing."

"What kind of fish?"

"Whatever bites."

Rusty thought that was funny. He smiled. He thought the spear looked more like an arrow, and he wondered where the boy's bow might be. Feeling more comfortable now, Rusty joined his brother on the other side of the flames and stood closer to the mystery Indian boy.

Upon getting closer, Rusty studied the boy's face. There was something familiar about it. He thought for a second that maybe he went to school with him at one time, but he didn't think that was it. The boy had a face full of freckles. The bridge of his nose and his cheeks and his forehead were covered, as if he'd spent many days out in these woods being kissed by the sun. They were lighter than any other freckles he'd seen, some of them almost red. Ruby had freckles on her nose, but hers were brown.

"What do you do with them when you catch them?" Bo asked.

"Eat them."

"Why don't you go home to eat?"

The boy shrugged and looked away.

"Are you an Indian?" Rusty asked, needing to know. "Do you live out here? Where's the rest of your tribe?"

"I already told you," Bo said, his tone firm but not as convincing as it had been when he said it the first time, as if he wasn't so sure anymore, "there aren't any Indians out here."

"Are you?" Rusty said.

"No, I'm not an Indian."

Rusty deflated a little, dropping his head. Out of the corner of his eye, he saw Bo's shoulders grow straighter, taller.

The boy smiled and said, "But that would be cool if I was, wouldn't it?"

CHAPTER TWENTY-FOUR

They all became fast friends. The boy's name was JT and he was eight-years-old. Rusty was nine; their birthdays were less than a year apart, just as he guessed. Although he insisted he wasn't an Indian — Rusty still had his doubts — JT did live in these woods. He made tools and weapons and shelter and used the resources in the forest to stay dry and fed and alive. He caught fish and squirrels and raccoons and skinned them and ate their meat. He washed in a nearby pond. He drank the water from the same pond, one boiled pan full at a time. He built umbrellas with fallen oak trees. His whole life was in the forest; the forest was JT's home.

The nearest town center was a mile or two through the forest to the west, according to JT, and he'd go there when needed. He made the trail himself. The men in town didn't ask many questions. They all seemed to ignore the fact that JT, an eight-year-old boy, would be in town all by himself, and would look the other way and pretend not to see him walk back into the woods when he left town. Goods were traded in exchange for cash or supplies, and that was all they cared about. Like everyone else, they had their own problems to worry about.

JT would save the skin from the raccoons and squirrels he caught and sell them to the taxidermist in town. He'd walk the abandoned dirt roads where the high schoolers would discard their empty beer cans, dip containers, and used rubbers, and he'd collect what he could in his satchel. The local supermarket had a bin for recyclables, and they'd pay up to a dime per can collected. Once a week, a resident would volunteer to pick up each container and drive his pickup to the county dump a few towns over, and he'd collect all the money and reimburse the supermarket. There was a little cash involved for everyone, although it took collecting a lot of cans to make any real money. JT collected a lot of cans.

The most expensive supply — and trickiest to transport — JT collected was wood. Cords were expensive, even in the off-season, and he could only carry two or three logs at a time. But he had a lot of time on his hands. His biceps were bigger than Rusty's.

"How'd you do it?" Bo asked.

Rusty could tell Bo was truly interested in all JT said, the excitement in his voice obvious. It was as if he were trying to determine the feasibility of permanently living out here. Rusty was just amazed someone younger than he could actually do all that.

"I had some help."

"Obviously," Bo said. "From who?"

"I made a deal. Let's just leave it at that."

Silence fell.

There were so many questions to be asked, so many things Rusty knew Bo wanted to say. And so many he wanted to too. It was hard to decide where to start.

The pan over the fire began to shake. There was water filling more than half of it, and it was bubbling now. Rusty thought it smelled cleaner. He was getting hungry; his belly felt empty.

Bo and JT stood, so Rusty did too, although he wanted to sit. His pack was heavy on his back, weighing him down, and the sun was getting hot. It was like being in the tobacco field again. He thought he was done with that for good.

"Hey," JT said, "do you guys want to see something cool?"

"What is it?" Bo asked.

JT bent down and picked up the spear he was carving. "Follow me and I'll show you."

***

No more than a half mile through the trees was another clearing. It was past the big oak with the exposed roots and past the tarp with the stacked wood underneath it. Neither Rusty nor Bo explored much beyond the stacked wood, but if they did, they would have found what JT already knew. It might have changed things.

The pond was the most beautiful body of water Rusty had ever seen. It sparkled when the sun shone upon it just right, creating a twinkle on the surface that looked magical. There were rings of ripples that vibrated across the surface when something beneath swam. There were lilies of pink and white and yellow floating on the surface as if they were elegant. Many of them broke free from their pads and swam generously across the pond with liberty.

Rusty moved closer.

A bullfrog sat on the bank of the pond and croaked as if it were welcoming Rusty to his home. Water bugs skipped across the surface of the water, bouncing from pad to pad. A bright orange fish swam past. Rusty felt at peace. He wondered if this was happiness he was feeling; if so, it was wonderful. He felt his lips widen.

He leaned over the bank and gazed down at the ripples, seeing his own distorted face smiling back at him. He almost didn't recognize himself — he wasn't used to seeing himself smile. The water was the bluest he'd ever seen. And the cleanest. He wanted to reach out and touch the surface to see if it was real or if it was a mirage, but he didn't dare; he didn't want to ruin the moment, in case it was only his imagination. The blue surface was as smooth as crystal when the ripples faded, and Rusty wondered if it might actually be a pane of glass.

The water from the well was nothing like this. That water was brown and murky and smelled and tasted of iron on its best days. On its worst, he wouldn't even look at it. Even the stuff from town that his father bought wasn't like the water in the pond, and Rusty doubted anything would be. The pond water was as pure as he ever imagined, as perfect as he would surely ever taste. His mouth began to salivate as he thought about what that might be like.

Rusty remembered what JT said about drinking the water — he could get sick if he did without boiling it first — but he didn't see how that was possible. In comparison to what he was used to, this water would taste like gold. Rusty made a cup with his hands and dipped them beneath the surface. The temperature was just right and it helped to soothe his chapped skin and sore palm. His fingers floated just beneath the surface. Everything about it was perfect.

Rusty brought his hands to his face and examined the pond water up close. The only imperfections he saw were the ones his own hands made, poisoning the purity with inadequacy. Droplets beaded on his palms as the water seeped through his fingers and fell back to where it came from. His hands shook as he thought about how flawless it was.

Little dots exploded from underneath Rusty's skin as if they were hungry mouths begging to be fed, and he felt his body tingle as he splashed water on himself. He hadn't felt something on his skin that was as smooth as this — he was used to the feeling of being wrapped in a wet towel all the time, unable to get completely dry, after he showered with the hard well water; the filmy residue left behind never seemed to go away.

Until now.

And Rusty couldn't take it anymore.

He wanted to dive in the pond and let the natural springs rinse him clean and cleanse the stains of his life from him. He wanted to splash water in his hair and scrub underneath his fingers and wash the crevices around his member. He wanted to soak his toes and his feet and his ankles. But most of all, he wanted to know what it felt like to drink fresh water, wanted to know what it tasted like as it filled up his cheeks and slipped over his tongue and went down his throat. He wanted to know what it was like to feel good.

So he tried it. Despite JT's warning, Rusty cupped his hands again and pressed them to his lips before the water disappeared. He did it over and over and over again until he was moving so fast his heart was drumming in his chest. He drank so fast and so long that his belly began to twist, and he thought he might vomit if he kept going. But it tasted so good. So fresh. So different. Even better than he dreamed it would.

When Rusty stood up, Bo was right behind him. He grinned from ear to ear, his face lit up like a string of holiday lights. It was as if he knew what Rusty was experiencing, as if he already knew how wonderful it tasted and was happy that Rusty finally got to have some. Bo didn't say anything about needing to boil the water before drinking it, which Rusty was happy about. He didn't care about that. He had no regrets over drinking the wonderful water, no matter what the consequences might be later on.

Further away, JT stood next to the edge of the pond, leaning over the water and aiming his spear at something. Rusty felt

Bo's strong hand rest on his shoulder, squeezing only slightly, so he turned his head around to check what was wrong. But nothing was wrong — the opposite, in fact. Bo still smiled at him, the bottoms of his front teeth sticking out like sugar cubes. Rusty wasn't certain what Bo was smiling at, but he had an idea. So he smiled back.

Rusty whipped his head back around once he heard a splash. JT made a noise that sounded like gibberish, and he was on his knees and elbow-deep in the pond. Ripples covered the surface of the glass again, and there was a lot of commotion near where JT was. There was a slapping sound that rang through the air when JT pulled out of the water, but before Rusty had a chance to guess what it was, JT showed him.

"Ta-da," he said, thrusting his spear toward Rusty and Bo. With a huge smile on his face, he looked like a little boy seeing his birthday cake for the first time. Rusty had a birthday cake once, he remembered, but it was just once. He didn't remember much about it, though. JT seemed to be excited to show someone else what he caught.

"Are you kidding me?" Bo said, laughing.

"Nope."

Attached to the sharp end of the spear was a forest green largemouth bass, its body bending like a pretzel as it tried to dislodge itself from the spear. Its fin swung back and forth like a propeller and its body viciously jerked. The underbelly of the bass was white and spotted, and Rusty recognized it as being the official state fish of Kentucky. This one looked to be maybe four or five pounds, but Rusty was only guessing.

Just about every boy he knew at school talked about the spotted bass, bragging that the one they caught was the biggest of them all. But Rusty knew the truth — they all did — and that was that none of them were the ones to actually catch the bass. Many of them were too scared to take the hook out of its mouth, and some of them weren't even strong enough to reel it in by themselves. It was really their father's fish they were talking about, but no one ever admitted it. Rusty hardly ever joined in the conversations when they happened because he never caught a bass in his entire life. He never caught any fish before actually, because his dad never took him fishing. Not even once. JT's fish was the first one he ever saw up close, and Rusty found it remarkable. Maybe next year he could join in on those conversations at school, now that he had a story to share.

"How did you do that?" Rusty said as he inspected the fish. The bass's gills were flaring, showing off some red meat that looked spongy under its scales. Its brown and black eyes were unblinking, its body still flopping. The bass closed its mouth and clamped its lips together, but the one on the bottom stuck out further than the top, as if the fish were angry. Rusty felt bad for it, but he didn't really want to touch it to let it go, either. Its skin looked slimy.

"That was unbelievable!" Bo said. "How did you learn to do that?"

"It was nothing," JT said, brushing it off, the smile on his face holding firm.

"What else do you know how do to?" Bo asked, his eyes wide and his teeth showing.

JT shrugged, holding a tight grip around the spear. He held it like a trophy — beaming with pride. The bass tried to wriggle its way free once more but was unsuccessful. It still had three or four inches before it would reach the top. Rusty kept hoping it might make it.

"So," JT said, "are you guys hungry, or what?"

CHAPTER TWENTY-FIVE

The phone rang just before lunch time. The timing was less than ideal. Beverly had just made hot sandwiches for everybody, and the table was set. Ruby emerged from her cave at the smell of buttered toast and melted cheese, and Earl could tell by the tremor in her hands that she'd already surpassed hungry. Earl was glad to see her. She'd locked herself in the bedroom since last night, as if something spooked her.

Earl excused himself from the table and grabbed the ringing phone. The cord was stretched and the coil had twisted in on itself, and it looked more like a corkscrew than a horseshoe like it was supposed to. Sheriff Cletus was on the other end.

"Is now a good time to talk?" Cletus asked. His voice was distorted and distant, as if the wind was coming in through an open window near his lips.

Earl made eye contact with Beverly and nodded. She quickly rose to her feet and walked over toward him with eyes that were widened. Her high had long since vanished.

"What do you got?" Earl asked. Beverly leaned in close to try to hear too. Her hair smelled as pleasant as it usually did on days she showered.

"I don't even know where to begin. It's complicated."

"Explain."

"Let me start at the beginning. We've got some problems here, Earl."

"Like what?"

"For starters, you aren't in Lenny's will. You get nothing, not even the land."

"But, he was my son. We lived on the same property."

"And you live with his ex-wife on that property."

Earl cringed. It sounded bad spoken out loud like that.

"Would you put you in if the roles were reversed? Think about it."

Earl didn't want to. "Yeah, yeah," he said, brushing it off.

"But that's not all. Not even close. The children get everything."

"Is that a problem?"

"Lenny is."

"Excuse me?"

"Your son is the problem."

Earl looked at Beverly, whose eyes were closed as if concentrating on trying not to miss a word of the conversation. Earl thought he must have been missing something, because Cletus wasn't making any sense to him. "I don't follow what you're saying here, Clete."

"Without a body, we can't get a death certificate for Lenny," Cletus said. "And without a death certificate, the will can't be executed."

"So make it happen."

"Not that easy. The coroner declares death, not the sheriff."

The phone cord was making Earl's fingers purple. He started to pace as far as the cord would let him. "So, what do we do? Do we get the—"

"No, that's not an option."

"Why not? You said it yourself, the will can't be executed without a death certificate. And without a body—"

"No, Earl. We can't do that. The second that body is analyzed by the coroner she'll know there was foul play. Then there'll be an investigation."

Earl forced out a laugh. "But you're the sheriff."

"No, no, no. You're not getting it. A homicide will go straight to the state police. We're not equipped to handle a homicide investigation locally. We can barely handle a runaway cow." Cletus paused, took a breath. "If this was somehow brought back to me...It would be so easy...With the money, and—"

"All right, all right. I get it. What do we do then? Report him missing and wait a few days?"

"That's the other problem."

"What?"

"The missing aren't presumed dead for seven years."

Earl felt the blow in his gut. "We have to wait seven years?"

"Listen, Earl. This is where there's good news."

"How is this good news?"

"Lenny didn't trust Beverly with anything. Especially not his estate."

"Didn't you just tell me it all goes to his children?"

"If you'll just shut up and listen..."

Earl made a fist. He hated being talked down to like that. "Fine. Go ahead."

Cletus took a deep breath. "This is where he trusted you. And this is our only chance. In the event the children were all minors at the time of his death, he noted you as being the guardian of their inheritance. Meaning you'd have full control over the assets until the children were able to take over."

"Which they are. Minors, I mean."

"Yes, but that goes back to the seven years again. Without a body, there's no death certificate. And without a death certificate, we have to wait seven years for Lenny to be pronounced officially dead and for the will to be executed."

Earl sunk. "And Bo is thirteen. He'll be an adult by then and will have full control."

"Right."

Earl felt weak. He wanted to sit down to try and wrap his mind around it all, but he settled for leaning against the linoleum on the counter instead. The phone cord wouldn't be long enough to make it to the chair. "Where in there is the good news?"

"There is one way around all this, which is where you come in."

Earl stood up straight. His back felt better. "I'm listening."

"I have to warn you, you're not going to want to do this. But it's our only chance. You get that, right?"

Earl sighed. He thought he knew what Cletus meant, and he was prepared to do whatever it took to get this done. "Just tell me what I have to do."

***

After hearing everything, Ruby snuck out of the kitchen without eating and locked herself in the bedroom again, breathing heavily. She was trembling all over, her entire body shivering as if she were freezing. Her chest ached from the pain of her thundering heart working so hard. She didn't know everything that happened, but she knew enough. She wasn't safe here.

The only window in the bedroom looked too small for her to climb out of. There was one in the bathroom that, strangely, was larger, but Ruby wasn't sure she could make it there before her mama and grandpa realized she was gone. And she knew she wouldn't make it to the front door in time.

Ruby felt trapped. Scared and trapped.

And from what she heard her grandpa and Sheriff Cletus talking about on the phone, it sounded like Bo was in serious trouble. He sat between her grandpa and Sheriff Cletus and some money, and Ruby knew money was a big deal — she heard her daddy talk about it all the time. She heard him say once that his tobacco field was worth more than any other property in the entire town, but she didn't know if that was true or not.

Ruby sat on the bed and tried to think of a way she could warn her brothers. She hugged her knees and felt a coolness on her face as tears began to fall. A light breeze flew in through the open window at her back, sending her loose hair into a shallow funnel. She held onto her ponytail and tried to think, rubbing the strands between her fingers, just like she'd do with Lucy's denim. There had to be something she could do, but she was quickly running out of time.

A knock came from the bedroom door.

Ruby froze.

"Ruby?" It was her grandpa's voice. "Ruby, are you in there?"

Ruby bit her lip and said nothing. She squeezed her fingers tighter around her hair and held on as if it were a rope that could lead her to safety. She thought of her favorite movie and wished for the strength Princess Merida had. Since their hair color was the same — that was why Ruby liked her the most — Ruby hoped that meant they could have the same strength too. If only she had a bow and arrow, she could fight her way out of here.

The door handle jiggled.

Ruby held on even tighter.

"Come out here, please. I need to talk to you."

Ruby bit her lip harder until tears fell.

"Your lunch is getting cold."

Ruby closed her eyes and pinched them as hard as she could, but could think of no way to escape and warn her brothers. She tried to imagine a bow in her hand, and she thought she felt it. But when she opened her eyes to check, there was nothing there — just a clump of her hair. Time was running out, and she was out of ideas.

"Last chance." Her grandpa didn't sound angry through the door, but Ruby knew he was just pretending to be nice so she'd open up. But she wasn't going to fall for it.

The door handle jiggled again. Then there was the sound of metal clanking against metal, and the button on the door popped out. Ruby clutched a pillow against her chest and slid back as far as she could on the bed, the muscles in both arms as stiff as stones. She closed her eyes once more and tried to think. When she came up blank again, she opened her eyes, terrified at what she might see. And when she did, that's when she saw the knob on the door start to turn, and she knew it was too late.

CHAPTER TWENTY-SIX

The weirdest part for Rusty was that the bass kept its eyes open, even after it stopped convulsing. Even longer after its insides were cooked by the boiling water. It's as if the bass wanted to see where it was going, although Rusty didn't understand why. It was off to a bad place.

It didn't taste so bad. The meat was stringy and tougher than he expected, but it wasn't as leathery as he'd been led to believe, either. Even so, Rusty thought something didn't seem right, and he wondered if JT might have cooked it too long.

"It may not taste great," JT said as if he were reading Rusty's mind, "but it's better to cook it too long than not enough. Kills all the bacteria that way."

"It ain't so bad," Bo said. His head was turned to the side and he was chewing with his molars. "Right, Rusty?"

There wasn't much flavor to it, but Rusty was glad to be eating something. He didn't want to complain. The best bites were those that had some juice in them, but he only had a couple of those. The pond water tasted like nothing after boiling, but the wetness of it helped to wash down some of the dry pieces of meat. It was better than nothing.

"It's good," Rusty said.

The three of them ate the rest in silence.

Bo's pack was still full of food that actually had flavor, and Rusty craved some beans. The kind their father bought were brown and covered in some sort of gravy that had chunks of bacon in it. That was the best kind.

As he chewed, Rusty looked around the fire. Bo had a hand on his belly and belched into the air. The sound that resembled a croaking bullfrog echoed off the oaks and lingered in the forest, the tops of the trees shuffling as a pair of crows scurried from their nest. JT delicately licked his lips as if he were savoring the flavor on them. His eyes were closed while he did it, and he used a knuckle to clean out the corners of his mouth where his lips met. He licked the knuckle when he was satisfied he'd gotten it all.

"Get enough to eat?" Bo asked. He was only looking at Rusty.

Rusty hadn't, but he didn't say anything. Both Bo and JT appeared to be satisfied, and Rusty didn't want to appear greedy or ungrateful. He nodded and told Bo he had.

Silence fell again. It was almost awkward this time, like they were all strangers who just met. Somehow there was nothing to say.

"Hey, can I ask you something?" Bo finally said, directing it to JT.

Rusty was relieved that Bo was the one to break the silence, as he knew he would be.

"Sure."

"Why do you live out here?"

It was a good question. Rusty wondered about the same thing, but he didn't want to be the one to ask. He looked across the fire pit at JT and gauged his reaction. His eyes were open now, and he didn't look quite as comfortable as he had been just a few minutes ago. He was fidgety.

"It's kind of a long story."

Bo looked around and shrugged, holding his arms out to his sides.

"Well, I guess I can tell you," JT said. "It's not like we have anything else to do out here, right?" He forced out a laugh, but he was the only one. Rusty tried to smile, but it didn't feel right.

"When I was a baby, I was put into foster care."

"Why?"

"I don't know. I had a mom and a dad, and they were still together and everything."

"Then what happened?"

"Like I said, I don't really know. When I was older I asked my case worker about it, and she told me it was something to do with addiction or my parents being unfit, or something like that. I don't really remember."

"How old were you?"

"When what?"

"When you were taken."

"A baby, I guess. I don't remember it."

Bo shifted his weight on the log and made a face. Something was on his mind, Rusty could tell, but it was like he was holding it in for some reason. Bo used to make the same face when their father was yelling at him over something that seemed insignificant, if not completely irrelevant.

"I've lived with more than a fifty people. I've lost count. Some of them were nice, others weren't. My case worker tells me it's only temporary, but I don't know what that means anymore. She tells me there's still a chance I might get to live with my mom and dad someday." JT looked down. His shoulders hunched, his eyes sunk. It was if all the life got sucked out of him.

Rusty knew that feeling.

"Do you ever get to see them?" Rusty asked, surprised at his own question. When he did, he immediately felt both sets of eyes on him, studying him. It always felt that way when he spoke for some reason, and while he liked people to listen to him, he didn't particularly enjoy the attention. He much preferred to just blend into the background when he could.

"Who?" JT asked.

"Your mom and dad."

JT nodded. "Sometimes. I get supervised visits with them and my case worker one day a month. We get to spend an hour together in a locked room with one of those mirrors, you know? Those ones where someone can see in, but the people inside can't see out. It's hard to pretend you're not being watched when you know you are."

Rusty nodded, although he didn't really understand; he didn't know what that was like. He thought his own life was bad, but at least he got to see his parents. But that was before. He wondered if maybe things weren't as bad as he and Bo thought they were. At least they used to have a father.

"I get to see them for one day a month, then I have to go back to a family that doesn't want me."

"Why do you say that?" Bo asked.

"It's easy to tell. These people usually already have their own families, their own kids. They love their own more than they do me. It's the way they talk to them or look at them. Most of them don't even smile when they look at me. It's like I'm bothering them to be there." JT looked down again and shrugged. "But whatever."

More silence fell. But now it wasn't the silence of strangers anymore, but the silence of not knowing what the right thing to say was.

Bo, as usual, took the lead. "So, what did you do, run away or something?"

JT nodded like it was nothing. He didn't seem to think it was a big deal.

"What happens in the winter?" Bo said. "I mean, you can't survive out here in the cold, can you?"

JT shrugged. "Maybe not."

"What're you gunna do?"

"Don't know. Haven't really thought about it, I guess."

Despite his own problems, Rusty felt bad for JT. And by the look of sadness in his eyes, the way they drooped, he could tell Bo felt the same way too. Rusty was beginning to wonder if they made a terrible mistake.

"Where did you learn to do all this stuff?" Bo asked.

"Like what?"

Bo spread out his arms like they were wings and panned them around the forest. "All this. The cooking and the fishing and the shelter. Where did you learn to do it all?"

JT shrugged again. "You just learn. Stay out here long enough, and you have no other choice. It's a matter of survival. It's not as hard as it looks."

Bo sat quietly, as if he were thinking. Rusty could tell by the way his mouth opened then closed again that he wanted to say something else, that he was unsatisfied with the answer. But Bo left it at that, and so did Rusty.

"Anyway," JT said, exhaling, "that's my story. What about you guys?"

"Us?" Bo said, taken aback.

"Yeah. I told you why I'm out here, now it's your turn. What are you guys doing out here?"

Bo looked at Rusty. His eyes were huge, as if he hadn't expected the question.

"Uh, well," Bo said, fumbling with his words. "It's kind of a long story."

JT crossed his arms. A crooked smile swept across his face, making him look even more mysterious than Rusty already thought he was.

"It's not like we have anything else to do out here, right?"

CHAPTER TWENTY-SEVEN

Much to Rusty's dismay, Bo told JT everything. He told him about the tobacco field and about how he and Rusty had to dig holes and weed plants and hoe soil all summer. He told him how their father would slap them across the face if they misspoke, or how he'd whip them with his belt if something went wrong with one of his tobacco plants. He told him about the murky water that was rationed, and about the fresh stuff that Lenny kept hidden for himself.

Bo told him about the shed and about how their father wouldn't let anyone else in there, and about the radioactive plant fertilizer that was so strong it could melt skin right off the bone. He told him about Ruby and about what happened to her, and about the shotgun Bo knew was there since he was JT's age. He told him about telling Ruby to stay in the shed until someone got her, and about how she didn't listen.

As Bo told JT about what happened in the trailer and about the events leading up to it, Rusty's recollection of it all returned. He remembered how strong the wind gusts were leading up to the trailer, how much the grains of sand hurt as they shot into his bare skin like bullets. He remembered how he felt, how afraid he was that something bad might happen to Bo, about how close he was to not going in at all.

Rusty remembered the smell of burnt toast on the counter, and the way the crumbs in the bottom of the toaster always made it smell that way. He saw the brightness of the screen on the television and how it burned his eyes if he looked at it for too long. He heard the stupid voice of the game show host making a joke that no one understood or found funny. He imagined his dull suit and ugly checkered tie and his greasy, slicked hair.

Rusty remembered seeing his father asleep in the chair with the remote in his hand, cradling it like he never did to his children. He tasted the stale beer that sat between his father's disgusting legs. He thought about the beer cans — all those reds and whites and blues that he grew to hate — and about how many of them he encountered over the years. His hand began to burn with the fire he felt when his father poured the stuff over his open wound. He thought about all the nights Lenny threw those cans across the room, about how many of them just barely missed hitting him or Bo or Ruby. Or their mom.

He thought about all of that and got angry all over again.

As Bo continued to tell the tale of what happened inside the trailer, then about what he did with their father's body afterward — and how they tried to find it again later, but couldn't — and what their plans were for getting Ruby back, Rusty felt something cold and wet on his cheeks. He knew they were tears, but he didn't care. He didn't care if Bo saw him cry, and he didn't care if JT did, either. For what he did, he couldn't help but cry.

Rusty's hands were balled into fists, the skin on his palm tugging at the edges of the scab — the Band-Aid was long gone, probably floating somewhere in the spectacular pond. He kept squeezing and squeezing because he had to, squeezing because it was the only way to make the memories go away. He squeezed until he heard a tear, until he felt the fire underneath his skin, until the warm liquid pooled in his hand and stayed there as if it were a cup. And when he looked down, the scab was split and his hand was bleeding, and the callus was screaming at him.

"Wow," JT said, shifting his weight, a grin on his face, "you guys are killers. I'm sitting with two murderers."

Rusty said nothing, and neither did Bo. The idea of it wasn't as cool to them as it was to JT, since they lived it.

"Who woulda thunk?"

The rage flew out of Rusty like a raven on the prowl, hovering over its prey, but the pain returned, as did the silence.

Eventually, as Rusty applied pressure to his again wounded hand, JT finally spoke. "Can I ask a question?"

"Shoot," Bo said.

"Which one of you pulled the trigger?"

A long, hard silence.

Bo cleared his throat. "There's not a simple answer to that question, really."

Except there was. Rusty remembered now. Somehow he remembered exactly what happened.

Rusty was back in the trailer again, his mind as clear as crystal. Bo was frozen in place, his eyes filled with a penetrating fear, the shotgun cradled between his overwhelmed hands. Rusty knew Bo wouldn't go through with it, so he took the shotgun from Bo and adjusted it so it was only inches from their father's head. He tried to keep it steady. He thought he had. But his shoulders dipped forward just enough to make the muzzle slip an inch, and when it did, it pressed up against their father's head.

Lenny woke up and grabbed the muzzle, spinning out of his recliner like a looney and reaching for Rusty's throat with more fury than he could imagine. His eyes were black and his nails were like bear claws ready to attack, and they did. Rusty felt the pinch of his father's nails against his throat, felt the claws digging into his flesh as if he were a meal. The pain was scathing.

Rusty remembered hearing Bo yell something to him, but the memory was only faint. He remembered closing his eyes and screaming, and clenching the muscles in his hands and squeezing his fingers, and he remembered the sound of the gun going off. It rung in his ears like an explosion had occurred inside his head, and at the time, he thought that was what happened. When he opened his eyes and saw his father stagger backward and press a hand to the open wound in his throat, that's when Rusty knew what he did. He still felt the pain in his pectoral muscle from where the shotgun recoiled. The vibration in his hands returned too.

Rusty remembered now. He remembered it all.

"It was me," he said, short of breath, the memories all too real as they replayed in his mind like a video on repeat. "I was the one who pulled the trigger. I was the one who killed our father."

***

The realization of what Rusty did, of what kind of human being he was, hit him hard. He was a cold-blooded killer. At nine-years-old. A killer. A murderer. And it was his own father. Rusty had to learn to deal with that.

JT was just as surprised as anyone when Rusty finally confessed, and although Bo would neither confirm nor deny Rusty's proclamation, him not saying anything told Rusty all he needed to know. Rusty had his memory back, and it was real. He, not Bo, was the one who pulled the trigger. He was the one who killed their father.

All this time Rusty had assumed it was Bo who did it, considering how he hid the body under the porch and refused to say it aloud as if he was ashamed of himself. Rusty thought that Bo took the shotgun from his hand and shot their father before he attacked Rusty's neck, that Bo was the one who pulled the trigger. But no, it wasn't that. Bo was just trying to protect his little brother.

His little brother, the murderer.

Rusty wanted to be alone with his thoughts, but Bo said he thought it wouldn't be best. Rusty argued only halfheartedly and lost. JT excused himself instead.

Rusty sat on the log and wallowed in his tears for a while. Bo stayed closed by and said nothing, just sat there for comfort. Rusty thought it helped. They sat there until the fire died out.

JT eventually returned and sat across from Rusty and Bo without asking, and he and Bo had a quiet conversation. Rusty kept his head facing downward, staring at a small ditch he dug with the heel of his boot. He was numb.

"Rusty," JT said, his voice gentle and even, barely audible through the howl of the wind that started. "Can I say something?"

Rusty found his sight through blurred vision and looked up. JT's shoulders were relaxed and his face was inviting. Rusty was glad he wasn't afraid of him. "What?"

"I don't blame you for doing what you did. I would have done the same thing."

Rusty said nothing. He just stared at JT, wondering if he really meant it.

"From the sounds of it, your dad was a real asshole who got what he deserved."

"You did the right thing," Bo added. "We both did the right thing."

"That's easy for you to say," Rusty said, using the backside of his wrist to wipe his nose. "I'm the one who pulled the trigger. I'm the one who killed dad."

"Only because I couldn't. If you weren't there, dad might have killed us both. You saved our lives, Rusty."

Rusty hadn't thought about it like that. What if he hadn't gone in there with Bo? What if he waited in the shed with Ruby like Bo said he could have? What might have happened then? Would Bo be dead? Would he? Would Ruby?

"You're so much braver than I am," Bo said, dropping his head. He was close to tears now too. "And I'm really proud of you. You stepped up like a man is supposed to, and I didn't."

Rusty was taken aback.

He just called me a man.

Coming from Bo, coming from his brother, it meant so much more. And if Bo said it, it must be true, because just about everything Bo said was true.

"You're a hero, Rusty," Bo said.

Rusty stood up, his knees shaking. Bo did too. They took a step toward each other and wrapped their arms around one another and squeezed until it hurt. The stink of dirt and sweat and unwashed hair hit Rusty's nose, but he didn't care. He just kept holding on, not at all embarrassed at what JT might think of him. It felt so good to hug somebody.

When they finally separated, Rusty saw something for the first time. The tears were unmistakable in Bo's eyes, creating a reflective glare that looked like a bubble about to burst. Bo's lashes were wet and the whites of his eyes had turned red. There was no doubt about it this time, Bo was crying. Rusty remembered hearing him cry twice before, but never saw it. But now, as he glared into the droplets of water that pooled in his brother's eyes, he knew it was definite this time.

"What, you've never seen someone cry before?" Bo half-joked, half not.

"It's just..." Rusty fumbled with his words. "It's just that I've never seen you cry before. I've never seen any man cry."

"So that means men don't cry? Is that what you're saying?" Bo wiped away his tears.

"It's true, isn't it?"

"No, it's not true. Who told you that? Dad?"

Rusty nodded.

"Screw dad. You showed him who the real man was." Bo turned to JT. "Have you ever seen a man cry?"

"My dad cries all the time. When my case worker tells us time's up, me and dad and mom — we all cry together."

"See," Bo said, turning back to Rusty. "His dad cries all the time, and he's a man. Men cry too."

Rusty was shocked. It was as if a Bo just removed a blindfold from his eyes, revealing the world in its true colors for the first time. The blindfold, he realized, had been on for so long. There was so much he missed. "But, what about grandpa?"

"What about him? I've seen him cry lots of times."

"You have?" Rusty almost smiled.

"Sure. I saw him cry just the other day. He was on the phone with some lady, and the next thing I knew he was crying."

"Really?"

"Really. Men cry all the time."

Rusty was astonished. Everything he thought was true about men and becoming a man was untrue. It didn't matter how long his member was or if he had hair under his arms or in between his legs. It didn't matter if he cried once a while or if he got blisters on his hands. What mattered is what he did, how he treated the people he loved. What mattered was doing things other men did, or wanted to but couldn't. It meant standing up for another man when he needed help. It meant sticking up for yourself when no one else would.

It meant being a hero to save your family.

Rusty looked between Bo and JT, who were both smiling at him, their teeth showing. They were both men. Even though JT was younger than he, JT made tools and caught fish and built shelter. He could make a fire and cook for himself and make decisions and sell raccoon fur to the taxidermist downtown. Being a man wasn't being a certain age or being a certain height. No, being a man was doing what you have to do to survive.

Rusty was a man. And for the first time, he actually believed it.

Rusty grinned the biggest grin he ever grinned. His grin turned into a smile, which turned into a laugh, which turned into a belly laugh. Because it was contagious, Bo started to laugh too, then did JT. All three of them laughed until they couldn't breathe, until their insides hurt. They laughed until they could no longer stand. It was just three men in the forest, laughing like old friends.

Luckily for Rusty, he didn't have to pee, because he remembered what happened last time he laughed this hard. Now that he knew what it really meant to be a man and was officially one, he'd hate to find out what other men might do to him if he peed in his pants. For all the things that made a boy a man, peeing in your pants wasn't one of them — Rusty knew that for sure. He decided he'd keep that little incident to himself for a while.

The laughter eventually quieted down and Rusty and Bo and JT pulled themselves off the ground. There was a small rock lodged in the skin in Rusty's elbow from how he landed during his laugh attack, but it didn't bother him. He just smiled and flicked the rock away, just like a man would.

"I'm really glad I met you guys," JT said when they all cooled. He had a smile on his face still, but Rusty could sense he really meant it.

"Us too," Bo said. "You're a cool guy."

Rusty nodded in agreement. He agreed with both of them.

"And I want to help you," JT said.

Rusty didn't know what JT meant by that, and by the blank stare on Bo's face, Rusty didn't think he did, either.

"Help us with what?" Bo asked. He used his hand to swat a fly away.

"Your plan. I want to help you get your sister."

CHAPTER TWENTY-EIGHT

Earl waited until nightfall to do what Cletus suggested. There was a way around this messy situation, and the way Cletus described it, Earl thought it might just work. Cletus was right; Earl didn't want to do it. There were so many memories that would be destroyed, so many things that would be difficult, if not impossible, to replace. Objects can be replaced but memories can't, and that bothered Earl at his core.

But on the other hand, it was the only way, and Earl suspected it might just bring the boys of out hiding. In the meantime, Earl hoped Cletus knew what he was doing.

There were still some supplies left in Lenny's shed that Earl could use, but he didn't want to go out into the dark empty handed. The M3 was in the closet in the bedroom, so he grabbed it along with some extra ammunition from the top shelf just in case. He didn't have a good reason for needing extra ammo, but the old military man in him always feared the worst once darkness fell. Darkness was when bad things happened. And darkness had indeed fallen. He didn't want to have to come back for more.

Earl stopped in front of the children's bedroom door and listened for Ruby. He thought he heard some movement inside, but he didn't go in. Ruby flailed her arms and screamed obscenities at him when he went in uninvited earlier, so he didn't dare try again. He only wanted to deliver the grilled cheese sandwich Beverly made for her, but he settled for leaving the plate on the corner of the bureau instead. He just wanted Ruby to eat something; he was getting worried about her.

Something was definitely bothering Ruby, and Earl figured it was the uncertainty about her brothers. It was unlike her to lash out like she did. He wanted to promise her that he'd find her brothers, but he didn't want to break a promise either. They didn't seem to want to be found yet, and you can't find someone who doesn't want to be found. But that would change before long. Eventually they'd come out of hiding; there was no way they could stay hiding forever, not at their age.

Ruby was a sensitive little girl, and she had Lenny to blame for that. Lenny did such a poor job of raising those kids. Earl could never forgive his son for that. As much as Lenny hurt Beverly, he was even worse with those kids. Earl wanted to find the boys for Ruby, to help to ease her mind. She was too young to understand what was going on around her, so Earl hoped that maybe she'd forget it all someday. And if her brothers were around to comfort her, maybe they'd help her do that. Earl really did want the best for little Ruby-Sue.

Earl moved past the bedroom and continued down the hallway and into the kitchen. Beverly sat watching television in the living room and called out to him when she spotted the M3, but Earl quickly dismissed it by telling her not to worry and to go back to her program. She did, just as Earl knew she would. He didn't think she'd be okay with what he was about to do, and he wasn't about to ask for her permission. She'd forget all about it when they were finally able to move out of this trailer one day.

The door on the screen porch pounded against the wood as Earl passed through it, and his feet sunk into the softness of the grass as he started to walk. The flashlight he held was dim, but it was good enough to get him to where he needed to go. There was only one way to get there, and he'd know it even if he were blind. But it never hurt to have a light, just in case.

Earl passed through the low hanging branches of the plum tree, swatting one away from his face as he walked into it. His back felt much better now, the pills he took doing their job to perfection. In some ways, he understood why Beverly took them so frequently — they dulled everything. And with the lives they were living, being dull and feeling numb to it may not have been the worst thing. But that phase of his life was over. He stopped using many moons ago. If Beverly didn't stop too, they may never get custody of those kids. And worse, they'd never get access to Lenny's fortune.

The moon overhead was bright and almost full, making his son's trailer easily visible in the not so far distance. Stars lit up the sky. Lenny's shed wasn't more than a few hundred yards from the porch. Earl headed toward it.

Cletus's instructions were vague. He said it didn't matter how it happened or why, and that he'd take care of the rest. All Earl had to do was make it look like an accident. He thought that'd be easy enough.

Lenny's body was gone, his skin burned off and his bones tossed away like garbage, slowing disintegrating in an old oil drum behind the trailer. The green goo that Lenny fed to his tobacco plants was toxic for human skin, which made the idea of him forcing his children to be around it even that much worse. Lenny would never touch the stuff himself, not after what happened to his chest when he accidentally splashed some while he was creating the concoction. The skin was burned off in seconds, leaving a hole the size of a marble in the middle of his chest. Skin eventually grew back over the hole and the muscles recovered, but his chest was permanently scarred, his confidence deformed. As far as Earl knew, the children hadn't ever seen what happened to their old man's chest, nor were they aware of the potency of the concoction they worked with on a daily basis. If Lenny did one thing right, that was it — telling the boys would have only made things worse for them, realizing how much danger they were in. It only made sense that Lenny's body was being eaten by the stuff in death.

With Cletus's help the day before, Earl found some of the fertilizer in the shed and used it on his son's corpse. It didn't take them long to find his body. The most difficult part was trying to make himself fit through the crawlspace under the porch while not spilling the bucket. Earl did eventually make it, but it was a slow descent beneath the surface. It reminded him of crawling through the foxholes in Vietnam.

Earl had seen more dead bodies in his lifetime than he cared to think about — he had the war to thank for that — but he wasn't fully prepared to see his son like that. He thought he could handle it, that it'd be no worse than all the others. But he was wrong. He was so wrong. It was a good thing he was on his knees already when he reached the ravine, because it would have hurt a lot more had he fallen to the earth from his feet. He'd never before had a panic attack until that moment, and it overtook him like an unexpected tornado; he simply wasn't prepared for it to happen.

His elbows buckled as he tried to catch himself when he fell forward, and he found himself lying face first in the dirt. It was warmer than he thought it might be, even in the shade, and he felt his own breath in his face, trying to suffocate him. It took some time for the pressure in his chest to subside, and it took until then for Earl to find the strength to lift his head up and breathe normally again.

All Earl saw was the bottoms of Lenny's feet. The rest of him was wrapped up in a carpet — the one with the red swirls that was missing from the living room, not so surprisingly. His once white socks had turned brown, and they were stretched out and covered with holes. Lenny's skin looked pale through the tears.

On his forearms, Earl crawled toward the carpet, just like he did on a daily basis during the time he spent overseas. It brought back memories he tried to forget, reminding him of the horror that was the battlefield. The screaming he heard in his mind was the loudest when it was dark, and the light underneath the porch disappeared. The crescent on his ear itched then, but Earl knew better. He knew it was only a phantom, and he refused to give in to his subconscious as it played tricks on him. As much as he hated it, he tried to concentrate on his son.

By the time Earl reached Lenny's body, Cletus was through the tunnel, a shovel in hand. Cletus showed no reaction upon seeing Lenny's body up close — he didn't flinch, didn't squirm, didn't make a face. Earl thought maybe he became hardened to it by the years working in law enforcement, but part of him wondered if he just didn't care. Sheriff Cletus associated with Earl for monetary purposes only — he looked the other way while Lenny did what he had to do to get the tobacco to market, and in exchange, Cletus received a portion of the profits; without the sheriff in his back pocket, Lenny would have been shut down a long time ago because so much of what he did was illegal. Cletus's reason for associating with Lenny became painfully clear to Earl at that moment. As much as Earl didn't approve of the way his son behaved, even the worst type of people need a friend in this world. Because of that, Earl hoped he was wrong.

Earl's guts lurched when he and Cletus unwrapped Lenny's body. The hole in his throat was as big as a ping pong ball, the crusted blood surrounding it almost stygian black. Even with his eyes closed, Lenny's face look strained. It looked as if he'd suffered.

As much as Earl disapproved of the way his son treated his family, Earl blamed himself. He blamed himself because he treated his first wife — Lenny's mother — the same way, and he wasn't much better to his son. But he grew up as he got older, he thought Lenny would learn from his mistakes as a father. But he didn't, clearly, and he paid the ultimate price for it. And it was all Earl's fault.

There were so many times when Earl could have gotten those boys help. He could have called Child Protective Services or told the boys' school or confronted his son himself, but he didn't. He didn't because he was handcuffed, stuck on Lenny's property rent-free, and leaving would mean never seeing the children again. It would have devastated Beverly, and she would have blamed him for it and made his life a living nightmare. And as much as she disgusted him sometimes, she was still his wife.

Then there was Ruby.

Poor, innocent Ruby. She didn't deserve the life she was given. She didn't choose the life she had. More than anyone, she deserved better.

That's where Earl failed the most — with Ruby. He accepted he couldn't protect the boys — they were old enough and independent enough to make their own decisions, and to live with the consequences of those decisions — but Ruby was different. She was different from them in so many ways, and she had no idea. Neither did the boys.

Those were the thoughts on Earl's mind as he doused Lenny's body with the tobacco fertilizer, waterfalls of tears streaming down his face.

It took hours for the fertilizer to melt the skin off Lenny's bones. Even longer for the meat. The smell was horrendous, repulsive, nauseating. The concoction worked like acid. Cletus broke Lenny's bones where necessary and tossed them in the drum in the back of the trailer — the small ones splintered easily, while some of the stronger ones took some real effort. Cletus was a strong man, as it turned out, a physical freak in some ways. Earl didn't know that about him.

While Cletus took care of that, Earl dug a hole as deep as he could from his knees and buried the carpet under the porch, plus whatever else had remained of his son. He wept as he filled the hole with dirt and smoothed the surface with the flat end of the shovel. He knew that was the last time he'd ever see his son, and that was hard to deal with. A parent wasn't supposed to see their child die, not ever. Life was cruel like that sometimes.

Earl shook away the memories. The weight of the five-gallon bucket pulled on his shoulder, twisting on the joint as he hauled it up. With the M3 in his other hand, he lumbered toward Lenny's truck first. Broken glass crunched under his boots as he approached, the shards popping like firecrackers. Earl leaned the M3 against the back wheel and used two hands to grab the bucket. Swinging his arms in unison, he tossed some of the fertilizer into the cab of the truck through the broken window, then he poured some into the bed. He was careful not to get any on himself.

Inside the trailer, Earl started in the back bedrooms, moved down the hallway, into the living room, and finished up in the kitchen. The cabinets were open and most of the food was gone, which told Earl this would all be over soon. The boys were close — they had to be — and they'd come out of hiding once they saw what was about to happen. Or if not, they'd run out of food sooner than they probably thought. Earl made sure they weren't inside the trailer before he went back outside.

With what was left of the fertilizer, Earl turned the bucket over and covered the stairs that lead up to the porch. He went back to the truck, grabbed his M3, and tossed the empty bucket into the bed of the truck.

When Earl was far enough away from the trailer, he turned and faced it and took aim. There was no scope on his M3, but the target was huge and his shooting was still good — he was an expert marksman once upon a time — and he had plenty of ammunition. Earl squeezed the trigger like he was a younger man and emptied the magazine. His body rocked as he fired and hit the truck's fuel tank, sending it soaring into the air with a brilliant explosion. Streaks of oranges and yellows and blues lit up the sky like fireworks, and the flames caught. The field roared with a thunderous boom, causing the drums in Earl's ears to ring. The ringing kept on for several minutes, worsening before it improved. The metal from the truck frame slammed into the ground and screeched, then collapsed once the flames completely engulfed it.

Earl jammed a finger in his ear canal and shook it, trying to stop the noises, the voices. They eventually stopped when the field fell quiet, but a slight hum remained, as it usually did. Earl knew he couldn't handle much more of this before it drove him completely mad.

But he wasn't done yet, not even close.

He changed the magazine and took aim at the trailer this time. He hesitated for a moment, getting one final look at the trailer that made so many memories, so many enemies. So much hatred. Earl braced himself and squeezed the trigger again, taking aim at the staircase where he poured the rest of the fertilizer. It didn't take much for the flames to catch there either, but Earl emptied the spare magazine just to make sure. He found some satisfaction in it, actually. It felt good to shoot again.

He stood and watched with the smoking hot M3 dangling at his hip, his shoulders and wrists and fingers vibrating, his ears buzzing again. The voices returned, just as Earl knew they would. Except this time, he let them talk. He was tired of them controlling him.

Lenny's truck burned to a crisp in minutes. The trailer took longer. When Earl saw that the flames had begun to suffocate the trailer — glass shattered from the inside out, black smoke seeped out the holes where the windows were, the walls started to give way — he started back toward the plum tree.

As he passed through its shadow, the heat from the monstrous flames at his back, he followed the porch light home. He looked up and saw Beverly and Ruby standing on the stairs, predictably startled by the explosion. Both of their jaws were dropped, their eyes wide, and Beverly had Ruby pressed against her legs.

"What happened?" she asked as Earl approached, her voice trembling.

Earl walked past them. "It's okay. This will all be over soon."

Earl walked into the trailer and tossed the M3 on the kitchen table. It was still hot. Earl was exhausted. He dropped into a chair and let out a sigh before looking at the clock. He noted the time and leaned back, and decided he'd wait a while before making any phone calls. He'd call Cletus first and let him decide what to do next, who to call.

Another explosion rang out from across the field, louder than did the first one, rattling the trailer to its bones. Earl closed his eyes and imagined his son's skeleton in that drum, and he wiped away a tear over the regret of what he did to cause all this. He didn't necessarily agree with what those boys did to their father, but he understood it.

It would only be a matter of time now before they came out of hiding.

CHAPTER TWENTY-NINE

The plan was simple; there was no plan. Rusty suggested they try to get Ruby out through the window in the bedroom, but Bo shot that down by reminding Rusty the window was broken. Breaking the glass and going out that way would make too much noise, he said. The same went for the bathroom window. They were going in the front door instead; it was the only other way.

Rusty and Bo left their packs underneath the umbrella oaks at the base of their root beds. They'd be waiting for them when they got back — all four of them. Rusty thought Ruby might be frightened to see them, spooked by having someone wake up her in the middle of the night while she slept, even if it were her own brothers. To combat that, Rusty fished through his pack and found what he was looking for, then asked JT if he would carry it for him. Lucy fit perfectly in JT's satchel, as if she were made for it. JT insisted the satchel wouldn't slow him down at all.

With no flashlight to lead the way — Bo left it under the porch of their father's trailer when they got out in a hurry — Rusty and Bo and JT started across the clearing. The bushes made sounds like they did the first night — small wings flapped, and hungry, blood-thirsty beasts howled through the darkness — but Rusty didn't feel the same way about them this time. He didn't flinch, he didn't scream, and he certainly didn't fall to the forest floor again. He felt different now, like he'd grown up in the past couple of days, like he was no longer worried about things that probably were exaggerated by his imagination. Ruby was on his mind — that was all — and getting her out of their grandpa's trailer was his only concentration.

A series of loud pops echoed from somewhere beyond the trees. The pops hung in the openness of the night for longer than they would have if they were surrounded by oak trees that stood taller than those cities up north. Rusty had never seen one in person, but in the books and movies, it seemed every major city had those types of buildings. All they had in Plum Springs were trees. Lots and lots of tall, beautiful trees. Because of the way the pops hung in the sky, Rusty knew they came from somewhere on the other side of the tree line. The forest tended to swallow sounds like that.

The first series of pops came and went in a matter of seconds, followed by a short delay, then a huge explosion went off, sending vibrations through the air that Rusty swore he felt rock the earth. Then more pops came in rapid succession. And when that popping stopped and silence returned, nothing else happened. It was as if the night paused itself, the pops taking a breather. Rusty held his breath and listened for more.

Bo and JT kept moving in front of him, paying no attention to the explosions. Rusty thought it may have been dynamite that was set off by the way each pop was stringed after the other in a perfect sequence, but he didn't know why someone would ever need dynamite out here. Despite his curiosity begging for him to stop and listen more, Rusty kept moving, afraid that if he didn't, he might lose his brother and JT to the darkness. Their pace was frantic, and the height of the oaks surrounding him weren't Rusty's ally — the moon was hidden somewhere behind the tops of them.

When they got to the clearing, a sea of color illuminated the other side of the field, opening up the sky above it with a trail of black and gray smoke. Rusty began to sweat, the heat from the flames so hot he thought he might melt. It took him until Bo spoke to realize what he was looking at.

"Holy shit!" Bo said. "Dad's trailer is on fire!"

Rusty slid in beside Bo and looked out toward where the trailer should have been. JT was on Bo's left side, standing silently.

The longer Rusty stared at the fire, the better his eyes adjusted. As the flames rose higher and higher and light shone off the structure beneath them, Rusty got a good look at what was happening. The trailer he once knew was blackened like charcoal. The glass from the windows was gone, leaving nothing but rectangular gaps in the side of the trailer, each forming a black hole that he thought might suck him in if he stared at it for too long. Metal began to crunch, just like his father's old truck off to the side, and Rusty found some irony that it rested on its roof, smoldered in char while this was happening.

There were sounds coming from the trailer that didn't make any sense, sounds that didn't seem to fit the scene. Something began to whistle. Something began to hum. It went silent for a moment. Then, as if three or four dynamite sticks were stuck together and set off all at once, something behind the trailer exploded.

Rusty hit the ground as the brightest light he'd ever seen shone into the night. The entire field lit up in an instant. Rusty saw the greens from the rows and rows of tobacco plants, the purples from the plums hanging from the arms of the plum tree, and the faded browns of the wood that painted the outside of the shed, which was still standing. Rusty worried what might happen if the shed caught on fire too, considering the plant food that was kept in there. He wondered if it would explode and cause an earthquake. Or worse.

Bo and JT hit the ground next to Rusty, and the three of them stared at the light show across the field. The roof of the trailer dislodged from the top of the structure and disappeared inside it, the walls swallowing it whole. The walls eventually gave way too and fell forward, and everything came crashing down like a house of cards. Rusty shook his head. He had nothing to say.

"It's gone," Bo said from his backside, "the trailer's gone."

Rusty nodded, although nobody was looking.

"Just incredible."

"What do you think that explosion was?" JT asked.

"Dad kept a couple of oil tanks in the back of the trailer," Bo said. "It must have been those."

Bo and JT stood up and brushed themselves off. Rusty stayed on the ground for a while longer and continued to stare at what was left of the trailer. All of their stuff was gone. Everything they ever owned was burned to ash — all their clothes, all their school supplies, what few toys they had. The memories of the living room that filled Rusty's mind with terror, gone. The thoughts of the pain that came from behind Lenny's bedroom door, gone. Everything was gone.

"Do you realize what this means for you guys?" JT said, his tone spiked, leaning toward excitement, his voice higher than usual.

Rusty watched the silhouette of Bo's head swivel and look directly at JT. Rusty's mind was doing cartwheels trying to figure out what was happening. He was glad he grabbed Lucy when he and Bo went into the trailer the last time.

"What?" Bo said.

"If your dad's body was still in that trailer somewhere…"

"Yeah?"

"Well, it's not anymore."

Bo stood silent for a while. Rusty stayed on his backside, overwhelmed with emotion. Tears filled his eyes, but he wasn't sure why. He thought he might cry, or scream, or jump for joy. He wasn't sure how he should react. His emotions were a mixed bag.

"Any evidence of what happened is gone too," JT said. "You guys might actually get away with this."

***

The three of them sat on that for a while. The new information was life-changing. Rusty and Bo sat next to each other on the dirt and said nothing. Rusty was in awe of what this meant, though he wasn't sure he fully grasped it. He still had to live with himself for what killing his own father meant, whether there was proof or not. He wondered if Bo felt the same guilt he did, but neither of them spoke of it.

JT gave them their space. He sat on the other side of the clearing with his knees against his chest and his hands interlocked, his thumbs twirling. Rusty glanced at him every so often, and he seemed to be enjoying the sights and sounds of the night — JT wouldn't stop smiling. Rusty couldn't imagine why JT was happy during a time like this. Or maybe he could.

The only rule they all agreed upon prior to going after Ruby was that they'd wait until the porch light went off on their grandpa's trailer. Their grandpa was usually the last one to go to bed at night, and he always shut off the outside light before he went to sleep — Rusty saw it through the bedroom window on so many occasions as he sat on the bottom bunk, in the dark, wondering if life was better on the other side of the plum tree;

he always told himself he'd live over there one day, where he was wanted, but he never actually believed it would happen. Knowing what he knew now about his grandpa, he wasn't sure what to think anymore. His grandpa and his dad were much of the same, and his mom wasn't much better — she could have protected him and Bo and Ruby if she wanted to.

Rusty wondered if he'd ever find happiness and peace. He was starting to doubt it. He was happy in the moment in the pond, he recalled, but it didn't last. It was simply a moment of ecstasy, nothing more. And he couldn't stay in the pond forever. Rusty thought of his mom and wondered why she abandoned him. He was young when she left, and he hardly knew her at all. Even when Lenny allowed them to spend time together, Rusty never felt as if he knew who she was, or if she even cared about him. He began to wonder if he'd ever find someone to love him. Bo and Ruby didn't count — that wasn't the type of love he was missing in his heart.

Until the porch light went off, the three of them would stay put. They all knew there was no way of getting access to the trailer until everyone inside was asleep, so they had nothing to do but wait it out. Rusty knew his grandpa had guns, and he knew he liked to use them too — it was yet another example of how alike he and Lenny actually were. And more evidence that Bo knew what he was talking about. Their grandpa always talked about getting revenge for what happened to him in 'Nam, as Rusty often heard him say. He was pretty sure that was a place.

The porch light stayed on for hours. Their grandpa didn't emerge from the trailer, not even when the two fire trucks showed up, or the police car afterward. Rusty and Bo and JT all moved out of the clearing and slid into the thickest underbrush near the tree line, and that was where they stayed until the fire was put out. They eventually took turns sleeping as the black smoke on the other side of the tree line billowed toward the moon. The echo of the sirens went on long past when they were gone.

When it was Rusty's turn to rest, he made a pillow out of some branches and vines and lay on his side. There was a boulder buried beneath the ground where he laid that dug into his hip and kept him from sleeping. He kept his eyes shut anyway, though, because Bo told him he really needed to try to get some rest. He thought about the horse fly, wondering where it would be sleeping tonight. In some ways, he missed it.

Bo and JT started talking once they thought Rusty was asleep. He didn't stop them, even though he was still awake. Coyotes howled at the moon somewhere deep inside the forest. It must have been approaching midnight.

"Can I ask you something, JT?" Bo asked. His voice was sullen and sounded a bit lonely. Rusty wondered what the matter was and thought maybe Bo did feel guilty about what happened, like he did.

"Sure."

"Did it really happen the way you said it did?"

"Did what?"

"With your parents."

"Yeah. Why?"

"I was just wondering. It's just…"

"It's just what?"

Bo sighed. "It's just that there's something familiar about your story. There are just a lot of little things."

"Like what?"

"Oh, I don't know. It's probably nothing."

"What is it?"

"Well...Okay. But like I said, it's probably stupid. It's just that the same thing kind of happened to us."

"What do you mean?"

"When our parents split, we went to live with mom and our grandpa in their trailer, right? But we were only there a couple of weeks before someone came to the house and looked around and said she couldn't keep us anymore."

"Really?"

Rusty caught himself beginning to open his eyes, but he stopped it. He didn't remember ever living with their mom and grandpa, and he wanted to hear more. Yet, for some reason, another part of him didn't.

"Yeah," Bo said. "We had to go move back in with our dad. This was before Ruby was even born. Rusty was just a baby, so I don't think he even remembers it. But our mom, she's been taking these pills for a while, and that was one of the reasons why we couldn't stay with her."

"There are a lot of kids whose parents are doing stuff like that. I've met lots of them."

"Yeah."

"I'm sure what happened to us has happened to a lot of kids, you know?"

"Yeah," Bo said, but he didn't sound convinced. "But there's something else too."

"Like what?"

"I remember that our mom was pregnant not long after Rusty was born. He couldn't even walk yet. I was small too, but I remember her belly getting really big. This was a couple years before Ruby. No one ever said anything about it — not mom or dad or grandpa. It was as if nothing was even going on."

"What happened?"

"Mom went off for a while — a couple days, I think — and when she came back she wasn't pregnant anymore. And there was no baby."

"No baby?"

"I know. I always thought that maybe she just had an abortion or something, you know? But now, I mean, I don't know. It just seems so familiar. You seem so familiar."

"Yeah, well, I don't think so." JT laughed. "My dad's older than my mom is. By a lot."

"What are their names?"

"Who? My parents?"

"Yeah."

"I don't know. They're mom and dad to me. I don't see them much."

"Yeah."

It was a challenge, but Rusty forced himself to keep his eyes shut during the silence that followed. He stayed really still, not wanting to do anything to ruin the momentum. His heart was beating briskly.

"Can I ask you a question now?" JT said, now a lot quieter.

"Okay."

"Remember that time you said your grandpa was talking on the phone and started crying?"

"What about it?"

"Do you know who he was talking to?"

"No. Why?"

"I just thought that maybe if you knew who it was, that maybe if you knew why he was crying…"

"Then what?"

"Well, I was just thinking…Because your mom and grandpa live together, you know? And my dad's—"

"Yeah, but I don't know who he was talking to or what he was crying about, so…"

"Yeah."

A long silence fell, longer than any silence yet. It was dead silent. Rusty could hear himself breathe. He could hear himself think. And so many thoughts kept running through his head.

JT had freckles. So did Ruby…
Mom was pregnant…
JT was taken away from his mother as a baby…
Mom came home without one…
It wasn't possible, though. JT said it himself — his dad was a lot older than his mom.
But mom and grandpa do live together. Maybe they…

"Can I ask you one more question?" Bo said, breaking the heavy silence.

Rusty could hardly keep his eyes closed now. He had to see if there was a resemblance.

"Sure."

"What does JT stand for?"

"Those are my initials."

"What's your real name?"

"Justin."

"Justin what?"

Rusty dug his nails into his thigh, grinding his molars together as if chewing. He knew he had to keep his eyes closed or he'd risk interrupting the conversation and ruining the moment. If he opened his eyes and Bo saw, they may have never found out Justin's last name.

What if it's…
What if he was their…

JT said, "Look!"

"What?" Bo said, frantic. "What is it?"

Rusty kept his eyes closed.

Travis...

What if his last name is Travis, like them?

What if they're...

Rusty felt Bo's hand on his ankle. "Rusty, wake up," Bo said, shaking his leg. "Wake up."

Rusty snapped his eyes open. He tried his hardest to not look at JT, but resisting actually made his eyes hurt. He let one eye wander and sneak a little peak, but he tried to be discreet about it. He had to see JT's face.

"What?" he said.

Bo pointed through the trees. "Look."

Rusty sat up and looked where Bo pointed. That's when he saw it, and he gasped too. Butterflies instantly started fluttering in his belly and began twisting. His heart thumped like a tomtom.

The porch light on their grandpa's trailer was off.

CHAPTER THIRTY

Earl watched through the kitchen window as the firemen came and went. It didn't take long for the flames to get under control. It was impossible to tell the damage from this distance at night, but the report from the fire department was all that remained were piles of ash and crooked metal. They said no one could have survived the fire. The fire marshal personally offered his condolences for Earl's loss.

It was perfect.

Cletus showed up shortly after the fire trucks arrived, and that was by design. All was progressing swimmingly.

As sheriff, Cletus had some special authorities under certain circumstances. Cletus knew one way to bypass having to wait seven years for a missing person to be legally declared dead. The coroner's office was the one to officially pronounce someone dead under normal circumstances, but there were those times when doing so wasn't possible.

Such as when there was no body, for example.

Or if a victim's house burned down while they were inside.

The sheriff made the official pronouncement of death in those cases, and it was considered official — a death certificate would be generated.

Earl knew by doing what he did, there'd never be closure. There'd be no formal funeral because there'd be no body, and there'd be no certainty about what happened to Lenny outside of a select group of people. Earl could count those people on one hand. But Earl had no choice in the matter. His grandsons killed their father, and he participated in the dismemberment and destruction of the body. He was just as guilty as those boys were. And it was his fault any of it even happened in the first place. If he was a better father to his son, Lenny would have been a better father to those boys, and none of this would have ever happened. It was only fitting that Earl finished what he started. Those boys deserved a second chance. They deserved to be forgiven.

But it was done, and Earl made his peace with it. Much of what was to follow would be in Cletus's hands. Earl trusted the sheriff to make the right decisions since he was a part of it too. He had personal stakes in it going according to plan.

Cletus rapped on the porch door before letting himself in. Earl sat at the kitchen table, his back throbbing again, washing down the pain meds with a warm beer. It had been a long night.

Sheriff Cletus came into the kitchen and stood across from Earl, hanging his hat over the arm of the chair like he owned the place. There was nothing different about his appearance — his brown uniform was as crisp and clean as it usually was, his neck was mostly unshaven, his lip was packed with dip — and he looked as if nothing even happened. To Earl, it seemed as if what happened tonight had no effect on Cletus's state of mind whatsoever.

"Where's Bev?" Cletus asked. He made a sucking noise with his tongue and spat in the sink.

"She and the girl went to bed some time ago. They're both out for the night."

Cletus nodded. He looked down and fidgeted with the gold watch around his wrist.

"Where do we stand?"

"You did good," Cletus said. "You did real good."

"What now?"

"It's open and shut, really. The marshal found the white bucket with some residue in it that matched what they found all over. It was the clear igniter."

"And?"

"And as far as he's concerned, there was an accident while Lenny was cooking up some fertilizer on his porch. He figures Lenny was probably smoking a cigarette and got too close. Happens all the time, he says."

"So, that's it? What about the bullets?"

"Don't worry about the bullets. The few casings they found near the truck were just thought to have fallen out of the bed when the truck flipped over. Lenny had all kinds of weapons on the property — everyone knows that."

Earl nodded. He felt confident, like it might actually work. "What happens next?"

Cletus leaned to the side and spat in the sink again. "I've already made a call to the coroner's office telling them what happened. Tomorrow I'll fill out the necessary paperwork and drive it over there myself. I'll explain that children are involved and I'll get a rush on processing. They may call you to go down and sign something."

Earl nodded. He could do that. "Then what? What about the custody situation?"

"We should have a death certificate by the end of the week. Until then, I know a judge I can get you and Bev in front of for an expedited hearing."

Earl shifted his weight, feeling uncomfortable.

"Don't worry. This one's conservative as hell. Won't even grant a divorce unless there's proof the wife tried to poison her husband or something. You and Bev will get those kids. There's no doubt in my mind."

"What about after?"

"After when?"

"You said this would only be temporary, right?"

"That's right. Once the paperwork's final there'll be a hearing for permanent custody of the children. Like I said, with this judge it'll take a hell of a lot to put those kids in the foster care system. Especially with living relatives. Their mother, even."

Earl nodded again.

"Bev isn't still…Is she?"

"Well, that's the thing—"

"She better stop now, then. Like today. That'll be one way to screw this all up."

"I know. We both know."

"But, just so you know, there's more to it that just that."

"Meaning?"

"Meaning the boys are probably old enough to make their own decision. Bo definitely is."

"Where else would they go?"

Cletus shrugged. "Just something to think about."

"I don't see them leaving Ruby behind."

"Better make sure you get full custody of her then, huh? Don't screw it up."

Earl thought about that hard for a second. He wished Beverly was out here to hear it directly with her own ears, but he also thought she knew how dire the situation was. She had to choose sobriety if she ever wanted her children back.

"Children aside," Earl said, "what about the rest of it? What about Lenny's will?"

"That doesn't change. You'll be the guardian of the estate until they're eighteen, regardless. Or at least until Bo's eighteen, then he'll take over. But without the boys living with you, good luck managing the estate without a lawyer stepping in."

"What do you mean?"

"Think about it, Earl. If Bo chooses to live with someone else, that family will be privy to his situation and all the money he's coming into. You don't think they'd hire a lawyer on his behalf to ensure you don't mismanage the assets? You'd never be able to make any transactions without the approval of the court if that were to happen."

"So, how do I do it?"

"Get custody of Ruby. Once you do that, everything else will fall right into place."

***

An hour went by and the clock struck midnight. Earl grew impatient, and he was tired and cranky. He hadn't eaten in many hours. Cletus was almost asleep in the chair, his head back, and his neck bobbing to one side. The night was at its darkest.

"I don't think they're coming," Cletus said. His hat covered his face as he slouched in the chair, smothering his words.

"They'll come."

"When?"

Earl stood up. Even though numb, his back was still stiff. Walking over to the sink was an adventure. He leaned against the sink and scanned the field. The porch light made a path about half way to the plum tree, but he could see nothing except complete darkness outside of that. He really thought the boys would come out of hiding once they saw their father's trailer in flames, but he was starting to think he might have underestimated them. He still had a hunch they were staying somewhere close by, though.

As he scanned the darkness, an idea came to him. He used his hands to push off the sink and limped his way toward the porch. He reached around and flipped off the light switch that hung near the door, then he went back into the kitchen and killed that light too.

"What are you doing?" Cletus said, removing the hat from his face.

Earl sat at the table in total darkness, the green illumination from the microwave clock the only light. He felt a grin make its way across his lips, and he didn't fight it. "It's only a matter of minutes now. They'll be here real soon."

CHAPTER THIRTY-ONE

The boys waited five minutes to make sure the light stayed off. Once the tense, silent minutes passed, they climbed out of the underbrush, leaped into the darkness, and took off toward the trailer. All three ran together.

The air felt cold as Rusty ran, and his lungs burned like chilled ice. He quickly fell behind. Stars blanketed the darkness above his grandpa's trailer, some of them winking, others dimming. Their work was nearing completion for the night. Clouds would be taking their place in mere hours, then the sun. Rusty wondered where the stars went while they slept.

Bo and JT were waiting for him at the trailer when he finally caught up. Both of their backs were pressed against the vinyl, and their chests rose and fell in unison.

"You okay?" Bo asked, panting.

Rusty nodded, too exhausted to speak. The inhaler in his pocket pressed awkwardly into his thigh, offering a reminder. He didn't think he needed it, but he felt better knowing he had it with him. He hadn't run as much he had in the last two days in his entire life, and he could feel it. Everything was sore.

"What do you guys want to do?" JT asked. His attention was on Bo. So was Rusty's.

"Now's it," Bo said. "Everyone's sleeping, so now's our chance."

JT looked at Rusty and nodded, and Rusty nodded back. With their eyes fully adjusted to the dark, Rusty noticed a strange look on JT's face, maybe excitement, maybe worry. He also noticed how crooked JT's teeth were.

"If you want to bail out," Bo said, "now would be a good time. We wouldn't blame you."

Rusty nodded at JT when they made eye contact, and JT let out a small sigh. Rusty thought he was going to take Bo up on his offer, just as Rusty almost did before this all began in the first place. Just as Bo had said, Rusty wouldn't have blamed JT at all — it wasn't his fight.

"We've come this far, right?" JT said, forcing a smile.

Bo smiled back, Rusty too, and they all nodded. They were in this together.

Then the all too familiar silence returned. It came with a vengeance. The next step wasn't as easy as the previous one.

"So, what do we do, Bo?" Rusty asked. He was breathing easier now, his chest feeling lighter.

"I say we go in the front. No more talking. Complete silence. What do you guys think?"

"You guys go," JT said. "I'll go around the back and check it out."

"You sure?"

"You go. I'll be right behind you."

Bo nodded. He nudged Rusty with his shoulder and pointed toward the front of the trailer. Rusty kept his lips pursed and followed Bo toward the porch. A loud drumming pulsated in his ears as they neared.

***

Earl heard some noise outside, some distant chatter outside the window. He leaped up from his seat and crept toward it. There was a tremor in his leg that only showed up when his adrenaline kicked in, so he flexed his quad to slow it.

He heard voices. Real ones this time.

Using the edge of the stainless steel of the sink as support, Earl stood on his tiptoes and looked down through the glass. The window was closed, which muffled the voices, but the sources of the voices were there. Through the glass, Earl saw the tops of their heads — three boys, two with hair, one without; the one without had his head buzzed to the scalp — and their backs were pressed up against the trailer. Their voices were soft enough whereas Earl couldn't hear what they were saying. But it didn't matter.

They were here.

When two of the boys pushed away from the trailer and took off to the front, Earl got a good look at their faces. He knew it. He knew they'd come eventually.

The other boy turned his back to him and went around the backside of the trailer, showing only more of the skin that bled through his hair. The mystery boy looked to be around the same age as Rusty. Earl assumed him to be a friend from school, which is who they must have been staying with. It made sense. They couldn't have been staying the forest this whole time.

But what were they doing here?

Earl backed away from the window and turned to face Cletus. The tremor in his legs kept increasing, now attacking muscles all throughout his body as if it were cancerous. Earl's finger shook as he pressed it to his lips, the words he wanted to say not to be spoken.

"Where?" Cletus whispered as he rose to his feet with a jolt of energy. He looked younger all of a sudden.

Earl held up two fingers and pointed toward the porch. Then he held up one finger and pointed down the hall.

"There are three?" Cletus said, louder than he should have.

Earl nodded, pressing a single finger over his lips again.

Cletus nodded back, grabbed his hat, and took off down the hallway. A hand went to his Glock as he disappeared into the shadows.

Earl made his way back toward the kitchen table and plopped himself in the chair. His heart raced while he waited, sweat forming a patch of moisture on his back he knew would leave a stain. He folded his hands in his lap and spun his thumbs around one another, refusing to address the itch that formed on the crescent part of his ear. He wondered what the boys' plan was and why they were trying to sneak into the trailer in the dark.

He stiffened as a slow creak sounded from the porch.

***

A soft, repetitive rapping on the window woke Ruby. Her mama's sleepy arm was draped over her torso, pinning her to the bed as if it were a vise. Ruby was groggy and confused at first, then she remembered where she was and what happened.

The flames were so bright.

Everything she ever knew was gone.

Lucy, her best friend, was gone.

She hoped her brothers weren't in the trailer when it happened. Ruby's eyes were sore from all the tears she cried thinking about it. The cuts on her face still ached.

The smell of her mama was different than it used to be. There was something stale about her, something hard, something toxic. She slept more than she ever used to, and it was a deep sleep. Ruby could move her arm and toss it to the side, or pinch her skin or wriggle underneath her armpit, and her mama wouldn't even flinch. She never used to be like that. Ruby felt like a prisoner, trapped underneath the weight of her mama's bulk, unable to escape, no matter how hard she tried. Being awake reminded her of how trapped she felt.

The rapping on the window started again.

Ruby was frantic. The rapping on the window couldn't be an accident. No one else lived out this way. The street was private. There were never any visitors. And it was the middle of the night.

It was her brothers, it had to be. She knew they'd come for her.

Ruby squirmed, trying to worm herself out of her mama's grasp. Her mama rolled over and grunted, wrapping her arms around Ruby even tighter, squeezing as if she'd forgotten Ruby were a child. Ruby could hardly breathe. She yanked and clawed at her mama's arm, using all her strength to try to push her away.

The rapping came again, louder and longer than the first two times, and it felt even more urgent.

"I'm here," Ruby called out softly, not wanting to wake her mama. She kicked her legs and squeezed her shoulders close together, and she was able to slide out from her mama's grip. She caught her breath and slid off the bed, then rushed over to the window and flipped open the blinds.

But no one was there.

She was too late.

Ruby wanted to cry again, to break down, to be angry. Being so close to seeing them and missing them was devastating, unfair even. She felt weak, incapable of taking care of herself. And she was learning her grandpa couldn't take care of her, and her mama certainly couldn't either. Because of that, she needed her brothers more than ever.

But she was too late.

She thought about sitting on the edge of the bed and weeping, allowing herself to feel sorry for herself, but then she thought about what Bo always said to her. Many times he told her to be strong and to always keep her chin up. He said that people may try to take advantage of her because she's a girl, and that she always had to stick up for herself. And most often, he told her to never give up.

So she wasn't giving up that easily.

If her brothers were outside the window just a minute ago, they couldn't have gone far. Ruby would go find them.

Her mama didn't even flinch from the bed when the bedroom door creaked open.

In the hallway, both ends were as black as midnight. And silent. Ruby's mama snored in the room at her back. Ruby stepped into the hallway, not being bothered by the darkness like she once was. She felt brave like Princess Merida and was ready to make her move, bow and arrow or not. She started for the kitchen, walking gently on her toes. Her socks easily slid across the floor as if they were covered with wax. She only made it a handful of steps before a light in the kitchen flipped on, and her grandpa's voice rose above the silence.

Ruby froze.

Then: "Hey, what are you doing up?" It was a man's voice, different than her grandpa's. It came from behind her.

She was about to turn and face the man, but then she heard something else. It was another voice, and it came from the kitchen. Tears welled up in her eyes at once, and she had no hesitation about rushing toward it. It was Bo's voice, which meant he was okay. He and Rusty were okay.

"Hey," the man behind her yelled as Ruby ran in the opposite direction, toward the light in the kitchen, almost slipping as she took the corner too sharp.

***

Rusty was on Bo's heels as they climbed the stairs leading up to the porch. The similarity of it to the one that used to be at their father's trailer was remarkable; the two setups were practically identical — the same colors, the same size, the same creaky top step. Rusty shook with anticipation.

Rusty let the screen door close delicately behind him, hardly making a sound as it landed against the frame. The night was quiet, the nocturnal beasts hiding. Without hesitation, they pressed forward. Rusty was ready to do this. He felt tough.

The porch was dark, and so was the kitchen. Rusty thought something smelled off — maybe sweat or old aftershave or underwear that needed changing. Or tobacco, their father's tobacco. Except their grandpa didn't smoke.

Bo led the way, walking on his toes as if he were a burglar. Rusty tried to imitate the best he could, but it was hard in heavy boots. When they were in the center of the room — darkness to the left, a single window to the right that provided just enough light to drop a small moon shadow across the countertop — Rusty heard a click. Before he had time to think about what it could be, the entire kitchen illuminated in a bright white.

Rusty cowered and covered his eyes with his wounded hand. The dried blood had clotted on the perimeter of the callus, forming a short mound on his palm that was sharp and had hardened edges. The sharpness of the edge pricked his skin as it made contact with his face unexpectedly. When his eyes adjusted, he opened them and looked up, dazed and confused. His hands shook as he held them near his face, ready to throw fists.

His grandpa sat at the kitchen table, his eyelids heavy, anger red on his face. "I wondered when you were gunna show up." The words came out slow and heavy, as if he were drunk. Except he wasn't — Rusty could tell the difference. He could tell their grandpa was exhausted.

"Where's Ruby?" Bo asked. His knees were bent slightly, but he still towered over their grandpa as he sat.

"She's in bed."

"We're taking her with us."

"You're staying right here."

Bo straightened his back and puffed out his chest like he always did when he was preparing for a confrontation. "No, we're not."

Their grandpa groaned as he used the table to push himself up. His arms shook as he did, his face strained. He worked himself to his feet and stood tall, stretching out his back and grunting. Bo's chest deflated as their grandpa now towered over him as if he were a giant. Rusty forgot how big their grandpa was until now, having not spent much time with him recently. He lowered his hands and sunk his shoulders once he remembered what they were up against.

From down the hallway, a voice yelled out. Rusty spun toward it, knew it was a man's, but didn't recognize it. Soft footsteps began shuffling, and Rusty stood motionless as they became louder. Rusty took a step toward the corner where the kitchen met the hallway, but was stopped in his tracks when Ruby appeared in the doorway.

She was shoeless, her white socks nearly tripping her as she slid into view. Her arm extended and pressed against the door frame, which stopped her momentum and kept her from falling. Water filled her eyes even before they met with Rusty's. Rusty's knees felt weak.

"Ruby!" Bo said, relief in his voice.

The ginger on Ruby's head was tied behind her, although much of it was loose. There was a red tint in her eyes where it should've been white, which, to Rusty, meant she'd been crying a lot. The thought of Ruby crying brought anger rising to the surface again. Rusty took a step toward her.

"Stop," their grandpa said, pointing at Rusty. "Nobody move."

Nobody did.

Just then, more footsteps — these ones heavier than Ruby's were — pounded in the hallway. A man appeared in the doorway and stopped just behind Ruby, towering over her. The man had a police suit on, and the hat in his hand looked as big as a sombrero. Rusty now knew who the man was.

"Where's the other one?" their grandpa said, looking between Rusty and Bo. "Who is he?"

Bo kept silent, so Rusty did too. He bit his tongue and kept his lips tightly puckered. If Bo wasn't going to say anything, neither was he. He hoped JT got away.

"I saw him through the window," Sheriff Cletus said. "He took off back around the front when he spotted me."

Their grandpa pointed toward the porch and moved his eyebrows up and down, which Cletus responded to by nodding. "Stay there," he said, then he took off toward the porch and disappeared into the darkness.

Rusty met Ruby's eyes again and took another step toward her. He noticed the abrasions on her face were starting to heal, but they still looked sore. She otherwise looked okay.

Their grandpa reappeared with something in his hand, but he was alone. JT snuck away, it seemed, and Rusty was happy about that. He felt relieved, actually. He liked JT.

"There's nobody out there," their grandpa said, talking to Cletus. "But I found this on the bottom step." His arm shook as he raised it, thrusting the object he found forward.

Ruby let out a wail when she saw it, rushing toward their grandpa and taking the object from him. He let her have it, looking at her like she was a wild animal on the prowl, his eyes wide and his lips curled.

Rusty felt his bottom lip begin to quiver. Thanks to JT, Ruby and Lucy were reunited again, and it felt so good to see her happy.

CHAPTER THIRTY-TWO

Earl and Cletus lined up three chairs in the kitchen and forced the children to sit. As long as Ruby was with them, the boys wouldn't put up much of a fight — Earl was confident about that. He had all the leverage. Ruby sat between the boys, the raggedy doll on her lap, and held a hand each. She clearly adored her brothers, which made this worse for Earl. Cletus set his hat on the counter. His Glock, thankfully, was still holstered.

"Who was that other boy you were with?" Cletus said.

Bo looked Cletus right in the eye and held it, unblinking, holding his ground. Rusty did everything he could not to make eye contact with anyone, instead choosing to stare at his boots as if they were of great interest.

"We know there was a third boy. What was his name?"

Still nothing. The boys held out strong.

"Let's try another way. Where'd he come from? A friend from school?"

"The woods," Bo said.

"Pardon me?"

"We met him in the woods."

"Is that where you were staying? In the woods?"

Bo said nothing.

"So, you met him in the woods," Cletus said — a statement, not a question; cop stuff. "What was he doing here with you? What were you boys planning?"

"We just wanted Ruby back."

Earl shifted his eyes toward Ruby. The tops of her hands were white as she held onto her brothers for dear life. Tears welled in her eyes.

"Why?"

"Because we wanted her with us."

"Out in the woods?"

Bo didn't respond, but the way he broke his eyes away said enough. He was old enough to realize the plan was flawed, if they even had a plan at all. Earl couldn't imagine Bo actually thought living in the woods would be an option. What about food? What about shelter? What about clothes? Next winter was closer now than last.

"You're not going to tell me about the other boy, are you?" Cletus said, crossing his arms.

"No."

"Not even his name?"

"No."

"Why not?"

"Because this has nothing to do with him."

"Then why was he here?"

Bo wouldn't answer that either.

Cletus sighed and looked over to Earl — it was his turn to try. There was some pain tugging at the muscles in his back, but he pushed through it and took a step forward. The children all looked at him when he did.

He said, "I think you guys have the wrong impression about what's going here. Nobody's in trouble." He tried to offer up a smile, but he thought the children might be smart enough to see right through it — Bo, especially.

Ruby sniffled.

Rusty shifted his seat closer to his sister, still holding her hand.

Bo didn't even blink.

"Then why is he here?" Bo said, referring to Cletus, but clearly intentionally refusing to look at him.

"There are some things we need to talk about, is all."

"Like what?"

"Let's just say there are a few things you all need to know. I think there's a way we can all help each other out here."

"What happened to dad's trailer?" It was Rusty. He was still close to Ruby and holding her hand, but he was finally looking up. The question took Earl by surprise. The boy didn't speak much.

"That's one of the things we need to talk to you about. There's a lot more going on here than you may realize."

"But," Cletus said, making eye contact and cutting Earl off, "before we can tell you anything, there's something we need from you first."

"What's that?" Bo asked.

"The boy's name."

Bo thrusted himself backward in disgust, making the chair skid across the kitchen floor, sending a surprisingly sharp pain rushing through Earl's ear.

"He's just a boy, all right?" Bo said. "Just some boy we met in the woods. There's nothing more to it than that."

"His name?"

"It doesn't matter what his name is. He's just a boy."

"It matters to me."

Bo went mute.

Cletus took a step closer toward Bo. "The boy's name, now!"

"Fine!" Bo said, not backing down, his chest out. "He went by JT. That's all I know. That's all he told us."

Earl's throat went bone dry. His knees suddenly weakened.

Sheriff Cletus visibly lightened, his chest falling back into place as he exhaled. He took a step back and stood next to Earl. "That wasn't so hard now, was it?"

Bo leaned back against the chair and crossed his arms, huffing.

"How much does JT know about what happened?" Cletus asked.

"What are you talking about?"

"Skip the games, okay? We know what you did. We know what happened in your father's trailer."

Bo stiffened, and so did Rusty. They both let go of Ruby's hands.

"How much does he know?" Cletus repeated. Earl could sense Cletus thought he was close to something.

Bo looked at Rusty for a moment, then, without moving his head, he found Earl's eyes and said, "All of it. JT knows everything."

***

Rusty hoped Bo knew what he was doing. He wondered why Bo gave up JT's name like that, and he didn't understand why he told Cletus that JT knew everything. It seemed like Cletus would have bought if it Bo told him a lie. Rusty wasn't sure what was happening, but he trusted Bo.

"Where did he go?" Cletus asked.

"Don't know."

"Come on. You must know where he went."

"I don't know."

"What was the plan?"

"There was no plan."

"Bullshit!"

"Hey," their grandpa said, giving Cletus a dirty look. Cletus responded by holding up his palms and shaking his hands real fast.

"Sorry," Cletus whispered, barely loud enough for Rusty to hear.

"Forget about the kid," their grandpa said.

"Earl, if the kid knows something, that makes him a lia—"

"I said forget about the kid. Drop it."

Cletus shook his head at their grandpa, then he turned back to Bo. Rusty moved even closer to Ruby and put his arm around her shoulder. He almost forgot how little she was, and he felt like a man protecting her. She was still pretty upset.

"You boys should be thanking us," Cletus said, which made Bo laugh.

"For what?" Bo said.

"For cleaning up your mess."

Rusty knew what Cletus meant. The fire.

"How long did you think it would have been before someone found your dad's body under the porch? Didn't you think someone would notice him missing?"

Ruby stiffened under Rusty's arm. He wanted nothing more than to cover her ears so she didn't have to hear this, but then he thought that maybe she'd be better off knowing. He didn't want her growing up believing lies, like he did.

"You boys could go to jail for a really long time, do you realize that?" Cletus crossed his arms again. Rusty almost forgot that Cletus was the sheriff until now.

"You going to arrest us?" Bo said. "Do you have any idea what our dad to us? Did you see Ruby's face?"

Ruby put her head down and sniffled again. Rusty pulled her in close until her ginger tickled his nose. The scent of cinnamon was faint.

"I saw it," Cletus said.

"What about you, grandpa? Are you just going to let him take us away just like you ignored what dad was doing to us?"

Their grandpa's mouth opened, but no words came out. He looked hurt. Or sad. Rusty still couldn't believe he let it go on for so long without doing anything.

"I'm not going to arrest you. I'm not going to arrest either one of you."

Bo looked as if he were frozen, his lips stuck between touching and not. His throat made a strange noise. "You're not?" He seemed short of something to say, which was unusual.

"Like I said, you should be thanking us."

"Did you set the fire?" Rusty asked. He wanted to hear it. He had to know what happened. All eyes turned to him, and he felt the heat.

"Nobody set a fire," Cletus said, a mischievous grin on his face. "It was an accident. Your dad died in an accidental fire."

Rusty looked at Bo, not sure what this meant.

Dad didn't die in an accidental fire. Were grandpa and Sheriff Cletus covering for them?

"Why?" Bo said.

"Why what?"

"Why are you doing this?"

"Like I said before, guys," their grandpa said, finally speaking again after being quiet for a while, "there's a lot we need to talk about."

CHAPTER THIRTY-THREE

Everything was different after that. Rusty felt at ease knowing he and Bo weren't going to be in trouble for what they did, and he sensed that everyone else did too. Bo wasn't as uptight and defensive, and he answered Cletus's questions with honesty. Rusty sat in silence while Bo and Cletus talked about what happened, everything from finding the shotgun in the shed up to meeting JT in the woods. Their grandpa began to act strangely when the conversation moved to JT and why he was living in the woods, and Rusty couldn't quite decide why that was.

Ruby only shrieked twice during the recount of what happened, which Rusty thought wasn't bad. One time was when Bo described how their dad died — about the gunshot to the throat and about how he bled out on the carpet; and the second time was when Bo talked about why they did it, about what led up to it. The details were excruciating, the memories just as painful as the physical scars they left. Rusty thought everyone seemed a little sadder after that part. Neither their grandpa nor Sheriff Cletus admitted to setting the trailer on fire.

"I have a question," Rusty said when the desolation became overbearing. He felt all eyes on him again, and he wanted to shrink. But he had to ask. "Did we do the right thing?"

Cletus and their grandpa looked at each other for a while. There was a long silence in the room that Rusty felt getting heavier and heavier, almost as if no one heard what he said. He wasn't sure if he should repeat the question or not.

"What's right and wrong is complicated sometimes," their grandpa finally said, looking at him, releasing the burden that had planted itself squarely on Rusty's back. "There's not always a yes or no answer to a question like that."

"But what do you think?"

Their grandpa weaved his fingers together and rested them against his belly, then he pulled them apart and scratched various places on his face and head. He seemed to linger when he found the cutout on his ear. "I think you guys did what you felt you had to do, and I commend you for that."

Rusty wasn't satisfied. It was as if their grandpa was uncomfortable, as if he didn't really want to answer the question directly.

"It if were me in your shoes," Sheriff Cletus added, "I might have done the same thing you boys did. It doesn't make it right, that's not what I mean, but I understand why you thought you had no other choice."

A smile made its way onto Rusty's face. Hearing someone else say it out loud made him feel better about it. Maybe, after all, he'd be able to forgive himself one day too.

"How come you didn't come looking for us?" Bo said.

The smile on Rusty's face fell away just as quickly as it arrived. It was an important question.

"We did," Cletus said.

"No, you didn't. We could have died out in those woods. If it wasn't for JT, maybe we would have."

"But you didn't."

"How long would it have taken?"

"Excuse me?"

"How long would it have taken us to be missing before you tried to look for us?" Bo's face was reddening. Rusty knew that look.

"I just told you, we did look for you."

"You're a liar. You were more worried about getting rid of dad's body than you were about us. I know it was you who moved him, you know."

"What's your point, son?"

"My point is you don't care about us. Neither one of you. You don't care about me, you don't care about Rusty, and you don't care about Ruby."

"That's not true," their grandpa said. "You know that's not true."

"Isn't it? You could have come looking for us as at any time, but you never did. You would have left us out there forever."

"Not true."

"It is true! You never cared about us. You wouldn't have let dad do that to us for so long if you had."

"You don't know what you're talking about." Their grandpa was getting mad, his face scrunching into angry grandpa mode. "Some things are just too complex for someone your age to understand."

"What's complex about this? You guys were more worried about hiding dad's body than finding us. What's not to understand about that?"

"Watch your mouth, Bo. I'm warning you."

"What are you going do? Hit me like you used to hit dad? Like he hit us?"

A sharp intake of breath surprised Rusty. Their grandpa's face turned really red. So red, Rusty wondered if he might explode.

"What, you didn't think I know?" Bo said. "I know more than you think I do."

Their grandpa balled his fingers into a fist and raised his arm over his head. He took a step toward Bo. "You ungrateful son of a—"

"Stop!"

Their grandpa's fist froze at the sound of the voice. He turned — everyone turned. It was Rusty's mom, and she wasn't happy.

"Put your hand down, you coward." Their mom's voice was as deep and as scary as Rusty had ever heard. He held Ruby close — not only because he knew she was scared, but also because he was too.

"If you ever lay a hand on my children, I'll castrate you and shove your balls down your throat."

Earl slowly lowered his fist, keeping his eyes on their mom the whole time. The redness in his face worsened. His upper lip rose in the corner, making his face into a scowl. The tension was powerful, intense, almost overbearing.

"Why don't you take some more pills and go back to bed? Men are talking."

"Ruby, come here," their mom said. Ruby slipped from Rusty's grasp and rushed toward their mom. "Bo, Rusty — you too." Their mom hugged them all as they crowded in around her. "How dare you threaten my children?"

"Bev, I—"

"Stop it, Earl. I've had enough of you."

Their mom crouched and looked at them. When her eyes met with Rusty's, he felt something he thought he lost — or never had at all. His heart sped up. Tears welled up in his eyes, his mom's too, and they embraced. She smelled weird, but she was warm. Warm and safe. And loving.

Bo and Ruby joined in too, and it was like being a family again. Part of Rusty wished Lenny was there too, but then he remembered all that happened and brushed the thought away. For the first time in a long time, he thought he'd actually be okay, that he might be able to move on with his life.

"Give me the keys," she said, looking up at their grandpa. "We're leaving."

"Let's talk about this, Bev. I did this for us."

"Don't give me that." She stood up and pointed at their grandpa, then at Sheriff Cletus. "I know what both of you are up to. You think you're going to get Lenny's money? Ha! Over my dead body."

No one responded.

"Both of you are slime. That's all you are. Pure, cowardly slime."

Their mom pushed past their grandpa and Sheriff Cletus and grabbed a key ring from the counter. Both men hung their heads. She called for Rusty and Bo and Ruby to follow her, and they did. Rusty tried his hardest not to look at his grandpa as he hurried past, even though he wanted to. They were almost at the door when their grandpa stopped them.

"Aren't you going to tell them the truth, Bev?"

Their mom stopped and spun her head around. She was only steps away from the porch now. They all were. "What are you talking about?"

"The children. Why don't you tell them what's really going on?"

Their mom stood motionless. Rusty's heart sank, the loving feeling now lost. He just knew something bad was coming.

"Go on, Ms. Perfect," their grandpa said. "Tell them. Tell them the real reason why they had to live with their father all these years. Go on. Tell them!" He breathed heavily now, and looked angrier than Rusty had ever seen. "Tell them how you lost custody because of how you couldn't stay sober. Go on.

Tell them. Tell them!" Their grandpa addressed the children now, looking between them. "That's right, kids. Your dear mama couldn't quite stay off the pills long enough to pass a drug test, so you had to live with your abusive father instead. How's that for the truth?"

Rusty looked at his mom in disbelief. It couldn't be true. There's no way she would have let that happen. No woman would do that to her children. Her lip began to quiver as tears streamed down her face, but Rusty pulled away when she tried to reach out. They all did. Rusty and Bo and Ruby all backed away together, looking at their mother with hurt and disbelief.

"Since we're all sharing secrets here," their grandpa said, "how about we tell them that other thing, shall we?"

"Please, Earl, don't." Their mom sounded desperate, her tone high, her eyes begging.

"Ruby, honey," their grandpa said, trying to crouch down to Ruby's level.

"Don't, Earl!"

"Ruby, honey, there's something you need to know."

"Earl, please stop!" She was frantic now.

"I'm not your grandpa, honey. Do you understand?"

The sounds of crying and screaming and a loud drumming jumbled Rusty's mind. So many things were happening right now, and he tried to make sense of it all. But it all happened so fast, and he didn't know what was real and what wasn't. He pinched his eyes closed and tried to block it all out.

"I'm not your grandpa. I'm your father, sweetheart."

Their mom fell to the floor and began to wail.

The room spun.

"And those boys you're standing next to, they aren't your real brothers. They're only your half-brothers. You do have a real brother, though, did you know that?"

Their mom's screams were piercing. Rusty's head spun a thousand miles an hour, along with the room, and he thought he was getting dangerously close to passing out. He felt for his inhaler.

What did grandpa mean Ruby wasn't their real sister?

"Your real brother's name is Justin, and he was taken away as a baby, just like you all were. Your mama's a real whore, sweetie."

Rusty felt his heart break, heard the muscle tear in two. He felt the bones in his chest splinter, felt the pressure of it underneath his skin. He listened for the drumming in his ears to make sure he was still breathing, because he wasn't sure if he was. His inhaler seemed just out of reach.

Rusty felt Bo's hand on his shoulder and it brought him back. He looked deep into Bo's eyes, saw tears, and remembered where he was. He took a deep breath, caught his wind, and exhaled so hard it hurt. Ruby grabbed onto his good hand as it dangled near his hip.

Rusty knew it, he just knew it. JT was his brother. The freckles and the ginger hair, the way he laughed and the way he smiled. The similarities were all there. And the initials — those made sense too. The JT he and Bo knew was the same Justin their grandpa was talking about — Ruby's real brother. Which also meant JT was their brother too, at least somewhat. JT stood for Justin Travis, and Justin was their brother. And they had to find him and tell him before he was gone forever.

Amidst the chaos inside their grandpa's trailer — their mom was still on the floor, screaming; their grandpa, Ruby's real dad, hovered over her, yelling obscenities; Sheriff Cletus stood behind their grandpa, trying unsuccessfully to get his attention — Bo grabbed Rusty's forearm and pulled him out of the trailer. Ruby held on to Rusty's good hand still, and the three of them slipped out into the darkness, making a chain with their arms.

The tree line wasn't far, and they ran through the night as if they were being chased — and maybe they were; Rusty didn't look back. He'd never look back. He was never going back to that trailer again, no matter what.

Bo slowed before long and they began to walk briskly, no longer running. Ruby asked Bo what was happening, but he ignored her. Rusty could only imagine what was going through Bo's mind — even he didn't know as much as he thought he did, and that must have been hard for him to deal with. Rusty knew what that feeling was like.

As they approached the edge of the forest, Rusty smelled smoke. Then he squinted his eyes and looked past the oak trees, and he thought he saw the orange glow of a flame crawling toward the moon.

CHAPTER THIRTY-FOUR

A few months passed. As it turned out, the state of Kentucky preferred to keep fostered siblings together when possible. It took some time for the four of them to find a forever home, but it did eventually happen.

The night they had their world shattered, Rusty and Bo and Ruby left the trailer for good. They never went back, and nobody went looking for them. Whatever their grandpa and Sheriff Cletus wanted to happen didn't. Rusty didn't know what to think about their mom.

JT already had a fire started by the time they found him, and Rusty could tell he was lonely. JT looked sad as Rusty and Bo and Ruby approached — his hands were held out over the fire, a branch of leaves draped over his legs as if it were a blanket, his head was down — and he didn't seem to notice them right away.

Ruby asked a lot of questions about the things she didn't understand — about how their grandpa could actually be her daddy, about who that made Lenny to her, about what that made Bo and Rusty. Bo tried his best to give her answers that made sense, but Rusty could tell she still didn't understand what was going on. To be fair, neither did he, really, and he doubted Bo fully did either. Rusty wasn't sure if the new information changed anything between them.

"I don't care what grandpa said," Bo said, seeming to sense the hesitation in Rusty. "We're still Ruby's brothers."

It took hearing it from Bo to make Rusty get that, and he felt better afterward. Bo was right — Rusty still loved Ruby like a little sister, and that's because she was, regardless if their fathers were different or not. Technically speaking, though, he struggled to figure out what she really was — half-sister and half what? It was a strange, confusing time.

Bo was closer to JT than Rusty, so Bo was the one who told him the news. JT almost didn't believe it at first, but then when he saw Ruby and found out what their grandpa and mom looked like, he nearly collapsed into the fire. Bo caught him and led him to the log that was starting to lose its bark from being sat on so frequently, and he sat with him and told him everything that happened.

JT did the smart thing by running away like he did, Bo said, and everyone agreed that him being there might have made things even worse. Rusty couldn't help but wonder what their grandpa would have said if he actually saw JT. Would he have confessed at the start?

When Ruby met her real brother for the first time, it was a surreal moment. The two of them stood facing each other for a few long minutes and gazed into each other's eyes to see if they could see themselves. Rusty watched as Ruby rubbed Lucy's denim overalls in between her fingers, watched as she slowly worked up the courage to finally say something to JT.

"Thank you for Lucy," was what she said. They hugged for the first time not long after that.

Rusty and Bo and Ruby and their new brother stayed in the forest for a couple of days. They collected enough food and supplies from the trailer before it burned down to last for longer than that, but with the extra mouth to feed, it went a lot quicker. JT caught a few more fish from the pond, which helped.

By the third day, after being showered with pouring rain the night before and temperatures in the nineties during the day, they decided they couldn't stay in the forest forever. Ruby developed a little cough by then, and nobody thought it was a good idea to give it a chance to worsen. Even JT agreed, which Rusty found surprising — the forest, after all, was JT's home. But JT had a sister now, he said, and it was his responsibility to protect her. Both Rusty and Bo smiled at that, because they knew the feeling. Rusty couldn't speak for Bo, but from his own perspective, he was happy Ruby had another man to help look after her; because that's what JT was — a man.

Instead of going back out of the forest the way they went in, they all took the path through the woods into town. JT told his stories again about how he made the trail himself and about his experiences making deals with the townsfolks. Rusty beamed at hearing it again, and Ruby seemed to enjoy it too. Bo didn't say much.

In town, JT found Ruby a doctor. He seemed to know the right people to talk to and the right questions to ask, and he led them straight into the same doctor's office Rusty went to as a younger boy. The doctor looked at him strangely, as if he recognized him, but he didn't say so if he did.

Ruby was given a bag of cough drops and some children's cold medicine for free, and in exchange for the courtesy, the police were called. The name Plum Springs was written on the doors of their cars, but Rusty didn't recognize either of the men that showed up. He was just glad it wasn't Cletus.

The four of them were driven to the police station in two separate cars — Bo rode with Ruby so he could make sure she took her medicine properly, leaving Rusty with JT — and were interviewed individually that afternoon. By dark, they all showered and were fed and were given a change of clothes from a big box that sat in one of the offices in the back. They all slept together in the interview room that night, one forest green cot lined up next to the other. Rusty's pillow was flat and the blanket was scratchy, but it was far more comfortable than that cubbyhole in the oak roots. Ruby's coughing kept them all up for most of the night.

The next morning, a brown-skinned woman in a coffee-colored pantsuit came to see them. There were almost no brown people in Plum Springs, so that meant she was from out of town. Probably from the county office, and Rusty knew that meant it was bad.

The brown woman drove them all herself — Bo in the front seat with her, Rusty and JT in the back with Ruby in between them — to an enormous brick facility somewhere beyond where Rusty had ever been. The place had the greenest grass he ever saw and big windows and a crimson roof. There were tons of bedrooms and lots of kids — most of them around Rusty's age, some older, a few younger — and the food wasn't bad. There was school during the day and leisure time in the evening, and Rusty had a room right next to Ruby's. JT's was further down the hall, and Bo's was on the floor above them. They still saw each other every day.

Days passed, then weeks, then months. Eventually, Rusty settled in and started to like the place, and Bo and JT and Ruby seemed to be doing okay too. Children occasionally left with smiling adults, but most of them stayed. Lots of them never even had a visitor. Many of the children were pretty sad most of the time.

A few couples came to see Ruby and one of them wanted to take her home, but they didn't realize that taking one home meant taking all four of them — that was what Bo made the brown lady agree to before taking them there. The people who ran the facility promised they'd keep trying to find a spot for all of them, but Rusty didn't mind the wait. The physical scars on his hands were healing, but the emotional ones would take more time. They each saw counselors once a week.

A few days after Thanksgiving, the brown woman summoned Rusty downstairs to talk. He didn't know what to expect, since he hadn't had an individual meeting with her before — not since the first day, anyway. He had butterflies in his belly as he walked down the lonely corridor and descended the stairs, hoping he didn't do something to upset the brown woman. His new bedroom was starting to feel like home and he didn't want to be sent somewhere else.

The talk didn't go like he thought it might.

Bo and JT and Ruby were all waiting for him when he got to the brown woman's office. There were two other smiling faces in the room he didn't recognize — one man and one woman. The brown woman hugged them all and cried, and the four of them went upstairs to gather their belongings. There wasn't much — mostly just some art and new clothes they were given. Everything they owned before was burned in the fire. They were all going home, the brown woman said, and she was going to miss them. Rusty couldn't remember the brown woman's name, but he missed her from time to time. He even missed his bedroom once in a while.

***

When the boys took Ruby and left, Earl knew it was over. The children were gone, which meant Lenny's money was gone, and Beverly too. Everything was gone.

Beverly kicked him out.

The final irony was that Cletus was the one who made him leave.

Earl found solace on the streets. He had his truck and his wallet, but the truck quickly broke down and Beverly cleared out their bank accounts, so his wallet did him no good. He ended up selling the truck to a metal scrap yard in town for a couple hundred bucks and a meal ticket.

Earl spent the money on hard liquor and cheap motel rooms, but he was flat broke in less than a week. He walked for eight hours to go back to the trailer to find out if Beverly was done being mad at him, but when he got there, everything was gone. She cleaned out everything and left.

There was a note stuck to the door with tape that had a phone number on it, but it took Earl two days to find enough coins lying around the sidewalks to make a call using the payphone near the pharmacy downtown. The number connected to an attorney in Bowling Green who said he was representing Beverly. The attorney asked where he could send some papers for Earl to sign.

Sheriff Cletus found Earl in an alley behind the grocery store a week later.

"Have you seen her?" Earl asked when Cletus walked up to him. His hand shook uncontrollably as he signed the line that had his full name printed underneath. He was famished.

"Yeah, I've seen her."

"Where is she?"

"She doesn't want to see you."

"Just tell me where she is."

Cletus didn't. He just stood there with a packed lip and a hand in his pocket.

Earl finished signing and threw the stack of papers back at Cletus, who scooped them off the pavement as if it were an accident.

"The kids have been orphaned, you know."

"Where?"

"I can't tell you that"

"Then why say anything at all?"

"I thought you might want to know that they have a good home."

"What about Beverly?"

"She's given up all her rights as a parent to all of them. They're better off without her at this point — her decision. She's getting herself some help."

Earl grabbed a discarded toothpick and spun in between his fingers. "What happens now?"

"If it's Lenny's estate you're talking about, forget about it. The children will get control once Bo turns eighteen, just like before. The courts have put a hold on all assets until then, so you'd need approval from a judge before doing anything. You've lost all your power."

"And you?"

Cletus shrugged. Earl didn't think he needed the money anyhow.

"What about that other thing?"

"There's nothing more to say about that. Lenny died in an accidental fire. The death certificate has the proper signature, and the file's been sealed. The case is closed."

"And the boys?"

"I don't think we have to worry about them. The case is closed, like I said. I don't think they're going to admit to what they did at this point, do you? Let them have a fresh start. You should do the same."

"I have nothing left."

"Now you know how those boys felt all those years." Cletus tucked the papers under his arm and gave a curt nod. "Take good care of yourself, Earl."

"Will I see you again?"

"No, I don't think so."

"No?"

"I'm transferring. Heading north. Clean slate."

"Where to?"

"Just north." Cletus turned and started back toward his squad car as it idled in the street.

"Sheriff," Earl said, one last time. "Can I ask you something?"

Cletus stopped, looked back at Earl. "Shoot."

"What's your last name?"

Cletus smiled, and he smiled good, his teeth showing. He spat on the pavement. "Take good care of yourself." Then he walked back to his car and left.

Earl never saw him again.

Taking Cletus's advice, Earl made no effort to reach out. He tore up Beverly's lawyer's phone number and tossed it in a Dumpster in the alley. He knew what he just signed; he wasn't stupid. Not only was he now a divorced man, but he was also a lonely one — his worst nightmare. Like Beverly, he renounced his rights to parent Ruby. Poor Ruby. It was for the best.

There was one of two directions Earl could go with his life from here. He could go back to work. He could get a job as a janitor or a handyman or maybe even a landscaper. He wouldn't be able to lift decorative stones or bend over for too long, but he thought he might be able to help out with raking leaves or cutting grass. The work would only be temporary. He could save up some cash and get himself an apartment, or maybe he could buy himself another trailer; his credit was still good, as far as he knew.

But Earl didn't want any of that. Not anymore.

He was tired. He was old and sore and tired. And broke. Life had won, worn him thin, as it tended to do to everyone in the end. Beverly would be getting half of his military pension now. He couldn't live on the rest. He didn't want to. There was nothing left for him to live for, not even himself. He hated who he was, and he hated his life.

Earl went in the other direction. He made some quick money doing bad things for bad people he met on the streets, but he stopped once he had the money he needed. It didn't take much. He bought the one in the glass case that was on special.

Earl thought about going back to the property to look around once more with the hope of finding some consolation, some reason to keep on living, but he didn't have the energy. He feared he might change his mind if he had time to think about it.

There was a tree in the park that cast a shadow like the old plum tree did. Its girth was similar, its root structure raised and nearly identical. Apples hung from the branches instead of plums. Earl sat in the shade and thought about his life, reminisced about all the wrong he'd done, all the wrong he thought about doing, and all the people he hurt along the way.

He cried for the children. One of the boys he hardly knew at all, and the one girl thought he was her grandpa. The one boy he did know intimately — the one he helped raise and grow into a man, the worst kind of man — beat the hell out of the only grandchildren he'd ever know. His now ex-wife — once his daughter-in-law — hated him. The arrangement was never out of love to begin with, but of sheer convenience instead — together they could hide their secrets, while apart might be more difficult; and the children would be accessible to both of them. Their other secret love child bounced in and out of foster homes and lived in the forest behind their trailer, without either of them even knowing about it for God knows how long. By himself. At eight-years-old.

Earl thought about the many men he killed. He covered up the murder of his son, then tried and failed to take all of his money afterward. He drugged his son's wife and slept with her, making her an addict. Then they hid the child they conceived from Lenny, made him think he was a stillborn, when in reality, he and Beverly instead signed away their parental rights. Then they did it again, but they couldn't use the same excuse the second time around. So they made Lenny think Ruby was his, and Earl had to watch as his abusive son raised his only daughter from a trailer away. And while he knew what Lenny did to those boys, he could say or do nothing about it. Because if he did, Lenny would kick him off the property and he'd never see Ruby, his only daughter, ever again.

Earl knew he was a bad man. He had very little to be proud of, if anything at all. His life was a failure.

Earl retrieved the one photo he had of Beverly from his breast pocket — the one of her nude, the one he found in Lenny's truck — and studied it. He rubbed his thumb over her face, her bare chest, and her naked legs. He thought about how he treated her, what he'd do differently if he ever got another shot at it. He admitted to himself that he actually loved the woman, in spite of everything. He regretted not telling her. He kissed the forehead of the younger woman in the photo and slipped it back into his pocket, where it'd stay for the rest of time, resting against his heart.

Heaven seemed so far out of reach at this point. Beneath the earth's surface seemed like a more appropriate resting spot for him, his soul burning for all of eternity. He didn't know if he believed in all that stuff anyway, but it seemed irrelevant now. He'd find out for certain soon enough.

Earl bought one bullet — that was all he needed. For all the death he saw in his younger days, for all the death he was responsible for, he didn't deserve to continue living. If God was really up there, and if he somehow made it to those pearly gates for Judgment Day, he'd have some questions for the man. Life was unfair and he wanted to know why; he wanted to know what he did as a child to deserve the life he was given. The two of them would have a lot to discuss.

Earl closed his eyes and slid the casing into the chamber. The short cylinder felt cool in his hand, and he thought that was telling. If he were to spend the rest of eternity engulfed in flames and playing servant to Satan, at least the last object he held in his hand on earth was cool. Heat would forever be his destiny.

Earl cocked the pistol. He kept his eyes closed and pressed the barrel up to his temple. He breathed in slowly and tried to relax. He saw images of Lenny as a child, and of Ruby as an infant. He saw Rusty and Bo and Justin, playing in a field, laughing like children were supposed to. He saw Beverly in a white dress, dancing among dandelions and wildflowers. He saw smiles; he saw happiness; he saw tears. And when he was as relaxed as he could have possibly been under the circumstances, Earl pulled the trigger.

All the pictures in his mind faded to black.

***

For the first time in his life, Rusty knew what home felt like. His new parents were wonderful.

There was money coming to him and Bo and Ruby when they were older, he learned, but he rarely thought about it;

money didn't matter to him. Bo would handle that when he became a grownup.

Their first day at their new school came after the Christmas break. Pine Bluff, Arkansas was the home of the red and white zebras, and it was their new home now too. Everything about Arkansas was different. There were more kids in Rusty's school than there were people in all of Plum Springs. There were white people and brown people and black people. There were computers in the classroom and free internet in most places in town. There were even some of those tall buildings that Rusty thought only existed in books. Life was different. Disappointingly, though, Rusty had yet to see an Indian on this side of the Mississippi, either. But there was still time; he hadn't been in Arkansas for very long.

Rusty had a new backpack. So did Bo, and Ruby, and Justin. It was Ruby's first one ever — it was her very first day of school. She was nervous. JT went by Justin now, losing the initials after their last names all changed from Travis to Weaver. Rusty thought Weaver sounded more sophisticated. He liked it. They all did.

There were other kids at the bus stop. The neighborhood was full of two and three story houses, many of them with swimming pools and white or brown fences around the yards — theirs included. Rusty thought it was a castle when he first saw it. They all had their own bedrooms. There was a girl named Cyndi that lived next door that Rusty could tell Bo had the hots for. She was tall and blonde and the same age as Bo. Rusty thought they looked good together.

There were two other little girls around Ruby's age in the neighborhood too, and one little boy. Ruby was shy around them, but Rusty knew she'd adjust in time. He was glad she'd have a friend or two — Lucy didn't count, although she was still around. Rusty and Justin only had each other, but that was fine; Rusty had more than he needed.

The school bus pulled up and stopped in front of the street, its brakes squealing to a stop, and the lady behind the wheel smiled and welcomed them to town. Ruby climbed up the stairs first, the yellow bus swallowing her, making her look like a pebble among stones. Her backpack was as big as she was. Justin went next, then Rusty. Bo waited to go last, even after Cyndi.

Justin sat in the seat with Ruby, and Bo sat next to Rusty. Rusty held up a hand and waved at his new mom as she waved through the window of her minivan with tears in her eyes. He couldn't wait to get home and give her a big hug and tell her all about his first day. He looked forward to getting to know his new parents even better.

Rusty met Bo's eyes as the bus took off, its big wheels churning against the pavement, spitting sand behind the exhaust. They smiled, but neither one spoke; they didn't have to. They made it. And they'd be okay, they all would. Ruby's face had scars that would always be there, but she was still beautiful. There was a special cream she put on them before she went to bed at night, because the doctor said it would help. Rusty thought they were fading, but it could have been that he was just getting used to them. He hardly noticed them anymore.

Rusty looked back out the window and saw his own reflection staring back at him. His hair was shorter on the sides than it was on the top, and the parts that stuck up during sleep were combed down. His teeth were clean and his breath tasted minty. His face didn't have dirt on it. He almost didn't recognize himself. He smiled at himself in the window. His heart began to feel full for the first time, and he loved the feeling. He finally knew what it meant to be happy. And the best part was, he didn't have to find a hidden door and be transported to a mystical world to find happiness. Happiness wasn't just a fantasy anymore — it was a reality, his reality, and he never thought it would be.

As the minivan disappeared out of sight and hid behind the oak trees that lined the street, Rusty thought about what life was like before, and what it was going to be like in the future. He didn't think about it much because the past was in the past, and he was determined to move forward. He saw no use in dwelling on what used to be. He was moving on with his life.

Rusty wasn't the same person he was before, changed by the time he spent with his brothers and sister in the forest, and by the bond he and Bo would forever share. Whether he was a boy or man, he was still unsure, but he wouldn't rush it anymore; there was no need to grow up so fast.

What happened before didn't matter. All of that was in the past — his old life and his old secrets; all of their secrets — and it would be forgotten. All of those memories — all the hurt he experienced, all the misery, all the sadness — would be stored in his subconscious and kept there permanently, never to be revisited again. Just like his old life, his old memories would be forever buried underneath the rubble in Plum Springs.

Author's Notes

Dear Reader,

If you've gotten this far, you've already given me enough of your time, so I'll keep this brief. From the bottom of my heart, I want to thank you – thank you for spending your hard-earned money and invaluable, precious time with me. With all the sincerity in the world, you choosing to read my story over the millions of others out there is a great honor for me, and I could not be more grateful. If you enjoyed the story – or even if you didn't – I would be indebted to you if you'd consider jotting a quick review of your thoughts on either Amazon or Goodreads. Reader reviews are instrumental for authors, as it helps to bring attention to the book so other readers, like yourself, may become aware of it. Even if you didn't fully connect with it – which I'm sorry to hear, if that's the case – a written review would be greatly appreciated, as if for nothing else, it will give me some feedback about why that is, and what I can do in the future to be better.

Thank you again for your time, and if the desire strikes you to contact me directly or to find out more about me or my work, please visit: www.danlawtonfiction.com. I will respond personally to any and all inquiries that are received.

All the best,
Dan Lawton